RAGA

A Novel by J

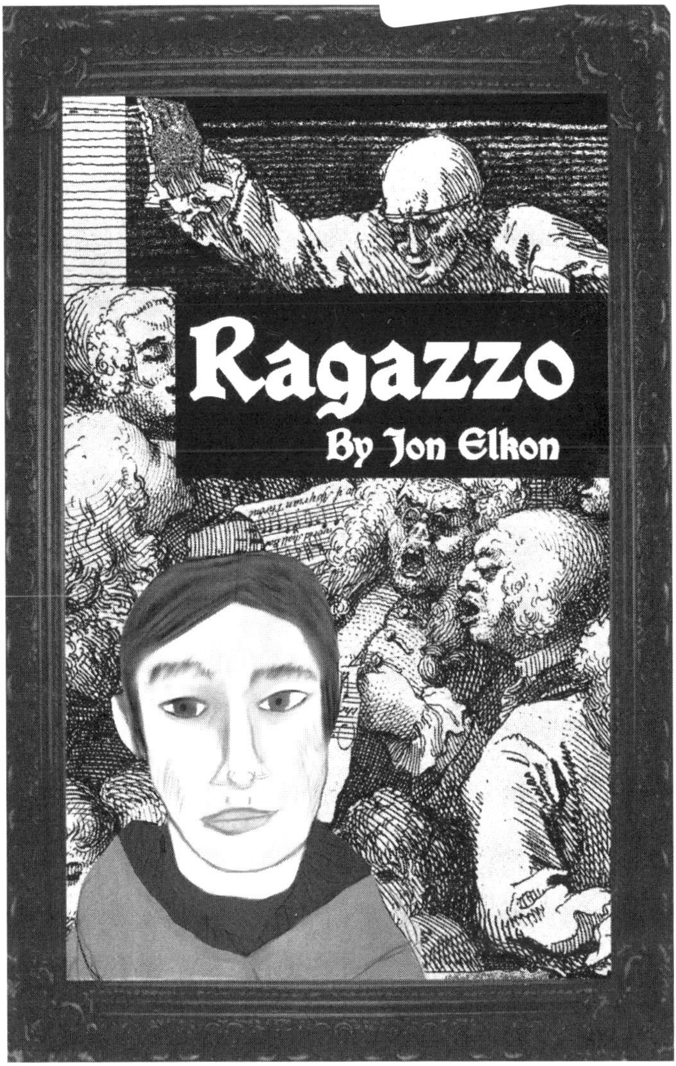

RAGAZZO

A Novel by Jon Elkon

ISBN: 978-1-7391474-2-6
Alien Rabbit Limited

Alien Rabbit Limited
www.alienrabbit.co.uk

Features Original Illustrations by Chris Godber

RAGAZZO

TABLE OF CONTENTS

Prologo

Welcome, dear reader, to my greatest production since my death!

This Opera Seria, this Opera Buffa, this tragedy, this comedy is the story of two millionaires whose wager destroyed an innocent boy, creating the greatest singer and the greatest killer who ever lived. It is also the story of how the greatest composer in history was relaunched in the musical minds of the populace.

Should you wish to sing any of it, feel free, but you will have to write your own music. I gave that up two hundred and fifty years ago.

1

ACT 1

Scene 1: The Seed Is Sown

Vienna February 1909

We are in a carriage. Motor cars futter and putt up and down Vienna's streets, but gentlemen still go to the Opera in a carriage. Even if it's not the famous Vienna Opera, but some ghastly amateur production in the suburbs, where sometimes a church lends its hall to wealthy members of the congregation who have the exceedingly foolish idea of producing an Opera.

This carriage is full of cigar smoke and to be rather more accurate, is conveying two gentlemen away from an Opera. And as far as both of them are concerned, it can't be quickly enough.

Eventually the portliest of the two bangs on the ceiling, hangs his head out of the window and shouts. 'Klaus!' he shouts, then again, 'KLAUS!'

The carriage comes to a stop. 'Ja Herr!' the coachman says.

'Wait here!'

---

[1] ***Illustration: The Baron's Castle***

A stopping in the night. Coachmen are quite used to this, as it normally means a passenger has to pee. Both gentlemen alight with a creaking of knees and smoke and mist from their breaths.

The redheaded skinny one, the one in the smoking jacket and spats takes the portly one by the arm and pulls him half a block along the snow-piled cobble-frozen street, slipping and skittering. Both men are rather drunk.

'Here! Here my dear Baron!' says Sebastian, the skinny one.

'Here?' the Baron replies.

'One, two…three..now!'

And both men let out the greatest highest longest scream ever heard in these prim and prissy streets.

And then, laughing and giggling like demented street urchins, holding each-other up, they make their way back to the carriage as windows burst open up and down the street and outraged Viennese poke their heads out to find out which army has invaded.

Scene 2: A Brothel

Welcome to the famous Viennese bordello, the Maison Grecque. This is the kingdom of the redoubtable Frau Sleister, famed for bondage and sadomasochism, for bestiality and every strange and wonderful sexuality imaginable.

Despite the name of the establishment, this is Vienna. We know the date is early 1900s, because while the bordello has a grandeur dating back to the Jugendstil of around 1900, which in the rest of the world they call Art Nouveau, it is just beginning to fade, like the Hapsburg Empire itself. Grand, pompous, flamboyant – but at its heart, tired.

Luscious bottle-green wallpaper lavished with hand-painted long-stemmed lilies, streaked with discoloured splashes of sprayed alcohol. Furniture whose lines mimic ferns and flowers, or the flow of golden hair in the wind. Green, gold and red. The gesso chipped, the velvet cushions blanched, the reds have turned to limned burgundy. There are paintings by Egon Schiele in this salon, evidence of his frequent visits. There is even a great and golden Klimt in which Frau Slappmeister herself is depicted as an overly voluptuous Eve, an apple in one hand and a whip in the other, her breasts glowing with gold. All overlaid with stultifying microns-thick layers of sienna, left by cigarettes, cigars and pipes.

Two middle-aged gentlemen, both obviously post-coital. They are scantily dressed but entirely at ease. Their bruises are evidence of the perfectly, exquisitely tasteful pain rendered to them at great expense by Frau Slappmeister's highly trained experts. Slappmeister, by the way, is what the regulars call the redoubtable madame. She doesn't mind.

The fat one with the mustachios smoking a Meerschaum is Baron Heinrich von Schweinstein. His companion is Sebastian Amore Geilis, a younger man, slim and military in bearing, spotted with freckles all over his body. He is strawberry blonde and gawky. His moustache seems like wisps of hair glued to a child's top lip

Baron: Ahhhh. Peace…our pipes, please Mitzi. . (Turns to his companion) Thank GOD for Slappmeister! I thought I would have bad dreams forever!
Sebastian: Oh come now, it wasn't so bad! They are amateurs, you cannot expect perfection.

Sebastian, dear reader, is not referring to the expert attention both men have received from Frau Slappmeister and her leather-clad team by the way. The two men have spent the earlier evening at a horrible performance of the Opera Rodelinda, before taking refuge in the one place they could have the memory excised. And the performance was so bad, only whips and chains would do. Now I am, not in favour of such extreme measures! Perhaps prison. With torture.

The friends had attended the performance for two reasons: firstly, Handel was hardly ever performed these days and the Baron had been excited to see an advertisement in the *Neues Wiener Tagblatt* for a performance of this rarity by an amateur Opera group, composed mainly of elderly ladies and gentlemen in absurd versions of mock-medieval costume. Secondly, he mistakenly thought Sebastian would be enchanted, excited, utterly entranced by my gorgeous music…

Meet my *Dei ex Machina* now, the two men without whom none of this would be possible. That is my joke you see. After all, I am the one without whom none of this would have happened. I am getting confused.

SEBASATIAN AMORE GEILLIS (baritone) is a flamboyant millionaire.

Around 45, he inherited his money and has never done an hour's work. His boredom is epic and is only kept in check by his main obsessions: his visits to Frau Slappmeister the bondage queen of Vienna, and of course music, in particular, Opera. In his case 'modern' Opera, from Strauss to Puccini and the emotionally draining *Verismo*, in which everybody dies.

...and his dearest friend:

BARON HEINRICH VON SCHWEINSTEIN: (bass) A big man, and wide. The scion of a family so old that their history has been forgotten. The inheritor of a castle and lands so vast they could form most of a country, somewhere near the borders of East Prussia and Poland. The Castle is so old that even the ghosts have died and their dust has clogged up the cobwebs. Our Baron is the last of the line, for the seeds of the family have long turned to dead atoms and given up the idea of progeny as being far too much trouble. His passion is Opera, particularly the flamboyant extravagance of the Baroque.

A scantily-dressed young woman drapes herself around his armchair, deftly filling and lighting a Meerschaum pipe and handing it to him. She then repeats the exercise for the Baron. I have no doubt that the contents of the pipes would not be legal these days.

Sebastian: Now go away. (She complies coquettishly.)
Baron: I can only apologise, my dear friend. Here I am trying to make you love the Baroque as I do, and I drag you to some amateurs shrieking away off-key, in what I can only describe as Opera Hell.

Duetto
Sebastian: (Chortles) Oh come now! They did their best.
Baron: My dear fellow! You are too kind to them. That soprano! Singing the hero Bertarido! Tits and trousers. Bizarre! The heroic King reclaiming his Kingdom. Never!
Sebastian: She was – almost – on pitch? Bah. Baroque Opera is so very superficial and complicated. I had no idea what on earth was happening!
Baron: Why not? Listen: Bertarido was thought to have died in battle and as he was King –
Sebastian: For God's sake do not try to explain yet again!
Baron: What's so difficult? The usurper Grimoaldo takes over, wants

wife, kingdom, everything. But aha! Bertarido is not dead –
Sebastian: You told me all this. I thought I understood! And then on the stage a woman is Bertarido and she loves another woman and she sings like a banshee and she is dressed like a man! No wonder we had to scream! My head is sore.
Baron: Ah but in Handel's day the heroes were sung by men. Think of that. I tell you Sebastian. Real men.
Sebastian: Castrati! Singing in upper register! Terrible!
Baron: Ahhhh my friend, if we could have seen the great Senesino singing Giulio Cesare or Farinelli in the eighteenth century, that was true drama.
Sebastian: Unnatural voices produced by an unnatural act!
Baron: They suffered for the art. And they had very happy lives too. Some made a fortune.
Sebastian: Ahh but without the pleasures of the flesh my friend. If Handel is ever to be revived properly, we will have to have women singing the heroic roles.
Baron: No woman could match the great Castrati! NO woman. In the great days of the eighteenth century, the Castrati were massive stars! They earned fortunes! Men and women fainted when they hit their high notes! You have no idea. If Handel is ever to be revived, only Castrati can bring back the drama. They would make your Madama Butterfly look like a dead insect. A dead insect!
Sebastian: (He is tempted to slap his old friend but knows the experience could be far too pleasant for both of them. He takes a deep breath.) Well my friend I for one am very pleased such things as men deprived of testicles have been left behind in the dusty past.

*

Of course I knew the greatest Castrati ever to live and I loved them. I made them into such great stars, they outshone the sun. Dead now, like me. Dead Senesino – I used to call him Sr Bernardi in private – I made him rich. Rich!

Except Farinelli, arrogant fool! Refused my invitations to London because he thought he was so great. Eventually he came, naturally! Left with his pockets stuffed with gold.

So many great heroes. Singing in that purest, clearest, high voice which makes women faint and men howl…. If you don't believe me, just visit Mr Google and type 'Castrati Opera' like so.

The seed was sown. Had it not been for this post-coital contention, lives would have been saved, and much suffering would have been prevented. This pile of words and history would have been stillborn in the annals of might-have been.

To these two men, living as they did in their own private Island of the Blessed, Handel was indeed like a God to them. Yes, both of them. Despite Sebastian's avowed contempt for the Baroque, he had great awe for Handel – as a young man, he had sung in church in the divine Messiah and had never recovered from the experience.

The Baron has been a fan of the Baroque since he was 12. His Music Tutor, the great Rudolf Grossmeister, had introduced him to the Operas of the Baroque with a passion and romantic flamboyance only a theatrically camp antique could express and be considered rather more 'artistic' than ridiculous. Ah, but Rudolf had lived at the end of the Baroque, had sung on the stages of the great Opera houses, had been applauded by the Crowned Heads of Europe, as he never tired of saying.

It is beneath my dignity to attempt to reproduce the manner of speaking of so extravagant a personage. I don't want to make him any more ridiculous than God made him. He had a beautiful soul, a sincere love of music and a dedication to his pupil which deserves our respect.

'*Ja liebe Kleinchen*!' the man would spout, using his affectionate diminutive pet name for the little fat boy who stared up at him with awe, 'This! Is the aria which had the Elector of Hanover in tears! The utter beauty of the divine Handel. Listen!' And flying at the poor innocent harpsichord, with its peeling marquetry and stained keys, he would sing his heart out. *'Lascia ch'io pianga'* (*Type carefully into Google or YouTube. You MUST hear this!*) he would weep as he sang, and little Heine (I don't like using the boy's name, because no-one ever called him anything but Baron. Just this once then) would see, as if he were there in ancient Jerusalem itself, the face of Almirena as she bemoans her terrible fate…Grossmeister could take the boy's heart and wring it like a lemon. This gave both of them great joy.

The Meister's ruined voice veered between alto and an uncomfortable falsetto. To Heine, it was pure joy. Once it was a thing of beauty but to us today, well we would have headed for the exit.

The man would tell his pupil all the great stories, all the epics of the past, and decorate them with the music of the Opera. 'Ahhhh and the most wonderful of the stories, Orpheus…so in love was that boy, when his beautiful wife died he followed her into death itself, to get her back. And when I was your age darling boy, I saw the divine Guadagni…singing Orpheus from Gluck as if God himself had come and put in him the voice of his favourite angel, I saw him! I heard him! This beautiful boy, this man born to inhabit Orpheus, to bring to life this perfect tragedy, in love with a dead girl. Beautiful boy. Beautiful like you!' and he would pinch the fat little cheek affectionately. 'Such a pity,' he would mutter under his breath, 'Such a pity you can't sing. Or play. Never mind. You are perfect in every other way!'

And the boy? Here in his moated world with its dusty emptiness of all joy and stimulation, he would look forward to his music lessons with his whole soul. Well, we may call them lessons – but in the main they were performances and lectures with the boy as the passive recipient of the great wisdom of his grotesque teacher.

'Ach Knabchen!' another affectionate pet name, 'For me, to have my heart broken as a boy and then when I get to the stage myself, to be made to sing Wagner! Such rubbish, all boum boum with huge breasts, HUGE. Breasts! Whips! Swooords! And arias which went on and on and on and on and never GOT anywhere.'

Interesting that later in his life the Baron rather appreciated big breasts and whips and even the odd sword. But suffice it to say that by the time Grossmeister died (the Baron was only fourteen) he knew every Handel Opera, practically by heart. And he had visited the great works of Porpora, Graun, Vivaldi, even Lully and Purcell and Gluck and on and on. The seventeenth and eighteenth centuries were his backyard. Italy, France, Germany England and Spain rang with choruses and arias in his head, filled with demented knights and gods, heroes and villains. His friends, night and day. And practically his only companions, for there was a distinct drought of Baroque Opera performance in those days.

*

'If only they would bring back the great Baroque operas!' Said the Baron, with a diva-like sigh. 'Some of the real culture of the Enlightenment.'

'You are obsessed!' Sebastian says, as he beckons the ever-attentive Mitzi over. 'Sherry?'

'Port, I think,'

'Sherry for me, Mitzi. Port for the Baron. The girl nods, disappears offstage.

'You could never mount a good Handel production these days', Sebastian continues, 'Too ridiculous. Bizarre. Women in tights! They only want Mahler here in Austria. Or Wolff. Or Wagner. Or Strauss, of course. Modern Germanic geniuses'

'Of course I am obsessed! Perhaps you are right. No mezzo, no female, no counter-tenor, no singer on earth could equal the Castrati of the eighteenth century.'

'Impossible to know!' Sebastian says. 'We will never hear a true Castrato. There has been no Castrato in Opera since Meyerbeer's time, round 1870 I think. It simply cannot happen.'

'Ah now, that's where you are wrong. The church had Castrati for much longer than that!'

'They would', Sebastian scoffs.

'A fellow called Moreschi left a couple of recordings apparently. He may still be alive. Very old now.'

'Perhaps - merely church music I'm sure. But what about Opera? With the drama? With the range! Stories! Love! Divine comedy? Your Castrati would look ridiculous. And sound it too.'

'Nonsense!'

Sebastian sighs deeply as Mitzi arrives with glasses, a bottle and a humidor on a tray. She pours out the precious port, and Sebastian removes two tumescent Cuban cigars from a cedar humidor and snips their ends with a silver cutter. He hands one to the Baron and ceremonially lights them.

'There is no way to settle this,' Sebastian says, exhaling pungent smoke. 'A truly great Castrato singer has to be trained from a young age. The Operation has to be when he's around 10, imagine getting a parent to agree - '

'Money, my dear friend,' the Baron says, 'money can do anything.'

The two men stare into their own thoughts, each ricocheting between the overwhelming desire to be proven right at any cost and the horror as to how it could be done.

'It will take many years,' the Baron states.

'I do not think it can be done these days.' his friend replies.

'Give me the time, and the right tutor…'

'Ridiculous. Dangerous. Illegal!'

'I would follow exactly what they used to do in the eighteenth century. Train him in all aspects of music. And culture. Languages.'

'What is the point! Any reasonable female alto or mezzo in

pants does the job as well.'

'Nonsense.'

'Really?'

They are thinking now, these devilish gentlemen in their tiny nasty little minds. Too much money, too much time, too willing to believe that with money and time, any crime can be justified.

Especially in the service of a bet.

'What are the stakes?'

A pause for effect.

'My castle.' Says the Baron.

'What!!! You are so confident you can do it? How will we measure the outcome?'

'We must have critics agree that he is the greatest in a Handel role. Ever. Greater than any female.'

'Which critics?'

'Uh, Foure? He knows and loves the Baroque. IF he's still alive by the time we've trained the boy!"

'Mannheim of die Zeit!'

'If he's still alive. Bah! Wagner lover'

'Pecarino! La Stampa!'

'Verdi lover….'

'At least three of them.'

'But the secret must be kept.'

'That he is Castrato? We don't tell them. Agreed.'

'Agreed.' And these two panjandrums shake hands.

The Baron suddenly laughs 'You know something – ' he says, 'I've just thought – '

'I doubt it' says Sebastian. 'If you thought, you would not have entered into this stupid bet!'

'No, listen. Do you realise that the boy, whoever we shall find, will be our Bertarido?'

'What on earth are you talking about?'

'The king! The returning king! Thought dead for so many years! He will take back his kingdom!'

'Ha!'

'And will you be Grimoaldo, the villain?'

'Ha. Again, Ha. We shall see.'

Perhaps you are accusing me of whispering into the ears of these contenders. For putting ideas into their woolly heads. But I swear to you, it was entirely their own idea. Entirely! Which was why I decided to watch this story unfold, and to record what happens.

2

Scene 3: The Boy and the Baron

Castle Schweinstein near the top right hand corner of Germany. October 1909

'My name is the Baron', he said, 'and I will make you famous. Adored. The most utterly proficient and perfect singer of this era and of all time that went before, and forever after. This is your fate, beloved boy! Guido, is it?'

The Boy stared at this looming monstrosity of a man, this bewhiskered gargantuan ogre smelling of tobacco and potatoes with

[2] ***Illustration - The Boy and the Baron***

his stained waistcoat and his florid language, and he burst out laughing.

'Oho so you don't believe me, is that it?' Irritated, the Baron assessed his new ward, bought from the slums of Naples and smuggled into the country by Hibert only that morning at very great expense. A slum boy. But a boy who sang like an angel at the Cattedrale di San Gennaro.

The *Ragazzo.* An Italian word meaning boy, implying ragamuffin.

'You are old and fat and ugly. I want to go home!' the Boy replied.

This conversation happened in Italian Neapolitan dialect (Guido) and very bad Italian (the Baron). So neither understood what the hell the other was saying. Especially as Guido, brought up on streets where everything was useful, had exactly the wrong idea as to the use the Baron had in mind for him. It took a while for the pfennig to drop.

*

Guido lived in this Castle for ten years.

He spent most of his first four months in the castle planning an escape, along with learning some basic German from the ever-looming Hibert and the other servants.

In the kitchens he discovered a grease-limned secret world where Frau Eberhardt stood over steaming pots swearing frantically as if imprecations alone could speed up the mysterious processes of reducing flesh to slush and fat.

'You fuck! You steaming pile of goose shit!' she muttered as she stirred the ragged remains of poor carrots and beets into the beaten remains of a goose, or a deer, or worse still, a pig, the trotters of which would protrude from the slush as if attempting escape. The creatures were usually freshly slaughtered in the kitchen outhouse, sometimes by the formidable Frau herself but more often by the ever-willing Janek, the kitchen and stable boy. This lithe sixteen-year old whose shiny black hair writhed with joy like an ecstatic rat, whose shirtless torso gleamed with filth sweat and blood, loved his job. Watched over by the Cook and her admiring acolyte Guido, the boy regarded every murder of a sentient creature as a performance. The subsequent flaying, gutting and butchering of the corpse being his grand finale.

Frau Eberhardt, a heaving mountain of woman, dressed in filthy lace-trimmed rags which had once, before being disassembled, formed the gorgeous silks of ladies of fashion, would then turn to the wide-eyed foreign boy sitting watching as if he expected her to transform into a cake and Janek into a prince. Then she would say 'Sweetie! Schatze! Do you want to give me a kiss?' And a chase would ensue through the pots and carcasses, the baskets of rotting produce, the bursts of steam and sizzles of fat until she would sit, farting on her stool and say 'You are a spitspot of a cuntish lump of turd and I love you. Here! Try my soup!'

*

Winter trickled into the castle within a month of Guido's arrival, and he didn't like it. He hated the cold outside, which was almost matched by the cold inside his cubicle of a room, in which while the fireplace resembled the glowing entrance to a passage to Hell, it magically emitted little or no real heat. He was bored, angry and depressed most of the time.

Eventually, on a night which had apparently retreated into a black space beyond stars, beyond Earth, he packed a small bag of his new clothes, some bread, a turkey wing he had accepted from Frau Eberhardt, and a compass. He was determined to find Naples, which he believed lay somewhere to the South. His plan was to sneak out, hide until dawn and then keep following the compass until Italy where the sun lives.

And so when the castle had sunken into its crumbling surly despondent silence for the night, Guido shouldered his possessions and slid out of the window. Quite literally, for the windowsill was connected to the ground by an ice-covered buttress, impossible to get a handhold upon in any way to slow his descent. Which ended with the sharp bite of pain as his ankle twisted beneath him, and he lay howling at the base of the wall.

He was rescued just before frostbite, despair and fury would have ensured an abrupt curtailment of all the Baron's ambitions for him by the lanky Hibert, the Baron's Butler and general factotum, who soundly caned the boy after gently bandaging the swollen ankle.

Guido spitting and swearing dragged by the hair to the dusty banqueting room where a feast lay on the scoured mahogany. 'You fuck! You scrawling scum of a French weasel, you –'.

'You hungry?'

'You spitspot of a cuntish lump of –'

'Sh sh dearing. Sh! Your dinner. Shush.'

Guido sat at the table heaped with beautiful food. 'You see,' Hibert lisped in heavily French-accented Italian, 'what you can have when you stay with us? Nowhere will you get such magnificence in this backwater. Now never go away again my pretty. We love you here.' And he dropped a kiss onto the top of Guido's head, which would have stung like a wasp's sting had Guido been bald.

And so Guido gradually came to the conclusion that perhaps life in the Castle wasn't so bad. Nobody had demanded any parts of his body for their enjoyment. There was so much to learn, so much to explore! He had the coziest bed he had ever slept in. The best food. Clean, comfortable clothes. No mama to keep throwing him out into the streets. Even the cold could be adapted to, with the right number of layers of cotton wool and fur. And he realized that if he did what the strangers wanted, he would be treated like the son of royalty. And as his grasp of the German language expanded, he became able to demand things.

Did Guido miss his Mama? Difficult to know. He certainly missed his band of brother Ragazzi. After all, he was suddenly almost entirely deprived of the company of peers.

There are letters from this period, found in the library of the Castle. They were never sent, possibly because Germany was at war with Italy. More likely Hibert cheerfully agreed to send them without any intention of doing so. After all Italy had just declared war on Germany and the Austro-Hungarian Empire, so while there was certainly post delivered both sides of the trenches, Hibert didn't know that.

I admit I thought the boy could neither read nor write when he was taken from Italy: apparently I was wrong. He must have had some rudimentary schooling, from the Church I presume. I cannot know everything!

'Cara mamma
Sono felice in un castello. Ora sono un principe e quando crescerò invierò il mio esercito per rapirti. E metterti in prigione per essere una puttana.'

'Dear mama
I am happy in a castle. I am now a prince and when I grow up I will

send my army to kidnap you. And put you in prison for being a whore.'

'Caro Dogface

Ora sei l'imperatore di Ragazzi perché sono andato in Germania per essere il suo principe. Devo essere famoso e ricco. Quando sarò ricco, verrò e sposerò te.'

'Dear dog face
You are now the emperor of Ragazzi because I have gone to Germany to be its prince. I am to be famous and rich. When I am rich I will come and marry you.'

'Caro direttore
Ti taglierò le mani quando sarò ricco e famoso perché sarò un principe e dovrai condurre il coro con il tuo pene'

'Dear director
I will cut your hands off when I am rich and famous because I will be a prince and you will have to conduct the choir with your penis'

*

Two months after his arrival at the castle the boy was given a sedative in his food and transported to a private hospital in a quiet suburb. Here he was deprived of those organs of which, until now, he had had no use. And as he had no idea as to the purpose of the Operation, he did not and could not complain. 'You were ill', Hibert said. 'You had to have an Operation. You must be grateful. We saved your life', and would say no more.

Thus, Hibert is an accessory to the crime committed against this innocent. Only he and the Baron in the Castle had this secret; were it to become known, even a man of such standing as a forgotten dusty Baron in a forgotten province would have been prosecuted, or at least reprimanded. Certainly his accessory would have been blamed and imprisoned for life.

Pain for three weeks. But Guido recovered as quickly as the young recover. At first the pain is the whole world. It takes over the world. And then, a mere two months later there is no memory of the trauma, as if it had been transformed to the gust of wind tickling the damask curtains in his musty room. Guido changed. His energy levels came back, but the discontent, the rebellious need to escape, seemed to have diminished. This apparently happens to cats, too. Not so surprising then.

The singing lessons commenced in tandem with an intensive program of education. The music tutor: Signor Alberto Gramaschi was a spinsterish spider-like man recently arrived from the Castle of Otranto or some such place - always dressed in a black suit and a shirt of shocking brightest orange. He had an apparent absence of most human qualities including patience and kindness. The boy was struck almost dumb with awe at this most peculiar confection, who knew so much about everything Guido wanted to know! Besides, he gave him the only attention he received in that echoing place, and a voice with which to speak and sing. There was also another tutor, the one Frau Eberhardt called *'The Spitzmaus'*, Henriette Maria, of whom much more later. She came from Hell. In the meanwhile enough to say she taught him English and German, reading and writing. He hated her.

Scene 4: A Viennese Waltz

16th January 1910. Sebastian's Apartment, Vienna. Evening. The Baron has been invited to dinner.

The apartment staggers over two floors of a pompous 1850's building in Slachthausgasse, which, despite the name, is not very near the Abattoir. It is furnished in a harmony of Jugendstil and Empire, each piece no doubt a treasure in itself but in this arrangement, every venerable expression of the proud craftsmanship of the artist is merely part of a perfectly conceived and intricately planned whole. 'Symmetry is everything' was Sebastian's command to Herr Geisler, the top designer in Vienna.

'So my friend,' Sebastian says, busily pouring out perfect glisters of finely crafted redness into rubicund glasses. 'how is it going? How is the boy?'

The Baron lifts the port to his cracked lips. 'The boy is fine.' He carries his drink over to a gilded chair with sphinxes for arms, and sits heavily.

'So tell me everything about the boy!'

'I told you he's fine! His education has been started. I have secured a marvelous Italian to teach him music. A signor Gramaschi. From Piave I think. Genius. His knowledge of the Baroque…'

'That sounds excellent! But can he train a Castrato? No-one living has ever done that.'

'He doesn't know the boy is Castrato. Yet. He thinks he is training a boy soprano.'

'Surely you should explain?'

The Baron sighs, irritated. 'Are you crazy? What we did is illegal! Do you want to go to prison?'

'Please do not imagine that could happen to either of us.'

'Of course you are right,' the Baron says.

*

We must now bid goodbye to Sebastian for a little while. He needs to go offstage, so that he can continue his flamboyant life. When the War comes, he needs to be an officer. In the Supply Corps, in an office in Bonn. When his mistress gets pregnant and goes off to hide in the Schwarzwald, we do not need to be present. She has no relevance to this story. She will take another name and disappear as surely as a pricked bubble. I made it, I can prick it. This is because the story now belongs to the Baron. And Guido.

But before I let him go, I will put him on the stage – because we shall certainly see more of him.

[3]

SEBASTIAN AMORE GEILIS: A LONG AND DUSTY PFAD.

If only we were immune to History.

In our story the person who carries most of the history of the time on his broad back is Sebastian. Not only History, but lumbago, rheumatism and a great chip on the shoulder too.

Sebastian grew up in the small but somewhat picturesque town of Graz, in the dusty old Austro-Hungarian Empire in the house of his grandfather Aleksander Geilis. The Grossvater was a vast monster with imposing mustachios, pink cheeks, the hips of a hippopotamus, a laugh as loud as a train and not a pfennig to rub together with another pfennig.

This lack of the means with which to make a decent pretense at a decent lifestyle didn't affect the outward appearance, at least, of a decent lifestyle. The family lived in a splendidly grand mansion in Feldkirchen-bei Graz, a leafy suburb in which the languid grand houses laze within bowers of trees, gardens, soft music and subdued laughter, as they have smugly done since the 1870s. Marble, oak, mahogany, sweeping staircases down which long dresses swished. Violins in the moonlight. Flirtations on the terraces. Fruit trees perpetually in blossom. What else. Carriages, servants. The panoply of

[3] ***Illustration: -A Long and Dusty Pfad***

fin de siècle Austrian bourgeoisie smelling of expensive perfume, roses, cigars. Perfect tiny dogs with high voices and a tendency to death.

Here Sebastian grew up ignorant of the mountain of debt upon which his whole existence was built. His pale and flaccid parents didn't know either. They lived in a miasma of misunderstandings. They believed, for example, that there was no need to work because Grossvater's wheat-trading business was happily and continuously scouring the world to make good and better deals, and so roomfuls bloated with cash were always there for the asking. They just assumed this. Also, they believed that the reason they lived with Grossvater was that the old man enjoyed their company. That Sebastian (their only child. I doubt if they had sex often. If at all. If so it would have looked like two dying fish in a basket.) went to the Hauptschule not because it was cheap, but because it was near and Grossvater hated him being away. That there was never much food because the old man needed most of it. (This was at least partly true.) That the maid was thin and angry all the time not because she was never paid, but because she was constitutionally thin and irrationally angry. That one day all the famous family jewellery which had belonged to Mutti (who had been dead for many years) was still in the safe and would be Geraldine's one day. That…

They lived in illusion purely because there was a huge gap in their reality. So big a gap it has to contain a ship. That ship was the Scheveningen.

Scene: The tiny attic room inhabited by Johanna, maid to the Geilis household. She is lying on the bed reading aloud to her pale son, who is riddled with a disease which is probably polio.

Johanna: 'It was a dark and stormy night,' she began. Johanna was the maid in the Geilis house. A whippet-shaped woman in her forties, she shared this room with her ten-year old son Karl, and had been there for fourteen years. As far as the family was concerned she was the faithful retainer who had always been there and would always be there. Her son, as far as they were concerned, was simply a sickly fact of life and they were absolutely uninterested as to how he had got there. They suspected that he had been given to the woman by a dead sister. Or relative. Or something. She had gone to stay 'With a sick relative' for two weeks, and returned with a baby. The boy was quiet, and that was the main thing. From the time he could walk he assisted his mother in the kitchen. He was good at shining shoes.

We know, as did Grossvater, that she was his mistress for many years until he grew too fat to fuck and she had become merely his assistant in his occasional autoerotic games. Right up to the day of his death in fact. But I am getting ahead of the story. We also know that Karl was Grossvater's son. Sebastian's uncle therefore. Sebastian didn't know this then either. He treated the boy as if he was an invisible but useful adjunct to their lifestyle.

Back to that dark and stormy night when Johanna sat at the side of Uncle Karl's bed as he sweated with fever, many years before she was to yield to her exasperation and strangle her employer.

DUETTO

Johanna: It was a dark and stormy night, The North Sea heaved like the stomach of a giant with hiccups. Like a snake tied with ropes. Like a hippopotamus that swallowed a snake which has swallowed a crocodile.
Karl: Heaved like the North Sea heaves
Johanna: The sea was as stormy as a dark and stormy sea can be and the good ship Scheveningen, a Dutch vessel of 14 tons, a crew of 16 and a drunken captain crept across its heaving surface like
Karl: Like an ant across my chest when I've got a cough
Johanna: Like a ship battling its way through a force 9 gale, its masts bending like whips, the funnel belching steam whipped away by the wind. A futile churning from the twin screws which rise, fall, rise, fall from the surface of the sea.
Karl: That's slightly better.

Johanna: Inside the Captain's cabin, a fight has broken out. A fight like

Karl: like

Johanna: a fight between two drunken men over. Over

Karl: A woman.

Johanna: Treasure.

Karl: Mama! This is not a pirate ship!

Johanna: A gambling debt. The ship pitches

(They start to sing)

Karl: The ship rolls

Johanna: The ship tosses

Karl: The waves foam!

Johanna: Blood is spilled.

Karl: The blood froths the waves. Death! The devil's breath

Johanna: Death. The Captain cries, the first mate is dead!

Karl: Damn his eyes he will never be wed!

Johanna: The ship on a wave as high as a berg

Karl: Rises, falls upon the Sjalberg rocks

Johanna: The crew scream and tumble to the seas

Karl: Which rips off their arms and shreds their knees

Johanna: (Sotto voce) That's a little melodramatic. There must be a better rhyme.

Karl: The screaming crew is flung to the seas

Johanna: Which tears masts like tinder and shreds the deck

Karl: Like cheese!

(They would have exchanged a high five if it had been invented)

Johanna: And from the hold

Karl: Spills the gold

Johanna: Which sinks like my dreams

Karl: While in Graz the man

Johanna: Whose desperate plan

Karl: Was clasped in the hold

Johanna: With Scheveningen gold

Karl: Went cold.

(Deep dark dangerous chords.)

Karl: (Speaks. Sighs.) Thank you Mama I feel better now...

*

Actually they weren't far wrong about the story in general, but the details were inaccurate. Based, of course, on what GF had told his mistress-maid. The true story: By the 1880s, the wheat trade was shrinking fast as American companies began to dominate the market. Imports were so much cheaper than anything that could be grown in Germany and Austria. One by one his offices closed. He sold the three houses, and even the Hotel. He was determined to escape the bankruptcy which was approaching the firm Geilis Pt like the inevitable approach of an Ice Age. He had never lived without vast amounts of money: the family firm had existed happily since his grandfather's day and now it was down to him to save it. But he had no ideas.

It was during a family holiday in Holland that Grossvater saw a possible chink of light in the darkness. There, leaning against a Dutch quay like an inebriated disheveled roué of an elderly uncle, the once proud Scheveningen, awaiting her turn to be broken up for scrap.

The Scheveningen was once the pride of the Van Dongen line. One of the fastest ships ever to cross the Atlantic with her revolutionary combination of sail and steam, she had carried the ridiculously wealthy, the most powerful politicians, as well as the crowned heads of Europe. The Russian Tsar and his family were on her maiden voyage. Her staterooms were marbled and mahoganied, her cabins paneled in rosewood. A sort of much bigger floating version of Feldkriechen-bei Graz. But now, beaten and battered, she resembled more an aged abandoned whore. So the Van Dongen family had decided that they needed slicker faster newer ships to compete with Cunard and the Americans.

So proud, so beaten.

Just like him.

'Marika,' he said to his beautiful wife. 'Look at her. Look at those lines, like an aristocrat in disguise.'

'Good disguise Aleks. So much dirt and rust. If you were so full of dirt and rust I would divorce you.' She replied.

'Marika, I see here the solution to our problems.'

'The solution? You idiot. I see somebody else's problem. Do NOT make it ours!'

'Don't you see Marika? Your father would help. We buy her – '

'Fuck off idiot!'

'Listen: we make her fine again – '

'I'm not listening!'

'We paint over the rust. We polish the brass. We varnish the decks. We float her proper.'

'La la lalalalal I can't hear you lalalalala…'

'We drive her to Ireland, pick up Irish to take to America. There are thousands fighting to go to America. We can jam her full. In America we pick up wheat. Bring it back to Europe – '

'I can't hear you – '

'And then we sink her.'

'I can't – what?'

'Fully insured of course.'

'What!'

'I said – '

'You stupid fucking shithead. It's brilliant. For once, brilliant!'

And so it was. The Scheveningen was bought with money borrowed largely from Marika's parents, refitted to a minimum degree and actually managed to float for a little while. Long enough to pick up 835 Irish men, women and children. Quite unlike the story he had told Johanna, the ship had been packed to the gunwales when she went down in a storm in the Irish sea. There was no gold in the hold, unless perhaps some belonging to the passengers who had wanted to make a new life in a new country. The Captain did, apparently, kill the first mate in that storm for reasons we will never know. And it's probably irrelevant. (Though: could they have had a dispute about the seaworthiness of the ship and its chances of getting across the Atlantic? Probably.)

And so why didn't Aleksander Geilis and Marika live happily ever after on the proceeds of the insurance? And go into old age with the specters of nearly a thousand people screaming at them from beneath the sea?

See Lloyds of London Vs Geilis, 1881 in the London Court of Sessions. It seems, owing to the efforts of Samuel Plimsoll, the 'Coffin ships' had had their day. No longer could magnates buy ships, insure them and sink them for the money – as had happened for many years, costing Lloyds of London and their insurers millions. Plimsoll had fought in the House of Commons for years for ships to be seaworthy, to have drawn upon their hulls his Plimsoll Line, showing the maximum load the vessel was permitted to carry. As a result, Geilis lost the case.

Good for the ghosts!

Bad timing for Herr Geilis, poor old fellow.

He didn't get a penny, and everything the Company owned was sold to pay a pittance of damages to the families of his murder victims.

The only reason he was able to stay in the Graz house was because he still had Marika's famous jewellery and handouts from her parents. She died three days after the court ruling, swearing with her dying breath that Aleksander was an arsehole and if he sold her jewellery she would haunt his ass. That's 836 people plus crew haunting the fat guy. No wonder he was murdered.

Of course he sold the jewellery. For a while the baubles (they were major baubles) kept the family in a much peeled-down version of the lifestyle they believed themselves entitled to. By the time Sebastian reached 14, the money had practically run out as had the patience of Marika's Papa.

*

It was as if the family lived in a house built of ice on an iceberg floating unstoppably toward the equator.

And it wasn't until *der Großvater* was found dead, apparently purpled by an autoerotic accident with a rope in his bedroom that everything just melted away, as if it had never been.

The young Sebastian witnessed his living ghost of a father dissolving into hysterical trauma as everything around him was sold, as the grand mansion in which both generations had experienced everything from first words to first orgasms was emptied. First of all its contents, and then of him and the near destroyed remnant that was his father.

Father ended up in an asylum. It turns out he was not merely broken, he was barking mad.

Sebastian was brought up by the mean and frugal Tante Beatrix, Aleksander's spinster sister in Innsbruck. Here she presided over the Calvinist Reformed Church like a bloated crow presides over the carcass of a mouse. She was also a gifted pianist, organist and piano teacher, as well as being an accompanist much in demand for well-known singers. She didn't give the young man any attention whatsoever. As soon as she could, she sent him away to the *Gimnasium*, where the boy consorted with the sons of rich merchants, the military, the petit bourgeoisie of the district.

When she died (Sebastian was 18) she left her considerable wealth to him. There are rumours as to how she acquired the money. But all the rumours are wrong. Including the one about her having been mistress of Franz Joseph the Archduke. True, they did have sex once, *droit de Seigneur* at a great ball in Vienna and the experience drove her into the Church.

The dull truth is that when their parents died their vast wealth was shared between the two siblings and while Aleksander lost the lot, Beatrix had squirreled hers away on 12% interest and lived frugally on her earnings as a piano teacher and accompanist.

Oh yes, and Marika's parents when they died left it all to him as well. Lucky for Sebastian that on both sides of his family, sex was infrequent – largely because it was undignified and messy.

Sebastian was determined never to make his grandfather's mistakes. So he invested in all the right places, growing filthy rich. What a guy. He even paid the asylum his father was confined in a good stipend, enough to keep him in whisky, laudanum and cigars.

By the age of 32 he had no need ever to work again. (This was the age at which he met the Baron at the house of Madam Slappmeister in the suburbs of Vienna.) It is also slightly possible that his four years working in the Supplies Office of the German Army in Bonn were rather fruitful on a financial level. I am not accusing, just surmising.

A SLICE OF HISTORY

We have intruded our ears and eyes into Sebastian's Vienna apartment on the evening of Wednesday the 13th of January 1909. Outside, the snow has piled up and turned to ice on the sidewalks. A few pedestrians are in the streets, wrapped in furs and wool, dashing carefully (can one dash carefully?) through this outer-city grand suburb, with its pompous apartment buildings and town houses. They were built when Austro-Hungary was the boastful self-proclaimed centre of an empire which was geographically at least, the second largest country in Europe after the Russian Empire.

In 1909, Austria was the hub of an immense Empire. Franz Joseph, the Emperor had ruled over this vast spread of land since 1848, and there was no reason to suppose this might ever change. So pompous was this fool, he would shortly involve the whole world in a war which killed millions. But for now Austria is inflated like a panjandrum stuffed to the ceiling by having eaten all his servants. And the belief that the Empire would be eternal was sunken into the very stones and streets of Slachthausgasse.

Germany meanwhile was also stuffed with complacency and self-satisfaction under the deliriously moustachioed Keiser Wilhelm. It seems to me that the whole of Europe at the time was under the domination of facial hair.

*

As Europe began to bubble with discontent, as the stench of oppression started to reek even under the moustaches of the rulers, Guido evolved from a slum kid from the horrible filth of Naples into a beautiful and articulate boy child. His intellect expanded exponentially, with a relentless curiosity about everything and anything connected with everything. He drove his tutors into a flurry of confusion. He almost forgot how to swear. Poor Gramaschi would reach for encyclopedias and dictionaries with the desperation a trapped zookeeper in a lion cage may feel in searching for meat to divert the hungry beast from ripping out his throat. As to *das Spitzmaus*, Frau Henriette Maria Eberhardt,, she began to feel more and more under siege by the demands of the boy's rapacious mind. Her strategy was to pretend to know everything and when she didn't, to resort to her 'little friend', a nasty bamboo cane which swooshed and stung when Guido questioned her or saw through her ignorance.

Eventually the boy caught up with and seemed to have surpassed his master in the matter of musical history and composition. By the time he was 13 he had read many of the books and studied so many of the scores in the Baron's huge library, the questions he had for his tutor were way beyond the man.

By the time he was 13, Europe was imploding.

*

The Library was a cave of wonders, a Pandora's box, a saucerful of secrets. His researches there into the classics, the stories behind the operas he was growing to love, into poetry and literature fueled his intellect and fed his soul. Having read a book or part of a book, he would wander up and down the shelves, allowing his hand to reach in and pull out another.

The Baron's father, Fritz had been an avid collector and a lover of the Orient. Apparently, he had learned Mandarin and Japanese too, for Guido found a collection of manuscript translations of Eastern classics. The Pillow Book, for one. Deeply disturbing, almost stifling, it took him into the mysterious world of the Japanese court more than a thousand years ago. Musashi's Book of Five Rings made him dream of ancient oriental warriors. And in dusty drawers and cabinets, Fritz' collection of Japanese antiquities. Netsuke and Okimono, Meiji and other metalwork, cloisonné scent bottles, and scroll paintings. And also, a Tanto. Asleep in its lacquer sheath a four hundred year old Samurai dagger, scalpel - sharp and shiny as lightning.

Guido wanted to be a Samurai. The Tanto connected him viscerally to that lost world of honour and grace, in which death was a gift of the warrior to his Lord.

Hunger for words as well as music! He plunged into the classics of Greece and Rome. Homer first, which drove him relentlessly through Xenophon and Thucydides and the wars of the ancients, to their philosophies, via their gods. Then Virgil, of course. Tacitus. Caesar, Plato, Ovid, Socrates… No better preparation could a boy have had for the Opera of the Baroque.

Guido wanted to be Achilles. Although he wouldn't have minded being Alexander. Or Xenophon, leading his 10,000 through the ancient warscape of Persia and Greece.

Guido only wanted to be a hero. Just like me.

*

Headlong into the operas.. Hunger for music! Watch this formerly ragged ragazzo curled around the phonograph with a libretto clutched in one hand swaying and perhaps weeping as the catastrophes of literature lived, died, loved, laughed all in song. How rich these worlds were! Compared to which the Church music of his youth seemed to be one-dimensional. But the paucity of recorded Baroque operas became an issue and as his musical knowledge grew, he curled head heart and hands around scores and manuscripts, of which there were thousands in this library.

Here, my own annotated scores for at least four of my greatest operas lay glowing like amber jewels with depths unplumbed, glittering with the petrified remains of my antique genius and others. Here were the scores of Bach's long forgotten operas, of Lucio Cilla, of Cavalli's L'Ormindo, of the once celebrated now forgotten Reinhard Keiser's divinely inspired Croesus. (I knew Keiser. I worked with him. An inspirational genius, even though we did have arguments. I had to leave Hamburg. More scandal.)

These were the ghosts of brilliance passed, of nights which two hundred years ago sang and danced with tears in their eyes. Astonishing, delighting and thrilling. Which died and were buried in the annals of the memories of Barons.

And then at the harpsichord (with Gramaschi playing, or playing himself) Guido would let the music flow, singing or humming or muttering with joy. He was Caesar! Or Nero! All-powerful with death in his hands. Bringing emperors, lovers and fools to life in the eyes and heart of a boy from the back streets of Naples who fell in love with the dead heroes of centuries past, with their gods and their adventures.

And then, their women.

Women. Creatures of legend, of whom he had so little experience, other than Neapolitan whores. There was Eberhardt, the cook of course. But she was more mountain than woman. Then there was the dreaded *Spitzmaus* Henriette Maria, who he hated, and if she represented all women would put him off for life. But there was also Magda, the pretty undermaid who sometimes spoke to him kindly. He could see her as Semele, Handel's heroine who seduced Zeus and was destroyed by him. Or even Cleopatra, vamp and victim who destroyed her own empire for love.

No operas there were in the Castle apart from the Baroque. As if all the nineteenth century greats had never been. No Bellini. Or Donizetti. No Wagner, for sure. And the upstarts Verdi and Puccini, banned. Pah! *Verismo* indeed! Even Mozart only there on sufferance.

Instead, *alles* Handel, all 42! and some of Gluck, Purcell, Monteverdi, Vivaldi, Hasse, Scarlatti, Terradella...this is not the whole catalogue. Shelves of hundreds of scores alphabetically arranged in an anteroom at the far end of the library with spines showing in parallel stripes loomed over the record player, which nestled in a noble oak cabinet in the French Rococo style. This shabby paneled refuge was once the Music Room of the Castle. The harpsichord still sat like a dying grandmother immobile near the French Windows which opened on to a short stretch of garden ending at a grassy ditch, what remained of the moat. At the far end a noble oak, always called the Guardian of the von Schweinsteins, maintained its sentry duty, surrounded by a grateful garden bench.

Guido adored this room. It was a place of such beautiful mystery, full of all the knowledge the library contained and more. As he listened to the small collection of recordings he would sing along to any tune he enjoyed, struggling to reach the high notes of the day's great sopranos - Nellie Melba, Amelita Galli-Curci, Lucia Tettrazini, Marcella Sembrich, Gallicurci, Lily Pons. At first it was hard work and he sang with strangled resentment as if his throat, in revolt at being submitted to compulsion, sat in a corner and sulked.

Bit by bit the gnarled and dusty soul of the tutor began to warm to the boy - and melted like powder exposed to moisture for the first time in a century.

'You will now sing boy,' the tutor announced, hands flying over the keyboard of the harpsichord as his predatory fingers sought the melody. Melody borne from the soul of the official Castle God, George Frideric Händel. 'You will sing 'Cara Sposa' from Rinaldo. This time, let it escape! This time remember what I have taught you! '

Intermezzo

Lots of Music here. Thinking music. Time passing music.

When Guido was 13 the War came. It knocked on the door of the Castle now and then. A platoon or a Company would camp nearby and a pompous Prussian would demand supplies. Then they would go off and have a battle, most would die and that would be it. Sebastian was nearly involved in the war. I will explain that.

Mostly, the war took place in muddy trenches many miles away while. Guido, almost unaware of the clashes of empires, sang his soul out.

*

For Guido years of sweat and effort, trials and tantrums. Rebellion, tears, canings. The boy learns English, German, keeps his Italian. He is guided, guarded and controlled not just by Gramaschi but also by the formidably evil Henriette Maria from Hell who teaches him languages as well as mathematics and history. Together they are good cop/ bad cop for even though Gramaschi is tall and dry, he is entirely lacking in evil. And Henriette Maria is a streak of purest evil.

Guido became determined to sing Opera perfectly, to release that trapped bird in his throat and fly with it because he so wanted to unravel the furrowed brow of the awesome Gramaschi. To make him smile with pride. After all, Gramaschi had opened the fabulous Pandora's box of Music for him, that magic which stole and carried his emotions and could make him soar. 'You sing every aria as if it was Ave Maria!', the Tutor would complain. 'Give me character! Give me power! Give me a *hero*!'

Guido could not satisfy him. In the Cathedral, everyone loved his singing. Here whatever he did was not good enough.

It was the same with Henriette Maria. Her demands of him seemed to make no sense. She wanted him to learn things he didn't want to know. To remember things he would prefer to forget. To be imprisoned in the expectations of someone he could never please.

And in the background the Baron, always with his firm hand on the controls. Demanding proof of progress from both tutors. Looming over lessons like a gargoyle in a cathedral. Demanding meetings with each. In which Gramaschi would appear indecisive and worried. And Henriette Maria, triumphant, in control and full of confidence. Taking responsibility for all progress. And no responsibility for the perceived failings of the Music Master. The Baron took to referring to her ironically, when carefully unpacking the progress of the project to Sebastian, as HM. As in Her Majesty.

*

Gramaschi doesn't know if the Voice is there or not. At best the boy's voice has a tinny sweetness, between mezzo and contralto, not even a true counter tenor. But no *expression*. No true timbre. He's just a boy! Gramaschi explains to his reflection in the Venetian mirror. A boy. Eventually the voice will break and all my work will have to start again.

Ah signor, you should have been told! This is a mission of madness! You would say. This is cruelty beyond reason! And you will fall into love with this boy.

You will be upbraided and threatened and told to do your job

And you will even fear for your life.

A Vignette

(Silent but for a solo violin, very quietly)

Guido is in the kitchen outhouse. Watched with amusement by Janek, also Frau Eberhardt, Guido is killing a hen with his Tanto. First he makes just a gentle slit in her throat, as she hangs upside-down in the kitchen boy's arms. Then he watches as the boy taunts and laughs. The blood trickles. Then he slits a little deeper, fascinated by the slow encroachment of death as the creature shivers itself to permanent sleep. Then, with a *kiai*, the Tanto slices laterally, sending the head of the hen flying and blood spattering.

Janek does a mad dance of triumph and joy, wipes his hands in the copious blood and daubs Guido's face with it.

Guido does not resist. He has been blooded now.

And after this blooding, dear reader, many were the sacrifices in the outhouse made to the god Tanto.

SEX

Of course Guido had a secret life, just as I did. There were times when his busy schedule allowed him library time and curling up on the grimy leather sofa with a book or a score or a libretto was his place of refuge. And this was how he discovered sex.

Sex was a subject not just hinted at in the classics he read-people 'fell in love' and then things got distinctly sticky. The 'falling in love' seemed to result in children and there was certainly a sticky part in the middle, between love, marriage and children.

And so Guido determined to analyse and understand the Sticky Bit. There was no point is asking his tutors - neither of them had ever managed to produce a child. The Baron, too, didn't seem to have reached the falling in love part. The boy's vague memories of his mother brought back the times he had to sleep in the streets, because mother had managed to persuade a man to spend the night and leave her with a few lire. Sticky times, judging from the sheets.

*

Here we need to discuss Castration. Kindly grind your teeth or cross your legs if you are a gentleman.

There are three basic types of Castrato.

'Throughout history, there has existed basically three types of eunuchs: those where were castrated before puberty, those who were castrated after puberty, and those who had their penis and testicles removed during the Castration. Those in the first group, who castrated during puberty, never developed mature sexual organs because they did not go through puberty. With the lack of mature male hormones, i.e. testosterone, their voices never changed, they had more feminine features, often gained weight very easily and lacked muscle tone, and they were totally impotent.

The second group, those who were castrated after puberty, went through puberty and though many took on feminine traits, it was easier for them to gain muscle mass, and they had the ability to get an erection. However, because of the lack of testicles, they could not produce sperm and therefore could not reproduce. They did however, have the ability to ejaculate, though instead of the creamy white ejaculate most men produce, it would mostly be a clear viscous liquid composed of the parts of their semen not produced by the testicles.

The third group lacked a penis and testicles and therefore were obviously not able to get an erection. Their bodies could remain masculine, if the procedure occurred after puberty, but since it was a highly dangerous procedure during the years before modern surgery, it was often performed on young men. '[4]

Suffice it to say (sparing those of a delicate disposition) that our Guido was Type 2, in that his (uh) testicles were removed at age ten. I did warn you. And so, capable of an erection but not ejaculation. Just the same as all the castrati I knew. Peasants called them 'Musico'. We composers called them 'castrati'! Though sometimes, 'evirato' when in more polite company

It seems to me, of the Castrati in my day, men like Farinelli retained their good looks and no person who was not present when he removed his trousers would have any idea.

Whereas Seneschino, I seem to remember, was the stereotypical

[4] ***https://closetprofessor.com/2010/07/15/the-sex-lives-of-eunuchs/***

eunuch, the type who appears in the classics. Too tall, too fat. For some reason their chemicals or hormones or such (I am no scientist) dictate that they become distorted. They may develop breasts.

Only one thing is certain about castrati: given the right training, nurtured in the right way, not only do they keep their gorgeous voice but they develop it. And some in my day became outrageously rich, famous and arrogant enough to enter into contretemps with me!

There is no doubt Guido developed an interest in sex. Close to an obsession. For three reasons: what he read, what he saw, and the strange phenomenon of the pleasant – it must be admitted – swelling of his penis, whenever he thought of or read about sex.

What he saw was Magda, the feisty maid who exuded sex, his Semele, who's blooming eighteen- year old body crackled with it. He couldn't take his eyes off her, and whenever he could he would take on the role of a secret agent and follow her through the mysterious dank and dusty corridors of the castle, his penis like an arrow pointing the way.

Eventually his reading and his persistence yielded solid gold. The sticky stuff itself! as he watched Magda being held up against a wall of the stable by the blank-eyed Janek, who, despite her cries for help then threw her to the floor and resisting her hysterical and tearful attempts to get him off, drove himself into her.

So that's what it means, thought Guido. She did not seem to have enjoyed it, despite what the novels said. Anna Karenina seemed to have enjoyed it. Madame Bovary too. Of course none of Jane Austen's heroines enjoyed it – but they didn't get sexed at all, according to the books. Yet Janik had a very good time, apparently.

He watched as the satiated youth farted and grunted with satisfaction, pulled up his pants, gave a brief laugh and left.

Magda lay sobbing a great deal until she eventually rearranged her garments and, still weeping, made her way back to her room. A puddle of blood stained the hay-strewn ground.

Guido did not enjoy this.

What did it mean? Was this 'love'? Or 'sex?' Or neither?

Could he *ask* Janek? Would he explain? But there was a great deal about the man he didn't like. In his visits to the kitchen, Janek would taunt him and bully him, goading him to use his knife properly when slitting a goat's throat, for example.

Guido realized this was probably jealousy: he was now indisputably Frau Eberhardt's favourite. Easy to tell: she reserved all her best swear-words for him.

Definition??? Perhaps, he thought, this sexlove thing is any activity involving the *schwantz* that isn't peeing. Judging from what he had read so far.

Yet in the books, there was kissing too. He's never kissed anyone, though he did lick stolen ice cream from Filippo Dogface's lips once as he held his friend down on the filthy beach.

For his Mama it meant bread on the table, a mere transaction, just 'work'.

For the Maestro del Coro at the Cathedral it meant a messy snuffling and a stroking, an infuriating abdication of dignity for a very small reward. Sometimes ice cream to take the taste away.

Research required! So he scuttled back to the library. Sex. What happens. How!

Difficult to research for a young man in those days, but faced with those vast walls of books, not impossible.

Research. Research. Obfuscation and part information. Babies happen. Why. How. Sometimes people do sex and babies don't happen. Why. Part information. Body parts.

Body parts.

Gray's Anatomy had an answer and a question.

Confirmed by Da Vinci and Michelangelo

Sobbing his heart out, the boy sat on the library floor until Gramaschi found him there.

'Eh! Guido! What are you doing? It's lesson time! What's the matter?'

'Leave me. Fuckoff Maestro.'

'My little one. What's wrong? What are you reading?'

'Nothing! Nothing! I am reading about nothing!' and Gray's great tome flies across the room and lands, face down, like Icarus would have done had there been an oak floor beneath him when he tumbled out of the air.

'Come, dry your eyes. We have singing to do.' Gramaschi takes him kindly by the upper arm, raises him so that they are face-to-face. 'Are you sick? Tell me. What.'

'If you don't know I'm not going to tell you!' Defiantly.

By the time they got to the Music Room and his lesson, something had gone pop! In Guido's head. He had, in one afternoon, crossed no-man's land

Scene 5 : Schweinstein-bei Oder July 1914

There were summers, of course there were. They intruded themselves arrogantly between the winters like flamboyantly dressed Baroque guests arriving at the palace of Mecklenburg-Vorpommern, laden with gifts. The first of which announced its presence from a high place on the Guardian Oak, the great tree at the edge of the moat. The recently returned wood pigeon, finding a high place in the tree from which she could shout mournfully for a mate, seemed to call to the boy suffocated under loads of books in the dusty library – with its mournful and desperate cry, which only other pigeons and the dead understand. 'Go away! Away. Come here! Here' it means. Now you know too.

Summer meant escape – with the first tentative notes from the miserable bird, Guido would look up in wonder, and note that for the first time in months, must and dust had given way to sunbeams streaming through the window. And today, being a Sunday when the Barone, Hibert and even the dread Henriette Maria would be in the tiny village church of Schweinstein-bei Oder, Guido felt free.

Guido had been excused Church. Two reasons: firstly, he was Catholic and the Baron and his household were Protestants of the Calvinist or Lutheran kind (Gramaschi too was Catholic. He spent Sundays reading and walking in the countryside. He would not work on Sundays); and secondly, the Baron preferred to keep the boy hidden until the time came when he would be ready to show his protégé off to the world as a world-class singing prodigy.

Incidentally, you probably want to know this: the Baron was not religious at heart. His religion was based on his belief that as the *der Schlossherr*, Lord of the Manor, as they would say in English, he would have to set an example. He did not agree with Henriette Maria who referred to Guido as a 'Papist' or the recently converted Hibert who said smugly, 'When he grows up the lad will see the truth.'

Besides, the Baron and Hibert were rather awed by Guido's extensive repertoire of pretty Catholic tunes, learned in the flamboyant Cathedral *de Santa Maria Assunte* in Naples.

*

Nobody near. Nobody to stop him.

He climbed the winding stone staircase to his bedroom. Here in the West Tower he had made the cubicle given to him into his own Cabinet of Curiosities. Here, some of the greatest treasures of the Late Baron Franz shone and gleamed, rescued from their rust and dust in the Library by the boy determined to release their secrets. He could hear the ghosts trapped in the silver singing as he polished the medieval silver spurs from Florence; or the scream as he liberated the sleeping violence of the flintlock pistol that had ended Franz' life, as he lovingly oiled and cleaned the lethal mechanism.

But his greatest treasure of course was the Tanto.

Silently, he went to the small oak table on which lay a bundle in a silk cloth. He bowed, once, hands to his side. Then reverently he unwound his beloved companion from its stifling prison. The *saya* – the black lacquered sheath – felt warm, as if it contained a living creature. A moment to slide the blade from the sheath, his hand as comfortable on the hilt as on a penis, the entrapped golden dragon of the *menuki* writhing on its abrasive rayskin to get free.

The blade skittered in the light of the new summer, winked, was returned to the sheath.

Then, with the knife strapped to his side Guido bounded down the stairs, out to adventure.

This boy needs a dog.

*

Schweinstein-bei Oder is a small ragged village bounded on one side by forest and on the other by the River Oder. Looming above on a rocky crag is the Castle, that crumbling former fortress turned into some kind of residence almost a thousand years ago or possibly more. If the Romans had reached this far East, there would be a strong suspicion that they were in some way responsible for erecting this forbidding edifice near the banks of the Oder as protection against barbarians coming over the river. It's possible. I can't know everything. If this were the Rhine, that would be the natural conclusion.

The only possible invasion in these days could come from what is now Poland across the river. As unlikely as Britain being invaded by the Isle of Man.

The boy sits on a crag, wiping the blood of a wood-pigeon off his Tanto, staring absorbedly into the streets and lanes of the village, laid out like a map before him.

The village church throbbing with devotion, an invisible halo lurking between the building and a wisp of cloud, inaudible hymns bending the air.

The cobbled village square with its grubby leaking fountain. Deserted for once.

Houses decaying into crumbling stone and half-timbered rot, chimney stacks leaning from cracked ties.

Spring flowers spurting. Rebel cornflowers cluster about doorways and intrude into plant pots. Of course there is edelweiss, this is Germany. Chamomile, pretending to be daisies. Spindle flowers on their craggy bushes make a brave attempt to smile at the passionless bees, far too busy harvesting to stop and admire.

'What are you doing here boy?' Guido looks up, startled. It's Janek, the stable boy.

'Nothing.' He says. 'I can't go to church. Why aren't you in church?'

'I said I have a stomach ache.' Janek laughs, sits next to him. 'Good view, eh?'

'Yes,' Guido says. 'Good view.'

'I'm hot,' Janek removes his shirt, lies back, crushes spring flowers, inconveniences ants. His body fascinates Guido. Lithe, muscled, browned. So unlike his own. 'Take your shirt off,' he says.

'Why?'

'It's hot,' Janek says. 'Come on!'

'Why?'

'Oh just take it off!'

Guido is very self-conscious about his body. Somehow he knows that it is not quite normal for a boy his age, even though he has never seen another naked. Already it is ballooning out, his thighs have grown with his waist.

Yet there is something – a mystery. He needs answers to questions.

He removes his shirt.

'Fuck!' Janek stares. 'You've even got tits!'

Embarrassed, Guido reaches for his shirt.

'No, leave that. I like your body.'

'I think I have to go,' Guido says, standing.

Janek snatches at his forearm, pulls him down. 'Just stay with me. Come. Lie down.'

Guido wants to go. But he is almost breathless with a confusion born of curiosity. He wants to know what happens next.

Reluctantly, he resumes his place. He maneuvers his shirt under his back, between him and the deaths of bugs.

The muffled sound of a hymn wanders up the hillside.

Janek is staring at him. An errant hand wanders over Guido's body. Exploring, wondering.

Then 'I think I have to fuck you.' Janek says, decision made. 'Come *liebe* freak. I want to kiss you!'

His head looms over Guido's, mouth approaches.

Guido writhes away but Janek has him by the hair. He is laughing. 'Kiss me freak!'

The scene in the stable. Magda's fear and anger. No, he did not want to experience what would happen next.

Tosca by Puccini. Act 2.

Did you forget the dagger, the lightning-sharp Samurai Tanto? Guido remembered it lying on the grass next to him.

*

Guido is utterly fascinated. He has just killed a man. A boy, really. Still handsome, lithe, Janek has a smile and an erection straining at the half-undone buttons of his flies. Guido undoes the buttons, stares at the penis, plays with it, turns it this way and that. He studies the testicles, holds them in a hand.

He kisses the dead boy on the mouth.

Sits back, stares.

Slices cock and balls off as easily as he slits the neck of a chicken. And throws them, trailing blood in the summer air, toward the church.

He has to decide what emotions to have.

*

Strange thing. Sad thing. No-one missed Janek, except for Frau Eberhardt. 'Where's that kitchen boy! Where's that lazy lanky peabrain?' she moaned, shouted, for a few days, until an exasperated Hibert brought poor demented Elias out of his retirement to do the menials. In a way it was good for him – he had been forgetting to eat quite frequently, and at least Eberhardt shoved food at him in great volumes. When there was food. Everyone assumed that Janek had simply run away, and they suspected they knew why. The rumour was that Magda was bearing his child, so being a rotter, he'd decamped. She had wept out the awful story of her deflowering to Frau Eberhardt, begging her to keep the story to herself. She tried, she did try. But. Such is life.

Janek's mother would have missed him if she wasn't dead. Now there's a story! But no, back to Guido for now. Maybe I will tell you later.

*

Guido's years caught in the stone-cold embrace of the ancient castle would have been lonely and bleak, were it not for the kitchen first and the dog Spitspot second. And for third, have I not explained that Guido, since his Operation, lives inside a castle of his own? I mean the one in his head. Built of stone. Stone cold anger. And sometimes, the dank intrusion of depression. Inside the innermost keep there skulks the prisoner: a frightened little boy, injured, former Captain of the Ragazzi, who once ran free and wild, laughing through the streets of Naples followed by his gang and often by a victim shouting give it back! Stop! Police! Now staring out through the arrow-slits of his fortress.

Guido is the victim of a terrible crime, and I have to think about that. In my time, I made my fortune largely from these mutilated men. How could I do that? I did not understand then. The Castrati I met and worked with were extremely happy people. Except perhaps Farinelli, who was always pursuing women – who once told me he had never coupled with a woman without her experiencing that ecstasy denied to him. I made some Castrati very rich. More rich than I was. They had wonderful lives.

I am musing too much. Guido certainly had a sense and a feeling that he had been badly used. And yet, and yet....what would he be without me?

I forgot to tell you about the dog! Spitspot! The companion, the co-conspirator, the replacement for the entire gang of Ragazzi. This also explains the terrible state of the Castle, throughout most of the War. So here is the story:

1914: DOG DAZED

Guido was not permitted to go into the village of course. Why? How could the Baron have imagined that a young boy full of boy-thoughts, energy, imagination, yearnings could be kept in a stone box?

At first he had a companion, Janek. But then he killed him.

He didn't miss the boy. After all, he had tried to rape Guido, and much as he would have liked to have known what being raped would be like, he had decided against it at the last minute. So Janek died. Just like Scarpia in Tosca. *Ach! Verismo!*

Guido made a monument to him of course. He was reading *The Iliad* at the time, so he decided that Janek should be honoured as a Greek hero. He was a kind of hero. His body had been that of a hero, all sinewy, a kouros at least, not quite Polykleitos.

He did his best to make the monument look ancient. He found a slab of stone (which I, being nearly omniscient, know to have been left on the hillside by the Romans. Guido did not know this) and dragged it to the exact place on the hillside where he had murdered the kitchen boy. Then he fashioned a crude pediment for the top of it made out of twigs and pebbles. Upon the surface, using a sharp flint he scratched the word 'ΠΑΡΕΛΑΒΟΝ', meaning 'received'. Received in Hades like a love letter. He couldn't find the word for rapist.

Today Guido is roaming free. Like me when I was his age, he had developed the ability to disappear. Not to become invisible, which would have been nice, but the capacity to slide through corridors like a ghost when everyone is busy otherways,

His reason: This morning at dawn he was woken to thoomp thoomp. Repeated many times. And he knew that noise meant cannon. Finally! The War had come to Schweinstein and he needed to see it. Up to now it had been miles away to the West and apart from minor shortages of this or that, the war was about other people.

The Baron was away in Vienna. His Tutors were asleep.

He was SO excited! War!

The ripping of bodies and the spatter of blood.

The charge of the cavalry and the cannon's dull thud!

And so he ran, sweating, ran out of the castle, through the Library, past the Guardian Oak, over the rubble-filled ditch which had once been the moat, and scrambled down the hill on which the castle lurked until he reached the monument to Janek, from which he had a panoramic view of the countryside and the village below.

And looking down, there was the corpse of Schweinstein-bei Oder.

Spilled viscera, shattered limbs. The church, roof removed as if swiped aside in fury, the Pastor lying face down on the stone slabs just outside the door, spreadeagled, a wooden cross in his hand..

He realised now how heavy the air was. Thick. Thick with blood-steam, cordite, the silent skeletons of screams.

Fascinated. His eyes scanned what were streets, looking for humans

Only a dog moved far away

Humans seemed to have been erased.

War. So. Very efficient.

He stood, shouldered his knapsack, tramped down the hill.

He had never entered the village before

How silent

This village was his now

The dog approached, whining, dragging behind him a bleeding, amputated bare forearm clutching his lead in a death-clenched fist.

Guido bent to examine

The dog sat on its haunches, looked up

Raised a paw, tapped him on the leg, look what I have here

Guido slipped the tanto from the sheath. I should kill this dog.

They eyed each-other

The dog lifted the dismembered arm in its teeth, deposited it at Guido's feet

What do you want, Spitspot. What am I supposed to do with that?

The dog regarded him quizzically. Then, having received no response to his offer, he settled down to chew at it.

Guido smiled, cut the lead and walked on down the rubble-strewn street. The dogs survive, he thought. And that's why.

The growl and grumble of approaching tanks

This was the bakery this was the village square, nice bread, just some gravel to brush off

He was hungry, sat on the step of the fountain which was bubbling blood and ate

A wrecked woman approached, hobbling, face almost blown away, no eyes

Zu hilfen zu hilfen she said through the hole that had been her mouth

(Mozart! Zauberflotte! Enter pursued by snake!)

'I will help you,' he said, and slit her throat, allowing her to sink gratefully to earth.

*

As he penetrated deeper into the village, more bodies.

Fascinating! The attitudes of death. Here a child all curled up like a snail's shell, no visible wound but certainly dead. The torso of a man wearing an apron – no head, the body registering astonishment. Then a young couple all wound up in each-other's last embrace, spattered with bullets or perhaps shrapnel. Pricks of red all over their bodies, clothes shredded off.

And in the bombed-out buildings, parts of men, women, children poking out of rubble. An arm. A head, mouth moving. Two perfect legs with feet still shoed, elegant, beautiful. Further down the street a horse on its back, legs in the air, stomach blown out. Almost comical.

*

Eventually the tanks were too close, they were entering the streets and Guido climbed back up the hill toward the castle. Looking down he could see that they were Russian tanks, with brigades of foot soldiers following.

He crouched down at the Monument to watch. Eventually the little figure of the small brown raggedy dog came happily up the hill, following him, bearing a large bone.

Impressed yet again, Guido welcomed him. 'Spitspot! Learn your new name you little shit. Come on boy, let's go home.:'

*

The Russian Army had almost destroyed the village casually, as an afterthought, like swatting a fly or slaughtering their imperial family, which they would accomplish in precisely three years. It was in the same spirit that they fired a couple of shells at what they thought to be a ruined castle on the hill.

The shells arrived just before Guido and Spitspot reached the Castle. So boy and dog watched in fascination and delight as an eruption of stone and fire leapt up from the Eastern Tower, and then, oh joy! A shell lands inside the curtain wall, and an eruption ensues, way up into the sky, flame and smoke.

Thrilled, they enter the Caste over the filled-in moat, through the garden windows, into the courtyard. Where what was the kitchen lies in smoking, flaming ruins.

Frau Eberhardt had evidently just left the kitchen carrying a basket of potatoes. Her body had been shattered into gobs of flesh and blood oddly reminiscent of a very large pomegranate squashed by a boot. The potatoes spattered the stone walls like bloody spit gobbets.

Interregnum

Three years pass, the years of the War. Boys kill each other. From the castle they sometimes hear the 'whoom, whoom of distant death. But mostly, the war is far, far away. The Russians come, then go off to have their revolution. Gradually, the village reinhabits itself. Miraculously, some of the houses seem to grow back. The church grows a new roof. The Baron helps with all this as much as he can. Having been abroad during the attack, he feels immensely guilty, as if he could have somehow diverted the shells, turned the Russian Army away had he stayed at the castle. To salve his conscience, he resolves to fix what is broken.

The castle flaunts its wounds. The Baron wants the injuries to his ancestral home to stand proud, like a defrocked cardinal, so he has the eastern tower repaired as it is, grimly replaced with a flat roof. The kitchen is re-established within the main building, its warm heart torn out.

The village boys leave and don't come back. The farms are silent. Old men and women pull at the teats of bored cattle, slit the throats of goats, sheep, and cows to feed the ragged remains of Germany. Now and again, a mother's wail rips the air, mourning the beloved son who was on the wrong side of history.

And the German people, bereft of hope, split into two.
Communists and National Socialists.

Scene 6: Die Jagd

April 1918

These were the starvation years. Even here, at Schloss Schweinstein, suddenly bereft of cook and kitchen – at least at first, food was a rarity. And so that ancient German custom, the Hunt became the key to survival. *Die Jagd*, Schweinstein style.

On a glorious early Spring day when the sun made a promise to one day bring Summer, the Baron gathered a collection of old men, women, castle servants together in the Baronial Hall and addressed them.

'My dear fellow survivors, what heroes have we been! We have fought off the English Empire, the Russians both Red and White, we have fought disease and now we face our greatest enemy: starvation.'

Much as I love this fat nobleman, who looks more like the Burgomeister of some provincial hellhole, he is such a liar. Look at him! He has not suffered even as much as the mice in the skirting boards. Or as much as the carved baronial escutcheon which lurks over the oak castle door like a corpse, dropping grains of sandstone drip-drop every time there is rain. Eventually the Baronial arms will look like a miniature representation of a desert, just dunes.

The suffering the villagers have had to bear is, it is true, great. But the village destruction was four years ago and since then there hasn't been the merest rumour of an army anywhere near the Castle. Yes yes I know. Four years ago when the Russians came Grossmutter was blown up. Klein Schupie was turned from flesh and blood into a simulacrum of an abandoned doll. Pieter Schaumann the Pastor was allowed to imitate Christ at last. Guido did at least get a dog out of it.

Forgive me, I am ashamed of myself for the above paragraph. It was war! War breaks people. I have many wars in my operas – it's because I write so well for trumpet, don't blame me. Blame the librettist. Metastasio. Haym! He loved a good war. Bononcini, the devil.

Who is the Great Librettist in the sky I wonder? Why does he so often write Opera Seria? Listen to my oratorios. The music is glorious, at least!

'…and so my dear friends, we will hunt! The table you see – ' he points to the table in front of him. It is laden with weapons: swords, knives, flintlock pistols and muskets, a priceless wheellock hunting rifle of the seventeenth century (one of only three guns with rifled barrels at the time), some pitchforks and a few black, bleak ancient pikes. 'is for you. Pick a weapon, my friends. And then, out we go! If it has four legs or wings it is meat! Cats and dogs are, of course, to be spared if they look healthy and useful. Or you know the owner.

'Kill kill and kill!' Applause. 'And bring back your kills, put them here on the table and we will gut slice and prepare the meat. Everybody gets meat!'

The remaining Castle staff were recruited to the task of

butchery. In the evenings, the table became laden with flesh and blood and there they sat: under the direction of Hibert - Gramaschi, Magda, Jonas the garden keeper, Elias the too-old-to work kitchen hand, and even Henriette Maria, Her Majesty who loved her arms up to the armpits drenched in blood.

Guido was kept away from all this. The Baron, remember, did not want his protégé to appear in public until he was ready. So every evening the boy sat high up in what had been the Minstrel's Gallery but was now a balcony adorned with gilt-flaking mock Baroque putti. Watching. Watching with utter fascination at the death displayed below him. Blood. Feathers. Skin. Eyes gone blank. While the humans ripped and tore the lifeless flesh. Often the tanto lay next to him, unsated while he experimented with masturbation.

Scene 7: Gramaschi's Dilemma

One day in a meeting with the Baron the threats and his feeling of creeping despair causes Gramaschi finally to erupt with 'But Barone you are paying me all this money to make a perfect boy soprano voice. And then what happens? The voice breaks! This can happen any day. He is approaching fifteen! – It is well overdue!'

The Baron stares at his rebellious minion as a cobra stares at a rat. And then using his fine voice like a blunt knife he says 'His voice will never break signor.'

'What do you mean will never break. Of course it will break!'

'No it will not.'

Gramaschi stares back at the Baron like a rat disbelieving in its own mortality. 'Baron every boy pupil's voice breaks. It is a fact– I will have to retrain the voice whether as tenor, or baritone, or bass, or even I have trained a counter-tenor. I repeat. It is not a problem.'

'His voice will not break.'

Here are the thoughts in that dusty machine of a mind which has for so long been the clanking and grinding engine of the Tutor: *This man is deluded. Perhaps he is living in the Land of Wishful Thinking. I could humour him but on the day the voice breaks he will kick me out. And what will happen to the boy. I will not succeed in explaining the facts of life. I do not know them. But I know more than this man. Who has never had a child. I have never had a child. I wish I had a child. Does he know something about this boy I do not know. I know most things about this boy. I know he is beautiful. And I know he is angry. There are secrets. I must keep this job. It enables me to hide.*

This is what he says: 'Baron you have hired me because you know I am a superior Music teacher. You chose me for the boy.'

'Do not seek to tell me what my motives are. I will tell you this: if you do not succeed in wringing from that throat the most perfect sounds ever to ornament the Opera, you will go. And the Boy goes back to the slums of Naples. *Capisc*?

Suddenly the rat knows the cobra is lethal. These thoughts*: it seems all I can do is delay delay delay. And when the voice breaks, run away.*

'Then I beg you one thing Herr Baron. One boon.'

'You can have anything. If you give me that voice.'

'Then I beg you let me do this in my time. I entreat you leave us to it, that you do not come near, or ask to hear until I say he is ready.'

Storms collect on the noble brow. Then, in a brief clearing of the clouds, 'You have nine months. That is the term for a birth, no? You will give birth to someone ready to be trained for the greatest roles in the Baroque. You will give me a Giulio Cesare. An Alessandro. A Bertarido!'

ACT 2

Scene 1: An Education

Gramaschi now understands his mission. For eight months he works the boy relentlessly. Not just the singing - the breathing exercises, the vocalises, the chromatic scales, the runs, the trills, all the tricks and tickles of the Baroque, but also playing the piano and the harpsichord, musical theory, Opera history and every aspect of composition. He was determined that even if he lacks the voice of a great singer, Guido could always earn a living with music. Should both of their arses hit the gravel outside the front door of the castle, they would at least have that.

And on this cloud-bothered afternoon when birds hide from imminent thunder, master and student face each other in the Music Room. Under the harpsichord, the dog Spitspot contentedly chews at the leg of the venerable instrument. This afternoon is different. This afternoon has never happened before in the history of the world.

*

The sun spatters the Music room through the wide-open French windows, bursting through the cloud, it pixillates on the harpsichord like unfinished pointillisme splashed by a careless giant.

Then, perfectly timed: lightning strikes. Coda! Synchronised with the first chord of *Cara Sposa* (Google. YouTube. You won't regret it!) as it flies from the talons of the maestro and explodes out of the cracked and dying harpsichord, a bolt of lightning smashes into the majesty of the Guardian Oak at the edge of the moat. Fire eats out its heart and sparks in the shattered branches. A great moan as if from the soul of a murdered giant goes up to heaven.

Suddenly from the depths of lungs and throat, shaped by palate, teeth and lips, made of crystal and blood, a sound no nightingale could have imitated, a voice unheard for two hundred years escaped the soul and the heart of the boy and from thence into the once dead heart of the teacher - and broke it.

Cara Sposa, he sang, dear wife, from Handel's Rinaldo. From the first note Guido seemed to have been invaded by the ghost of Farinelli or Senesino. Perhaps it had escaped from the heart of the oak tree in which it had lain imprisoned and jumped into his own. The divine voice soared, curled, soothed, ripped, teasing and cruel, as sharp as slivers of shattered stained glass.

And as he listened with tears in his eyes Gramaschi finally added One and One. One: this incredible voice, this soaring free thing with its lucid clarity and definition, at last viscera-red, shaped by loss and longing. Plus one, the Baron's confident assertion that the voice would never break. Plus another one: the sheer lung capacity of this boy's strangely grotesque growing body. For Guido had begun to put weight onto his hips and thighs, while his head did not seem to grow at the same rate. And there was a picture he had seen, who was it, that, that Senesino...the Baroque superstar, the Castrato. His body was like that.

…the boy had mentioned an operation long ago, shortly after arriving at the castle…

There could be only one explanation.

*

It was as if, once he had climbed to the pinnacle of his profession and his ambition, Gramaschi had jumped off. And while the fall did not kill him it rendered him permanently disabled, scarcely able to imagine anything resembling life without the boy. He had changed from Guido's master to his servant. And until the day he died he regarded Guido as his master and his guide and his light; for whom he would kill or die.

Guido, too, would never be the same. From the depths of his broken soul he had discovered a power, a secret gift, a weapon. He had finally learned to add the heart to the vocal organs. Suddenly he understood that the arias had to be acted as well as sung. Felt, as well as technically perfect. He knew, from his tutor's ecstatic face that all of a sudden he had found an intensity of strength and power which could shake a world.

*

Life in the Castle continued as before, at least on the surface. The singing lessons continued to astonish and delight the Tutor, who was finding it hard not to applaud after each performance

'Signor,' the boy would ask at each lesson, 'When will you let me sing for the Baron? I think I am ready now!'

'The Baron said nine months and that has almost passed. You will then be better than good. You will be great and we will soon have you singing in the most famous Opera houses in the world! Now give me your Cara Sposa again! Again!'

'But Signor! What if my voice breaks before then! I am fifteen. It must happen.' Why did Guido ask this question when he knew the answer.

A bird chirped outside. It was hungry but the need for a mate was greater than mere hunger. The chirp said 'Come to me! Come to me!'

The dry soul of the Maestro was suffused with tears. He hit the keyboard hard, as if the innocent harpsichord was the throat of the Baron, jabbed to shreds by his fingers. 'Sing!'

*

This last month of the gestation passed stuffed with busyness. There were events punctuating the strange routines of Guido's life. Occasional walks with the dog. But mostly breathing exercises, vocalising, learning, preparing.

Scene 2: Four Weeks.

November 1918

Intermezzo

Guido is fifteen. The War is four. Guido's birthday is on the ninth of November. Happy birthday Guido. Yes, Guido is a Scorpio for those of you who are interested in such things. And so is Germany, well modern Germany anyway. Because while Guido's birthday was being celebrated Keiser Wilhelm was abdicating.

The War had not gone well. Convinced initially that Germany would win, this puffed-up animated moustache actually believed that everyone would surrender to the superior German forces and the massive cost of the adventure would be met by an expansion of Germany eastward. The rest of the world did not agree. Doughty Britain. Beaten France and Belgium. The Netherlands. Italy. And once the Americans brought their beer, chewing-gum and amphetamines to the battle front, Germany was doomed.

Defeat after defeat. German troops driven out of their conquered territories. Millions dead. Populations starving, desperate, hopeless.

Angry. Revolutionary.

*

A note is delivered from the Baron to Gramaschi. It is sung by Hibert the butler, mezzo soprano. 'The date for the Concert performance by the boy Guido accompanied by Signor Gramaschi on the harpsichord is to be 9th November at 5pm in the Grand Salon. The programme will be made known to you three days before. Present for the concert will be the honourable Sebastian Amore Geillis, baritone, and a coterie of carefully selected guests under the aegis of our host, Baron Heinrich von Schweinstein. Thank you!'

Four weeks.

Meanwhile the hated lessons with Henriette Maria proceeded alongside the singing. Or more accurately, were interspersed with the music like unwelcome *recitativi secchi*.

A schedule of an intensity designed to leave no space in a growing mind for anything other than what was put into it and wrung out of it. 'The programme will be made known to you – three days before' Three DAYS! Impossible to know every possible aria…they could only guess. The Baron, they knew, loved Handel above all composers. But he could choose almost anything from the thousands of arias composed over two hundred years.

So there were fewer opportunities for exploring the library, or the castle, or meeting any other being except his tutors and the servants. Of course he began to love the singing. It allowed him to climb above himself to a place where, boosted by columns of air he would be impregnable; in control; ecstatically experimenting with timbre and colour and playing joyfully with the given notes, a personal conversation emerging between the singer and the composer, a conversation from which even his tutor was excluded.

How he loved the heroic roles! Especially the Handel heroes! : Alexander, Caesar, Tamburlane, Roderigo, Riccardo (Richard the lionheart) - these powerful macho characters all written for Castrati.

So different with Henriette Maria. This bleak expanse of thought and deed, self-serving at any expense, saw the boy as a tool designed for her own benefit - and at the same time, as a nuisance and an obstacle to her own advancement. As a result their lessons consisted of barrages of facts and challenges, accusations, denials and what we would describe as bullying.

'So I suppose you cannot tell me the basic theory of National Selection as I told you I would ask you? Did you even write it? No! I can see you did nothing since yesterday. You are so lazy!' Yes, she said 'National Selection'. She didn't understand Darwin's theory any better than he did. She assumed it was about the superiority of the white race.

Here she would slap him in his nearest exposed skin, whether a knee, or a forearm or a cheek. Sometimes she would slap him again and again in the same place. Never hard, but the sheer frequency of the blows would mount up into a collection of pain, a stinging which would last for days.

'Such a lazy boy! Now we will play your favourite game: der, die or das!' Which meant she would give a German noun and he would have to give the article, masculine (der) feminine (die) or neuter (das). Of course each time he got it wrong his reward was a slap.

'Freund!'

'Der!'
'Tisch!'
'Das'
Slap!
'Tisch!'
'Die'
'Löffel!'
'Der!'
'Messer'
'Die!'
Slap!
'Messer!'
'Das!
Slap!
'Der der der!'
'*Das!* Idiot!'
'I *said* das!'
"Idiot!' Slap! 'I'll tell you what you said!'

Despite the fact that she was often wrong, Henriette Maria enjoyed this game best of all. It enabled her to dominate this small spoilt creature, so that she could trumpet her brilliance to her employer and use her favourite phrase: 'If it wasn't for me....'. If it wasn't for her, she was convinced, the boy would be nothing. In fact, if it wasn't for her, she was convinced, everything would be nothing.

Guido of course hated this game as much as he hated Henriette Maria's name, her swirled-up greying hair with its pink bow, her fat hands covered in rings, each of which would scratch any boy's hand or cheek they happened to slap.

After a lesson with Henriette Maria Guido would sit in a deep shadow in his tower room. At his feet, Spitspot chewing at some part of the furniture. He was hardly breathing, his whole body still. Sometimes, perhaps I saw a tear in the corner of his eye. Such a lost soul, bruised, as alone in his shadow as a boy can ever be. Perhaps he was thinking, nobody can ever understand. Perhaps he was dreaming of revenge. Perhaps he was in an ecstatic dream of fame? No, I don't think so. Even I don't understand him.

ACT 3

Recitativo

The nine months had flown away like the birds in Keiser's brilliant Croesus. Or the nightingale in the Keats poem, which had been drilled into the uncomprehending head of the boy by his Tutor with a slap at each line.

And today is the Concert. The program had been decided at last by the Baron. And this was it, as it appeared on a flyer distributed to the locals:

The **BARON HEINRICH VON SCHWEINSTEIN** *together with* **HERR SEBASTIAN AMORE GEILIS** *invite you to a* **CONCERT DEBUT** *of the superb* **GUIDO della Roccaporca** *who will sing a selection of* **ARIAS FROM THE BAROQUE** *including:*

Ombra mai fu	*Handel - Serse*
Che farò	*Gluck - Orfeo ed Euridice*
Cara Sposa	*Handel – Rinaldo*
Come Nave	*Porpora – Siface*

accompanied by his renowned Tutor, Sr Gramaschi of Florence and Vienna on the harpsichord.

There will be a selection of free meats, beer and bread for all the guests

Schloss Schweinstein, 9th January 1920 at 5pm

The Baron had selected a selection of some of the greatest arias written in the Baroque period for Castrati. Chosen to display range, flexibility, control, tone, dramatic talent as well.

Guido practised relentlessly in the three days to the Concert..He became the driver. Poor Gramaschi, lost in his adoration for the boy, could only follow orders.

The biggest problem for Guido was the Porpora aria. Madness! Flourishes of fury! With larynx-busting bursts 'Again!' Guido would command. 'But slow down! I know it says allegretto but that's not how I sing it. It's controlled anger of a King, not a peasant raging!'

Which sums it up.

Guido was so deep in his conversation with dead composers, it was as if he and they collaborated on improving each work, primarily to make the aria more dramatically relevant to character and action. Closer, closer, closer to verismo, can the Baroque approach Puccini's vision of verismo, truth?

Scene 3: A Concert

This part of the story is presented as Opera Buffa, or the Comic Opera of the 18th and 19th centuries. Why? Because it is very painful.

The Grand Salon of the Castle was designed by the Gräfin Sophie von Schweinstein in 1743, because her husband who had imported her from Schleswig-Holstein was too busy delighting his favourite stable boy to pay her any attention and she was bored.

It was a fantasy of Rococo magnificence, based on Sophie's vague memory of Versailles from a visit she had made when she was twelve. Hence, this vast space (formerly a dignified medieval hall with oak paneling and a minstrels' gallery) was encrusted with florid gilded plaster curlicues, acanthus and fleur- de lis. Angels of every sort - putti, cherubim, fat babies with wings cavorted everywhere. Frescos painted in gaudy colours by an expensive talentless Italian imported from Ravenna hung gloomily from the suspended ceiling depicting impossibly muscled Greek Gods and Goddesses doing mysterious things in the nude. And of course, there were the mirrors. Expanses of rococo swirled around with gold, the silvered glass spotted with islands of tarnish, the gilt frames flaking like dandruff, all along the walls except for the French Windows which open onto the garden.

Bogus, broken Rococo.

Everything was flaking to some extent. Flaking, cracking, fading, biodegrading, covered in dust and grime.

A podium has been constructed at one end, upon which the tired antique harpsichord with its rattling keys and fading cracked marquetry sits, or rather, leans languidly in readiness. The journey from the Music Room has been rather demanding for this aristocratic antique.

In front of this raised platform five dusty Louis XV armchairs are lined up. Behind them there are lines of battered oak benches for the peasants and villagers. The Baron's program of education for the locals has consisted mainly of quarterly Opera and poetry recitals by himself. Compulsory, of course, for his tenants and servants, who are required to sit on these hard benches, provide ersatz applause when not sufferingin silence.

Enter Gramaschi, L. He is flustered and a little drunk. He carries a bottle which he conceals beneath the raised lid of the harpsichord. The Tutor is not a drinker. However he has decided to make an exception today. Exit L.

Enter the Baron, flustered, followed closely by his Factotum, Hibert (mezzo soprano) Hibert *is* a drinker, and will be making no exceptions whatsoever either today or on any other day. He is delightfully camp, about 70 years old and often very vague indeed. The Baron reluctantly retains him in honour of his late Mother, who adored the man. Hibert had adored her too, and there were rumours that this strange creature was in fact his father. Not entirely unbelievable, as the Baron's putative male parent spent so much time with mistresses in Paris that his infrequent visits to the castle were mostly spent asleep or in a clinic in treatment for syphilis.

Baron: Why only five chairs? Who are the VIP guests?
Hibert: I have no idea darling. You gave me a list. Don't you remember?
Baron: Sebastian and the Frau should be here already are they not? If there are trains. Old David, Madam Henriette Maria, the other tutor. Do we have sufficient benches for the audience?
Hibert: Enough room for hundreds dear. It's good for the boy to face a lot of people. If you want him to be Operatic, to face the Crowned Beards of Europe he needs some practice.
Baron: Well I want one more comfortable chair.
Hibert: Who for? You know how heavy these damned chairs are!
Baron: You know.
Hibert: Why? Yes I know. Der Geist.
Baron: Der Geist.

And so a chair is brought for the Ghost. It is better to ask no questions. Four more chairs are still unoccupied by 7.30 pm, the start time advertised. Missing: Sebastian and Frau Slappmeister, who had made the perilous journey from Vienna the week before through battered Austria and Germany, troop movements allowing - and David, an old friend of the Baron's father. Deaf as a dead dog, David has attended every concert the Baron has hosted as a matter of course. His presence is expected.

Gradually, the peasants filter in. Stern men and women, their best church clothes starched and smart. Mostly older men and women. Mostly terrified that the Baron might be about to recite some poetry.

The Baron beckons his factotum over to him.
Baron: (*Sotto voce*, to Hibert): Where are they, man? That blasted HM

should be here at least!
Hibert: (Whispering behind his gnarled beringed hand) No idea darling. As to that woman, fire her. She thinks much too much of herself!
Baron: (Testily): *You* are the one I should fire! A perfect description of yourself!
Hibert: All right darling, don't get nardy. I'll go and find her for you. (Exit R)

At that moment David arrives, pushed into the room by his equally old and deaf manservant Roger. With a great deal of fuss, he is offloaded into the Louis XV armchair like a sack of potatoes.

Baron: Alive, is he?
Roger: What?
Baron: (loud enough for all to hear) I said, ALIVE IS HE?
The audience of peasants and servants shrink in terror, fearing the poetry recital has begun.

Meanwhile Gramaschi and the boy wait impatiently behind a screen. Spitspot yawns at Guido's heels.

Guido: I need to pee, Maestro.
Gramaschi: You can't go now.
Guido: But I need to go!
Gramaschi: Why didn't you go before?
Guido: I didn't need to go before!

Enter Sebastian accompanied by Frau Slappmeister. He wears the uniform of an Oberstleutnant of the Supply Corps, she wears a ballgown in black leather, which has suffered a great deal in its perilous train journey through the collapse of the Austrian Empire and the imminent defeat of Germany. If I have time I will add it as an addendum at the end of this tale. But first I must find out and describe what happened next.

Sebastian: I cannot apologise enough dear fellow. Exigencies! Complications! Events! Wars! None of it my fault!
Baron: Dammit man, sit down! Cher Madame, I beg be seated. There is still one more to come…

Sebastian: (Seating himself as unobtrusively as he can. Frau Slappmeister sits next to him, between him and the Baron.) Thank you. So where is our prodigy?
Baron: He is ready. We can wait no longer. (Claps his hands imperiously) Maestro! Come!

Enter Gramaschi, who bows to the Baron and the audience which is now bemused. He makes his way somewhat perilously to the harpsichord and arranges his music on the stand. He strikes a stagey chord.

Baron: (Attempting applause. Sporadic, loyal applause follows from the crowd. Frau Slappmeister is clearly thrilled to have been invited to the Baron's castle at last; but the journey was perilous for her. The leather dress was extremely stiff, as was Sebastian most of the time. Being in the same first class compartment as his dominatrix was deeply thrilling for him and he was determined to take the fullest possible advantage of the situation. The *Gnadige Frau*, however, had not been out of Austria since 1910 and was so absorbed in the journey she scarcely gave him time enough to climax.

Sebastian (seating himself): so terribly sorry old fruit. Exigencies! Events!

Baron: Just in time. *Liebste Dame*, please take a seat.

Frau S (whispers): Say please.

Baron: I beg you.

Frau: Again!

Baron: (testily) Not here! Just sit!

Frau S takes an irritated breath and seats herself on the opposite side of the Baron to Sebastian.

Thinking to herself: The Emperor would NEVER treat me this way. The next visit this silly man will lick boots.

Sebastian: So where is he?

Baron: Well, where is he? Where is the boy? Come in, boy!

There is a shuffling sound and an abashed Guido emerges, doing up his flies. He had hoped to take a quick slash against the wall, but the Baron's summons was simply too imperious to refuse. He takes his place beside the harpsichord, where a tired gilded music stand leans, covered in sheet music. Guido is terribly nervous and dying for a pee. Gramaschi is terribly nervous, dying for a drink.

The Baron is just terribly nervous.

Sebastian: Ahhhhhh so at last, five years have flown by! How you have grown boy!

Baron: (growls) mostly sideways

Sebastian: Let me see you! Turn around...yes Baron..yes indeed....indeed! As described I believe.

Baron: I would not mislead you on this.

The Baron stands. A silent groan goes up from the benches.

Baron: my good friends, I welcome you most heartily to what my friend, Maestro Gramaschi here (indicates G whose hand had been wandering to the bottle concealed amongst the keys of his instrument) has assured me will be an evening of unique musical entertainment, not to mention, for some of you, enlightenment! And now (Aria:sings *a capella*)

Ladies and gents I present
For your respective joy
And enlightenment
The greatest secret never told
A boy whose larynx
Of purest gold
Will break
Every heart and make
Your broken dreams attend
To your deepest yearnings until
Mended, you instil
In your dreams

Your fill!

An awkward silence. David looks up from a brief snooze and applauds. Sebastian bravely says Bravo. And whispers, Hardly da capo!

More silence.

(Gramaschi has taken this opportunity to take some deep drafts from his bottle)

Sebastian (Aside): shall we remove his trousers? Just to make sure, you understand?

Baron: (Aside – testily): nothing to see! I will explain. Well boy, you have the program. Amaze us!

Guido is too nervous and uncomfortable to have taken in any of this exchange. But please note: Guido has a mind like a cabinet of curiosities or rather, the room of a compulsive hoarder. Even if something may be of no use whatsoever at the time, he would put it away. Which he did. Shelve it for now, take it out later.

Gramaschi too has taken these words into his dry old skull wherein they rattle around like broken pieces of glass, drawing blood.

His grizzled face like the surface of a fresh croissant flakes, almost cracks. But with a supreme effort he rearranges it so that it resembles that of a human.

Again his fingers plunge down to the keys. The first slow, ponderous notes of Handel's great *Ombra mai fu* flow into the room, as if invading from a country hidden in cloud. The boy suddenly seems electrified, his eyes spark and his body gives a shiver as the divine voice gathers, and then like a river of warm blood washes over the audience stilling their minds and invading their hearts.

The Baron's moist eyes are staring at the Geist's chair. The dead man concerned is the late Rudolf Grossmeister. For the Baron could never listen to, or play any Baroque aria without the face of his dead tutor appearing before his eyes. He would have been so proud! The boy Guido would have made him so happy! The Baron who had no pitch at all had always disappointed the man who had to be content with developing his pupil's ability to play the piano and the harpsichord to a rather bumbling amateur level. Grossmeister had surrendered all attempts to make a musician of his charge and had decided instead to make him a connoisseur, a *musicant*, an appreciative audience. And all the Baron had ever wanted to do for this old man was to make him happy. This evening, he would have been so proud.

It was Grossmeister who had found the body of Baron Franz

von Schweinstein, our Baron's father, the flintlock pistol from his antiques collection in his fingers and his face reduced to blood and pulp. This is the same pistol Guido so loves to clean and oil.

The song ceases.

Silence.

Even the benches have no idea what has just happened to them. Sebastian is sweating as if inflicted with a sudden ague. The Baron is frozen into his memories. Frau Slappmeister is immobile and expressionless. David responds to the end of the song with a heartfelt snore.

Finally, Sebastian applauds and the Benches, realising what is required of them, follow suit.

Gramaschi is pleased.

Gramaschi: Well thank you. That was Handel, and now we give you Gluck from the famous *Orfeo* in which the hero is lamenting his dead lover. *Che faro!*

Again, heart and soul combine in this incredible voice. Before the stunned audience this strange shaped boy-man laments as if he is a mythical magician of music crying out for his dead lover, his heart displayed raw. And as the aria reaches its climax his face is streaked with tears which in this light look exactly like blood

The Baron's face, too, has tears like blood. The Baron, cast by the voice and the song back to when he was twelve years old and stood before the four poster bed of his mother, his face smothered in tears. He can see his mother's dead white plaster face as if she is here, in this room. He can see the draped bed, the threadbare tapestries on the wall, the fluttering smoking gaslight, the silent women, the gap where his father should have been.

His mother had represented a refuge for him. She seemed to expect nothing from her son apart from the occasional bony hug and his presence at her rare convenience. Provided he remained silent. And in her sanctuary, the Sewing Room, he had found solace lying on the window seat with a book while she pretended to embroider, often accompanied by her huge gossipy friend Greta, who chatted and chatted and seemed not to care if she was heard or believed. Her stories were always lurid – ticklish scandals, mostly, in which crops were sold to the Turks for three times their value, or the Virgin Mary visited a neighboring castle – what a cheek - or villagers raped Cossacks.

Like a wart on the face of a much loved old hag, the sewing

room clung to an outer wall of the castle. Held there by projections of rotting oak beams, it had supplied a sequestered and safe place for the Castle's women for five hundred years. The only males who ever set foot there were its builders and the occasional boy child, and so generations of the castle's women had loved this place. As did the Grafin, until the very moment when a mild gust of wind dislodged the last remnants of the rotting oak beams supporting the edifice, pitching it and the whole room along with Greta, two porcine friends and the none-too lissome Countess herself into the dried up bed of the moat and to their dusty deaths. It was said by the Butler and others in the know that while the Sewing Room could take five normal sized humans quite safely, Greta plus four would taunt any oak beams to surrender, even if they weren't rotten.

And so it was that Orfeo's lament conjured up that sweet dead face and the Baron wept again, his childhood washing like a spring tide against the sea wall of his crumbling sanity.

Sebastian: Bravo! Yes actually not bad. Perhaps a little more legato.

The benches, realising applause is expected, respond.

Gramaschi: And now for this man wants his wife so bad, so a letter for a wife, called *Cara Sposa* by Handel, which means dear wife.

David is deep into his dream. He is ninety years old, and he has been on the fringe of death for the last ten years, but the actual flight of soul from body had not yet happened. Largely because it needed an excuse to leave. It was not enough, in David's case to say, well he died of old age. That would be a spurious and superficial reason for the translation of his flesh to maggotry.

His dream was what sustained him. Inside that noble edifice of bone and scant flesh there was a world in which David was a potentate in a palace filled with colour and light, where people with three-dimensional histories in time and space live and love and laugh. Here in this country of his mind he has a beautiful young wife, Griselda, who he adores and whose constant infidelities he is always desperately trying to subvert.

The dream weather is superb. Sunshine penetrates the walls of the Palace. In the fields below the cattle are so contented, their bellows and moos in divine harmony. At his side on the chaise-longue his beautiful Griselda reclines, open as a cracked oyster, her gown is chiffon and silk and lace, and she is gloriously drunk. His hand gently explores the glorious mounds of her perfect body and he can feel himself growing ponderously erect as she playfully teases and laughs.

'She is going to kill you tonight' someone is whispering. A shadow, whispering.

'Nonsense nonsense go away'

'She is going to kill you tonight!

Sorrow suffuses the echoing chamber of this mind, drapes the palace walls in black and red. Now he knows it is true.

He sighs. His dream says, 'perhaps that would be best...'

The music disappears into a vacuum in which even the gasps of the benches are still. There is no breathing in that vast room. The mirrors reflect nothing at all.

Until Sebastian, roused by the scratch scratch of a dog nibbling at the leg of the harpsichord, starts the applause.

Sebastian: Bravo little fellow. Not bad. (Aside, directed at the Baron) But watch that *vibrato*. Just a tiny bit melodramatic.

Sebastian alone of all there in the hall has remained above and beyond the power of the voice. He has been listening keenly, deeply critically, thoughtfully and cynically analyzing every note.

Sebastian's voice penetrates the Baron's emotional defences, bringing him back into this room to stare in near disbelief at the face of his friend. Could it be he did not feel the passion? Admittedly Sebastian is not a man to admit defeat. Is it possible that he is not swayed by emotions, any emotions? Perhaps. Were his tears in Tosca, or Cavalleria Rusticana, or Aida real or feigned, because tears were expected of him and needed in order to prove the superiority of Verismo to the Baroque?

The Baron feels the castle lurch, like a ship on a nearly still sea experiences a wave. He holds on to the arms of his chair. In an attempt to steady himself he visualizes the stone. The stone beneath the threadbare Aubusson carpet. The stone behind the flaking gilt-framed mirrors. The stone above the cracked plaster ceiling.

Gramaschi: And now we are coming to the final song in this short concert of Masters of the Baroque. And this is the most difficult of them all for my pupil Guido. I beg you listen carefully, he will amaze you. This is *Come Nave* by Porpora. (You MUST Google or YouTube this one! It is madness. Purest madness. Like Porpora...Cecilia Bartoli's version is closest to how Guido sang it. Just not as good.)

How correct you are, Maestro, the Baron thinks. Here is my final test for the boy. This aria is a drunken ship in the pelt of a storm, the helmsman with his feet on fire. This aria has driven men and women mad, at one performance a princess leapt over the balcony at the Vienna opera…if Sebastian fails to be moved I will have to kill him.

Gramaschi bashes the poor old keys of the poor old harpsichord again, which, loyal instrument that it is, yields up the last scraps of its soul. As its metal talons pluck at the ragged strings, barbed antique sounds from the great mind of the great Neapolitan rip like jagged knives, tear into Frau Slappmeister. It is as if each key stroke bares her – slices at her leather dress, lines of blood following each stroke and then, when the Boy begins to sing, she leaps to her feet in ecstatic agony

Writhing with each tortured note. Then, as the second stanza erupts from Guido's throat,

Basterà per tuo conforto
L'amor mio nella procella;

She tears at her clothes- opening the dress at her throat and snatching at the buttons of the blouse

La tua guida, la tua stella,
Il tuo porto egli sarà.

Her breasts burst from the pulled-down blouse, her long nails rip into her own flesh

And then it is over and Slappmeister howls, bereft, ripped apart, destroyed.

Silence.

The harpsichord gives up the ghost as its leg collapses, almost skewering a terrified Spitspot, whose chewings considerably contributed to the demise of that once noble instrument. Gramaschi's bottle spews onto the floor, turning like a Catherine wheel spraying fire.

Slappmeister: You! (Pulls up blouse and buttons dress). You MUST visit me in Vienna! (mock flirtatiously – but it's an order) You make sure Herr Baron, ja?

Silence.

Tableau Vivant

The Baron sits as if mummified.

Sebastian is silent, stunned and embarrassed by Slappmeister's behavior.

Guido is immobile standing at the corpse of the harpsichord. He has pissed himself. There is a yellow pond below his left leg on the Aubusson.

Gramaschi's head has descended to the keyboard. He is dead drunk, though not dead.

David is rigid on his chair, straight as a board. His erection protrudes like a tent pole.

From the benches, the peasants stare. Some are bemused beyond endurance. Some think of dinner.

Slappmeister is wholly unaware that her behavior was in any way extraordinary and has sunken back into her immobile self

Enter Hibert, L. He is very flustered, he looks as if beetles have colonised his underwear. He observes the tableau for a moment, trying to decide how to proceed. Coming at last to a decision, he goes up to the Baron and whispers.

David's manservant Roger enters R and examines his charge.

Hibert: (Stage whisper) Dear! You must prepare for some bad news!
Baron: (Shakes himself into awareness) What? What on Earth? What do you want!
Hibert: We have had a telegram. From your cousin in Berlin.
TRIO
Baron: Not now!
Hibert: But – the War is over.
Baron: The War?
Hibert: (is there an element of triumph in his voice?) Germany is defeated.
Baron: Defeated?
Hibert: And also, another news. The woman. The tutoress. The one you call HM. Henpecky Maria.
Baron: Yes what! Where is she?
Hibert: She is *dead*, Herr Dear. Dead! I found her! Blood galore! Deluxe!
Baron: (Shouts) Dead??? She is dead? His voice slurs.

Roger: Yes! No need to shout! He is dead!
Baron: Who?
Roger: (Points to David) Him!
Hibert: Her!
Baron: Germany!
Roger: (Arguing) Him!
Hibert: (Arguing) Her!
Roger: (Arguing) Him!
Hibert: (Arguing) Her!
Baron: Germany!
All: Him/Her/Him/Her et seq
Sebastian snatches the telegram from the bemused Butler's hand. 'Liebe Gott! I have to get to Bonn straight away!' Probably to burn documents. Quick hand-shake with the Baron and a 'We will discuss this after!' Off he goes, in as close to a panic as I have ever seen him. The Baron attempts to stand, perhaps to protest, or bid farewell. But he is unable to stand, for he has suffered a stroke. Hibert sees this right away. 'My dear!!!' he shouts. 'My dear!!!'

CURTAIN

ACT 4

Amongst the best-known clichés on the subject of Opera, next to 'it's only over when the fat lady sings' is the deathless phrase, 'Everybody dies.' Let's face it, in so many operas all the best people die at the end. But this is a comparatively modern innovation. In the Baroque operas, Apollo arrives in a glorious gilded flying phaeton and rescues the hero or heroine. Or everybody forgives everybody, and they get married. But in most of Verismo (Puccini, Leoncavallo and Mascagni especially) the lovers die to big fat chords and cadenzas, the audience applauds to the rafters and leaves with a severe case of PTSD.

Real life of course is different. In the case of this concert several people did succeed in leaving alive and there were in fact only two known human fatalities plus the harpsichord. The Baron himself was a casualty; the stroke eventually affected his speech, so that he could only slur. His right side too, was partly paralysed. So, in those other immortal words so beloved of novelists, he 'took to his bed.'

As to the peasants on the benches, I didn't check. I presume they survived. Millions didn't outside the Castle walls..

David's death was put down to Old Age. Obviously no-one knew that Griselda did for him in a dream. Guido blamed himself. The boy was gradually coming to the conclusion that his voice could be lethal. And that made him proud. Gramaschi was coming to the same conclusion. He knew that every time he accompanied the boy, he felt as if something precious inside him had been bruised, injured, slashed. And day-by day his strength depleted. He was being drained. It was his sacrifice to the magnificent tragedy of his incredible pupil.

Henriette Maria's death was not as easy to explain. She had certainly been murdered; a knife had pared and sliced her. She was found in her tiny room with its stifling perfumes, dusty books, canes of different sizes, jars of unguents and sticky makeup.

The only clue to anything at all was a letter.

Dear Henriette Maria

Now you know how much love I have for you. That everything you have ever done for me is appreciated beyond appreciation. That your spirit and your beauty has no rival and there is no release for me unless you die tonight.

Always yours

Q

Naturally, every effort was made to identify this 'Q'. The local police, led by the redoubtable Kaptain Schenky resolved to interview everybody with a Q in their names. And because no-one had a Q in their name, he left the scene of the crime without a single idea as to the murderer.

A week later the maid Magda was found hanging in her tiny, dusty little room. Naturally all assumed that she was the mysterious Q and could only guess at the full story.

ACT 5

Scene 1: Midnight.

A dented Hispano Suiza bounces and slides its way down a rutted lane. There are three people in this ship of the road. The chauffeur, or he would prefer to be called, the driviste, is our old friend Hibert, major domo of the Castle of the von Schweinsteins. On the back seat, buffeted by the freezing wind, Guido is curled uncomfortably under the arm of his tutor as the car breasts waves of road like a speedboat through an arctic storm.

Behind the car a terrified, bereft mongrel, half Jack Russel, bounds over the snow, yelping, Where are you going!!! Take me!!! Take me!!!

Sleet whizzes into their faces like the spit of ice gods. Each has a suitcase clutched on a lap, containing all that was permitted to accompany them from their last eight years in the Castle.

Hibert's voice floats back at them in gobs. 'Go! Leave! You won't break my darling! You rubbish! You Leave! You Go!' Repeated in variations the whole way to the fog-and sleet bound railway station where at last this terrifying sleigh ride slides into a wall with a bang, and Hibert leaps out to whip the door open and almost pull the passengers out by the scruffs of their necks. 'You go! You leave! You run away! I warned him! Now look what you've done! You go'

At which he leaps back into the driver's seat and with great difficulty reverses the injured vehicle from the wall. Shivering in the driving sleet, Master and pupil watch the car accelerate out of their lives and they trudge into the deserted station.

Guido: Where shall we go Maestro?

Gramaschi: (Sighs) I have an idea. Capodimonte! He was with me at the Conservatorio di San Pietro a Majella in Naples.

Guido: I'm not going there!

Gramaschi: No no. We are going to Berne in Switz. I had this letter. Capodimonte is directing in Berne. There is a perfect part for you.

Guido: A part? A part!

Gramaschi: A small one. A start.

Guido: (Claps)

Gramaschi: We will have to change your name…

Guido: But I like being Guido von Schweinstein! Will I not be *Adel* any more?

Gramaschi: You were never noble!....I have it. Translation. From now on, you are Guido della Roccaporco! That's the translation. You have been translated!

Coda.

A sad after note. Hibert, on his way back to the castle did not even notice as the wheels of the vehicle clumped over the desperate Spitspot, rendering him flat in the muddy snow and as dead as a dead dog. Guido hadn't even noticed the car was being pursued by his companion of the last four years, as he was well ensconced in the armpit of his tutor and the roar and rattle of the vehicle was loud. Add to that the swirl of the sleet and forgive him.

Did he think of his former friend now and then? Yes, now and then. But perhaps he assumed the dog was being looked after by someone at the Castle.

Scene 2 : The Berne Opera House, backstage

A group of young boys, all about fifteen, sit or stand pale-faced, accompanied by parents or singing teachers. They are auditioning for the role of the Shepherd Boy in Puccini's Tosca. Most are terrified.

One-by one they are called forth to sing for a row of steel-faced men and women, who occupy the fifth row of the stalls. In the middle of Row 1 sits the Director, Alfredo Capadimonte. He wears a ridiculous Tuscan feathered hat and a velvet suit. He has obviously researched 'Opera Director stereotype' and decided to conform to the limit.

'NEXT!' A thin blond boy shaking like a leaf staggers onto the stage and sings a third of Ave Maria.

'NEXT!'

Guido and Gramaschi huddle in a corner, waiting for Guido's turn. They both look gaunt and hungry. Gaunt and hungry is the only excuse they may have for auditioning for a bit part is this most *Verismo* of operas, this melodramatic feast of raw emotions in which the shepherd's solo at the beginning of Act 3 brings relief between the intensity of Acts 2 and 3.

Guido: I'm tired Maestro.

Gramaschi: I know you are.

Guido: I don't want to do this.

Gramaschi: Think of the money.

Guido: I am thinking of it. These are such provincials Maestro. They wouldn't know a great voice if they heard Caruso.

Gramaschi: Yes true. Or Farinelli.

Guido: Farinelli never went through this. Everything was easy for him, then.

'NEXT!'

Gramaschi: Ah! But your talent my boy, your talent will take you all the way. You will be as famous as he was. Just do this audition. Who knows where it will lead?

'NEXT! Mr Gramaschi! Bring this famous boy! Where are you!

Guido stands up and walks to the apron of the stage.

Guido: I will sing *Cara Sposa* for you.

And then, a capella, Cara sposa. Dear wife. At the start, perhaps a little wavery. Then Guido's eye falls on poor innocent Signor Capodimonte, and he knows that this man is his. This strange creature could shape his future. So his eyes seek his, fall in, and the aria becomes a duet between the two souls.

Poor Signor Capodimonte! He is like a mouse at the mercy of a snake.

Poor Capodimonte! Where there was once a heart there is now an empty throne.

[Deh! Ritorna,] a' pianti miei. (2)
Del vostro Erebo sull'ara
Colla face del mio sdegno
Io vi sfido o spirti rei!.

And in the emptiness of a life lived at the edge of belief, at the very edge of disappointment, there flashes a tiny spark of hope.

As always, whenever Guido has revealed his *Cara Sposa* to anyone, eternity gasps.

In the silence, a shiver of disbelief.

Capidimonte: (recovering) boy! Sing something else. Sing another one!

Guido: can my teacher accompany me? On the piano?

Capo: Yes yes play! Sing!

So maestro and pupil like performing monkeys unroll their repertoire.

Che faro

Gasp

Capo: Another one! Boy! Sing! Man play! The rest of you go. Fuckoff!

Intermezzo:
Garibalderdash!

Alfredo Capodimonte came from a family considered amongst the aristocrats of the Opera in Italy. As producers directors and managers at the Teatro alla Scala in Milan, at the Opera di Roma and the arena di Verona they had been amongst the most famous of their day for at least three generations. Capidimontes it was who first saw the genius of Raimondi and Gigli, who launched the careers of Mascagni and going further back, Bonaventura.

So now we must take you back nearly fifty years, to around 1880. Carlo Capodimonte (Alfredo's father) was one of the most successful Opera directors ever, and was in constant demand to direct operas at the greatest Opera house of them all, La Scala in Milan. Known to all as Da Capo, his successes were legendary; his production of Aida and *Ballo in Maschera* won screams of approbation from audiences and critics alike. He was feted by all and could do no wrong.

But then, disaster.

Signor Giacomo Calvi was a banker in Milan whose love of the Opera was expressed in his frequent visits to La Scala and his extraordinarily generous gifts to that institution. As a major donor he was given full access to every area including backstage where one day he met Capodimonte and confessed his dark secret: Garibaldi. His Magnum Opus. A Grand Opera in four acts. The obsession of almost twenty years, which he had kept hidden from everybody, even his piggy wife. (His original decision to concentrate on composing an Opera, by the way, was a response to her constant miserable persistent nagging. Usually for sex, an activity he detested. He was safe behind the locked door of his study.) Until today! Because at last he had finished it. Which was why, filled with the thrill of creation, he sought out the greatest director of the day.

'Yes of course Signor!' Said the Capo. 'I will look at the score and give you an opinion. But I warn you: if it is rubbish I will say so!'

Of course it was rubbish. It was ordure. It was melodramatic romantic shit of the worst sort. The plot was laughable: Garibaldi takes time off from uniting Italy to fall in love with a maid in the palace of the King of Naples but she is secretly his daughter and is in love with a handsome knight who is in love with...and so on. The usual Baroque Opera tosh. At least so many of those are made divine by wonderful music! In Calvi's case, sadly not. To make things worse, he was determined to 'revolutionise' the orchestra by the replacement of the entire string section with saxophones, the only instrument he could play. When the Capo read the score, he cringed in terror at every note.

Most unfortunately, before he was to meet Calvi to tell him what he thought, he met Vicenzo Dragi,, the Chairman of the Board at La Scala. Brimming with deviltry and delight, he began to tell this august gentleman about this Monster. 'You would not believe how bad it is!' He said. 'Everything! From libretto to score to orchestration…'

'It isn't.'

'Pardon?'

'Signor listen to me. This Opera is *not* terrible.'

'You have seen the score?'

'No.'

'Then how can you - ? '

'Signor Calvi keeps this Opera House from total collapse.'

'Collapse????' Capodimonte's gaping mouth could have admitted an entire gilded sky chariot with Apollo in charge.

His brain churned as his mind boiled. In his mind's eye he saw the grand lifestyle of Signor Dragi – the carriages, the mistresses, the houses in Paris, Vienna and Prague. Not just Dragi – the entire Directorial Board seemed to see it as a duty, and a reflection of the success of the Opera house to live lifestyles of extreme luxury and even debauchery. They also paid him very generously as if he was expected to do the same. So out of respect for his employers he wasn't slow to take on a vast array of mistresses, and indulge in some gambling too. In his mind's eye he saw the frequently full houses, the lines of people desperate to see the hugely elaborate productions La Scala was famous for. And in his mind's eye he saw liras, liras flowing out of the cornucopia that was the generosity of men like Calvi.

Largely into the pockets of men like Dragi.

For the first time in his life he met the Real World, and quite frankly he didn't like it.

'……Signor Dragi, what must I do?' He asked, desperately.

'Listen to me. You will tell Signor Calvi his score is brilliant, but of course will need some changes and fixing. You will offer to find a wonderful composer to do this. It will take a long time.'

'Yes.'

'A very long time. Years perhaps.'

'I see.'

'And then you will tell him how hard it will be to get wonderful performers of genius who are good enough to take on this work of genius,

'Yes.'

'And then, to mount such a production, to design such a production, to rehearse this – genius – work… do you get my point?'

'Will take years.'

'Exactly.'

'Years. I will tell him.'

'And then we will see which comes first: the production or his sad demise.'

'Brilliant Signor!'

'And if that doesn't work we will have him killed. No doubt La Scala features prominently in his will.' He laughed.

Capodimonte laughed nervously.

'And you don't worry dear Carlo. Whatever happens, I will take the blame. Ok?'

And so, filled with righteous apprehension, Capodimonte went off to see Calvi.

'Well?' said Calvi. 'I hope you can see the genius in my work?'

'Without a doubt Signore. The concept is very – high. The plot is very – original. The music is certainly different….'

'Different?'

'The saxophones. Very - unique'.'

'Exactly!'?'

'Indeed Signore. I believe – '

'It will cause a stir.'

'Oh, it will that!' Capodimonte said, 'It will that!'

'Good. I propose you get me a cast, arrange a date with the Opera, begin rehearsals! I am very excited!'

'Certainly Signore, we will do that. There are a few changes and edits I will need to make to the score – '

'What! You will not touch one note!'

Capodimonte shrugged. 'It is usual for a Direktor to make some changes, adapt to the production – '

'You will make not ONE single change. I have worked for twenty years on this score. Every line, every nuance, every note has taken my sweat and tears. This Opera will be produced and directed and seen precisely as it appears in my head, in my dreams.'

' – Signore – '

'I have even decided the cast!'

'The cast…'

'And soon. Very soon. You will tell Vicenzo.. The work will debut this season. Within six months!.'

'SIX MONTHS!'

'I don't care what Vicenzo has programmed.. The public do not need another bloody Puccini nonsense. Or stupid Verdi with camels. They want history, patriotism, exciting modern music. And they want it now. Understand?'

And so the legendary production of the Grand Opera Garibaldi by Giacomo Calvi came together like a modern motorway pileup. The lead roles were sung by hideously overweight aging stars, some of them retired, because Calvi had idolized them in his youth – and had 'always' visualized these has-been stars in his Magnum Opus. The sets were hastily and horribly assembled. Rehearsals were continually disrupted by Signor Calvi who invariably sat in the stalls with his saxophone, always ready to adapt, correct and guide the singing or the playing by what Capodimonte came to call contemptuously The Orgastra.

Incidentally, three mysterious attempts to assassinate Calvi took place during those six months – each one frustrated by the wall of armed men allocated to him by his bank. These men accompanied him everywhere he went. In rehearsals they would applaud every aria, almost every note of what they delightedly called Garry Boldy.

By the time the premiere finally happened, the Opera House was packed to the rooftiles. The press had built up a fervor – 'The Great Capodimonte's Thrilling New Discovery!' 'Banker banks on Capodimonte!' 'La Scala Banks on Banker and Da Capo!'

The curtain opened, and from then on the stage of La Scala became one of the most famous Natural Disasters in history. It eclipsed the eruption of Vesuvius. It made Noah's Flood look like a mere dribble of sputum from the lips of a child. And as you would certainly have predicted, Capodimonte's career was destroyed for life.

Is it necessary to describe the fury and hatred the La Scala *loggionisti*, the hooligans who lurk in every corner of the upper circle and the gods, directed at the stage? Not just imprecations and boos, but tomatoes and on the second night (there was a second night at the insistence of Calvi, who was convinced that the premiere had been hijacked by his enemies from a rival bank) the stage was pelted by dead ratsten minutes into Act One. The aged divas and fat tenors fled in terror and refused point-blank to return to the stage.

So what about the vaunted support the Chairman of the Board

had so generously promised poor Da Capo? Alas, that venerable gentleman died of syphilis, alcohol and opium two months after the discussion with Capodimonte. And as for Calvi, well he went home, shot his piggy wife (he had wanted to do that for twenty years) and then himself.

Carlo Capodimonte went off to found a company producing porcelain and pretty figurines and eventually made some money out of it. He never set foot in an Opera house again. It must have been devastating for him when his only son Alfredo went off to Naples to study Opera.

Scene 2: Berne

Back to our story, February1920.
It was Carlo Capodimonte's son Alfredo who now sat in the first row of the stalls at the Berne Opera House, ears straining for the ghostly echoes of the applause that had followed all his father's productions before the Calvi catastrophe. And watching as a magic boy made magic sounds like bells.

This was not believable. From the mouth of this beautiful, strange creature, came Handel as Capodimonte has always heard him in his head. Gluck as he always should have sounded. Graun, sung by a divine. Bach, in the dreams of the composer.

Capo: Enough! Stop! (Stares up at the boy on the stage. Stares up. Shakes himself. Shrugs. Makes a decision. Cancels the decision. Makes it again. To Gramaschi:) Your pupil, no?

Gramaschi: Yes he is.

Capo: He sounds just like I imagine a Castrato!

Guido: Ask *me*! Yes I am.

Gramaschi is overcome with surprise and shock.

Guido: (Turning accusingly to Gramaschi) So *why* didn't *you* tell me?

Gramaschi: Tell you?

Guido: That I am Castrato?

Gramaschi: When did you realize?

Guido: For heaven's sake Maestro, years ago! Look at me! Why did you treat me as if I was stupid?

Gramaschi: (Groans) Oh my poor boy

Guido: There is a book in that great library of his, it's called 'Gray's Anatomy.' There are many books in that library, also books on

Opera – many! Books on the Baroque - all Renaissance art! it did not take much research to find out why –

Gramaschi: Oh my poor boy

Guido: Where my voice comes from, why I have no body hair, why my voice didn't break…and *WHY*!

Guido is almost in tears. He is filled with frustrated anger, held back, suppressed for years since he had started to research into his condition.

Guido: Why they did THIS to me! Did they ask me??? – !

Gramaschi: If they didn't you wouldn't be here. You would still be in your slum Guido. Stealing apples.

Suddenly Guido stares straight ahead. All expression removed.

Lots of dramatic music here, perhaps even a cadenza. Or perhaps that is too melodramatic.

Capo: Are you finished your conversation? I could see straight away. I have never met a real Castrato before. I have read about. I have seen pictures. Now I hear you, and I see you, there is no other explanation. So you want to sing in this Opera? Puccini huh?

Guido: Yes please.

Capo: Why? With that voice, you go join a church choir, you sing Messiah all day and all night. They would love you

Guido: I want to sing Opera. I can act. I know all the Baroque –

Capo: *ALL* the Baroque?

Gramaschi: I taught him. He knows everything. He plays harpsichord, piano. He composes. He is a genius.

Capo: Enough! Both of you go away. Go sit in dressing room 16. You wait for me. I must finish auditions. NEXT! Spoletta!

Berne Opera House was also the *Stadtteater*Berne, also its Masonic Lodge, and its venue for dozens of provincial pleasures from concerts to amateur dramatics. The building itself is a *fin de siècle* extravagance, the entrepreneurial experiment of Hans Breir, the millinery millionaire. During its construction, however, Brier went bankrupt. His dream of being host to the Moulin Rouge troupe, of being in the front row with a privileged view right up those skirts where his favourite concatenation of legs and torso met, was dashed.

For twenty years the theatre sat there in the centre of this pompous little city like a deflated hot air balloon, gently degrading into its component parts. Until at last the new Mayor, Magister Hubris, decided that now the War was over it would be rather good for his legacy if he could squeeze a couple of million marks out of his Orphanage Fund for the greater glory of his city and himself. So at last the interior was decorated, seats were installed and the place opened for business with a grand performance of *Le Vent de Folie*, with the outrageous Josephine Baker of the Folies Bergere, star of the Ziegfield Follies, the 'Sensation of Paris'.

Scandal erupted! The influx into this *haute bourgeois* utterly strait-laced city of Mademoiselle Baker and her retinue of self-described 'Pansies', drag queens and other rather 'artistic' persons may have delighted the Mayor and his Companion Derek, but it horrified almost everybody else. According to all the local newspapers, the Ladies' Circle, the Masons, and the Church the production '...brought the City into great disrepute!' And '...caused *outrage* and distress to every decent, right-thinking citizen of our noble city.' And 'Such shock and horror has not been experienced in Berne since the Socialist Internationale!'

And so he began to realize that the only way to retrieve his reputation and retain his position as Mayor would be to move into the holy realm of Culture. And so he hired Alfredo Capodimonte, who was a rising young director in Naples to transform the image of his beloved city by bringing Opera to the place.

Tosca by Puccini was to be the launch of Berne as a city of culture and its theatre as an Opera House. This emotional cataclysm and hurricane of an Opera, always hugely successful although not terribly well-known in this part of Switzerland, was the obvious choice. According to Capodimonte, anyway.

For Alfredo Capodimonte, this was his chance to revive the family name and overcome its shame.

Entr'acte

Everyone has a backstory, dear reader and try as I might I find it so hard not to tell you everything. All of us are as we are as a result of what we have been. And also as a result of what our parents have been. And their parents before them. And of course this applies to everyone all concerned have ever met. And everyone those people have ever met and so on in ever radiating concentric circles. And once you factor in unexpected events like hurricanes and buses running over Aunty Annie, you have the whole of reality summed up in a paragraph! All for the measly price of this book.

As for the young Capodimonte, rebel, hellraiser, cynic, empty of heart and full of head - had life been a perfect symmetry of well-matched shapes each fitting cosily into the other - as naively suggested in the paragraph above - Alfredo would have run away to Naples because being a teenage rebel he loved Opera and music, because his father Carlo no longer did. In defiance of his father he would have applied for and been accepted by the Conservatorio di San Pietro a Majella in Naples, for the famous course in Opera production. Perhaps his father was furious when he discovered this. He would have fought with his father and run away from home just as I did. Maybe his mother sent him money to pay for the school and his maintenance.

As a typical carousing drunken student on Naples's back streets he could have met and had sex with - perhaps even fallen in love with - Guido's mother. Which would explain in some way the electric shock, almost, when Luigi found himself faced with the magic Castrato that was or was not his son, on the stage of the Berne Opera. Or perhaps it was just that voice. That killing voice.

I don't know. I present it merely as an intriguing possibility.

Scene 3: *Io de sospiri*

Dressing room 16, Berne Opera

Enter Guido, dressed as a shepherd, followed by Gramaschi. Guido has just performed. He is elated, flushed with triumph.

Guido: My God did you see that! They loved me!

Gramaschi: Yes they did. (Closes the door, reaches for a bottle in his bag)

Guido: Did you like it old man? Are you proud of me?

Gramaschi: Proud of you! (Drinks)

Guido: see! My debut! Even these provincial nobodies, never seen an Opera in their lives! Bankers politicians shopkeepers! They could see!

Gramaschi: (does not mention that Berne is after all the capital of Switzerland; that many of the people in the audience are sophisticated cosmopolitan business people, politicians and lovers of culture who no doubt would have visited Opera houses all over the place) (he wouldn't dare.) yes! Of course they can hear the quality!

Guido (Aside): Perhaps I don't actually care what you think old man any more.

The door bursts open. Enter Capodimonte, furious.

Capo: ...so you listen to me: don't you EVER do that again! How DARE you humiliate me!

Capo is puce with fury. He shakes, he spits, he writhes

Giulio: (hurt. Surprised) I sang it! I sang it beautifully!

Capo: *Maladetto*! Madman! The *shepherd* you were singing! The gucking SHEPHERD! Not Tosca. Not Cavaradossi. You are a BIT PART. You do not stand in front of an audience and act like you are the lead, like you are the star. And then come out and bow and again bow!

Giulio: But they loved my aria! They clapped me more than even *Vissi d' Arte*! That Tosca she can't sing. I could do it better.

Capo: Damn it boy! (Slaps Giulio across the face) If I wanted you to be a woman - if I wanted a soprano I will say! I am the Maestro here!

Giudo (furious): You hit me! I don't believe! You hit me! Come Signor Gramaschi! We are leaving! I cannot work with this man!

Capo: Yes fine you go! You leave me after the opening night with no shepherd! Fine!

Gramaschi stands reluctantly. Since we saw him last he has shrunk in stature and his confidence has left him. He has become a servile creature, Guido is his god, and alcohol is his constant companion. His function is to carry bags, play the piano, carry the money and take abuse.

As for Guido, he has grown physically into a strange misshapen man. Where he once had an eerie beauty and even allure, he now has a growing contempt for his fellow man. Inside him is an as yet not fully formed sense of grievance. His chest and shoulders have expanded quite out of proportion to his head and his legs. His hair is overlong, black and shiny but it looks unkempt, framing his angelic face and flopping around it like a sentient yet demented collection of living beings. His stark blue eyes still beam out from the darkness of his face, utterly disturbing all who dare to face him. A conversation or confrontation with Guido starts with a metaphorical disrobing.

Gramaschi: but! But..

Exit Capo in a huff.
Guido: (turns savagely on his tutor.) What but, idiot?
Gramaschi: All right all right! We have no money. We have nowhere to stay. I am sorry!

Guido: (punches the door hard. Then, suddenly, as if nothing has happened. Calmly): Yes, no money. Nowhere to stay.
Gramaschi: (anxiously) So what do we do?
Guido: Let me think.
The role-reversal is very poignant here. Whereas before the Tutor made all the decisions, now he seems to have ceded all responsibility to the pupil.
Guido: We will apologise.
Gramaschi: But – he has slapped you. He has insulted you.
Guido: So? And in what way does that inconvenience us? As much as having nowhere to sleep and no money?
Gramaschi: (Pretending to consider this. But he has had a great deal of experience, recently of the extent to which his former pupil adapts to circumstances. Sometimes he thinks Guido has no emotions – they are all pretense) Yes –
Guido: I will go to him.
Here Guido disappears into the maze of backstage at the Berne Opera, seeking the Director. As he seeks him here, seeks him there, we hear the soul-wrenching music and singing of the final act of Puccini's melodramatic masterpiece. The wracking thrump of the drums as the firing squad on stage line up to pretend to shoot the hero Cavaradossi. Then the Wakkkk! Of the muskets. Tosca's hoarse admiration, as she compliments her lover on how well he pretended to die…
Thrumppp thrumppp
And her horror as she realizes the bullets were real! The soldiers swarming up the steps to arrest her…
And then her scream of *'O Scarpia! Avanti a Dio!'* as she throws herself off the battlements and goes flomp! Onto the mattress next to the questing Guido. And bounces up! And down! And up! To the scarcely muted delight of the audience…
This is true. I was there. I saw it.
Perhaps the stage crew, sick of the Diva's rudeness, had replaced the mattress with a trampoline?

Curtain.

Curtain calls. The cast troops out in a line, first the minor roles, some applause, then the major roles, applause and cat-calls. The conductor does his bow, orchestra takes theirs. Guido stays behind the curtain, waiting for Capodimonte who, as Direktor has joined the cast onstage and taken a bow. Guido knows that if he goes onstage, the audience will probably give him a standing ovation.

There is no call for an encore. The dejected cast trudge back to their dressing-rooms, their costumes feeling like a clump of wet rag, make-up like drying plaster-of Paris.

'Maestro!' Guido pulls at Capo's sleeve.

'Boy! Why were you not on the curtain call?'

'I was ashamed Maestro.'

Capo stops dead. 'Ashamed? You told me you sang better than Tosca!'

'Maestro – ' Guido feels he cannot use the honorific too often – 'I am ashamed I was rude to you. I apologise.'

'You apologise??? Incredible. I understand. You have nowhere to go and no money. You want to keep your role.'

Guido fakes a self-deprecating chuckle. 'Yes Maestro.'

'Very well. But NEVER do that again! Or I will make you sing Tosca!'

ACT 6

Introduction and *mise en scene*

Poor Europe. Sometimes it takes a slap across the face to make a man take control of his fate, to wake up to reality, to regain his pride. Of course the war was far worse for Germany than a slap in the face; more like a kick in the balls, followed by a removal of the head (the Keiser) and the amputation of an arm or two. (The reparations.) And yet the German people were not easy to destroy, or even dishearten. Everywhere industry and trade began to pick itself up dust itself off and start all over again, in the words of a song that came quite a bit later.

As far as Opera was concerned, the Baroque era was not a favourite for performance in the post War period, as I have said before. This was an era of operetta, of Strauss, of Wagner, of Verdi, Puccini and eventually Rimsky-Korsakov and Stravinsky, and horror of horrors, the atonal monstrosities of Schoenberg and Alban Berg.

Except in a few corners of the world where some misguided dreamers had a fantasy of frock coats and crinolines, of lace and swords and bustles and even Castrati…and here is where I have to do what novelists do: lie a lot. But be sure, gentle reader, I lie in order to protect the feelings of those still living who will remember the characters I need to lie about. It is not something I enjoy doing.

But then Karl Federich Arshlock was an idiot.

Or that, at least was what his parents thought, his neighbours thought, and all his friends agreed. 'Feddy', as they called him, was crazy about music. He was certainly a Wagnerian character – not Siegried, as it happens, but Alberich the Dwarf. Four foot eight inches tall when fully grown, slightly hunched, with a big nose (which later he followed across the oceans to America where he wouldn't be called 'that Jewish Dwarf from Wagner') (to his face) In fact his enemies called him Alby, because they knew how much it infuriated him. Particularly since he hated the music of Wagner.

Growing up in the stifling world of a University town we'll call Fohlingen for now, Feddy (we like him so we'll use that name) was incredibly fortunate in having the opportunity to play his clarinet in the University orchestra from the age of twelve. There are several reasons for this. Firstly, blame his father who would do anything to get him out of the house and sent him off for a variety of lessons and activities. Poor Feddy had to try out fencing, horse riding, mountain climbing, football, boxing, any sport or activity which would 'make a man of him.' He made valiant attempts at mastering each of these, at least for the first ten minutes. After which he would come home, go to bed and snore loudly enough to cause his professor father nightmares. It was his father's contention that it was Feddy's constant farting as well as the snoring that made it impossible for him to complete his research into Eugenics.

Eventually it was his mother who suggested the clarinet. Her best friend Liesl's pasty son Peter had been learning this instrument with Herr Hassler for a year and seemed quite taken with it. And so Feddy was dispatched to the Hassler house, a case containing a Boosey and Hawkes clarinet borrowed from Liesl's Peter in his sweaty hand, one claustrophobically sweltering day in August.

As soon as the good Herr Hassler's door was opened to him, Feddy was in love. No, reader, not with the teacher, but with the daughter.

Gertrude was her name. She too was rather Wagnerian. Of the

stereotypically blond, stereotypically pigtailed, and fairly non-stereotypically exceedingly myopic type. In fact she wore glasses which were as thick as jam-jar bottoms and just as useful. As was she. When she opened that door, she was 12, a year older than our hero, and let's face it, half as smart and twice as fat. Her 'Ja?' was for Feddy an arrow straight from Cupid to the heart.

What made it worse was the fact that the beauteous Gertrude sat in on every lesson, obviously infatuated with her own father and determined to do anything and everything to delight him. Which made the naïve pupil believe, with every self-deceiving bone in his funny little body, that her passion was for him and him alone. Even when she would bring Papa tea and offer him none; even when she would stroke Papa's face as he tootled earnestly and not his; even when she would coquettishly plead for Papa to explain what her picture book showed right in the middle of an arpeggio which he, Feddy, was trying to master. He took his comfort from her determination to sing along with his attempts to delight the ghosts of Mozart and Weber as flirting with him, when it was her daddy she loved and desperately wanted to impress with her rather beautiful singing.

And so Feddy continued his lessons week after week. Eventually his surprised mother found herself buying Feddy his very own clarinet.

There was of course a fly in this very happy soup. The Professor.

Imagine the horrible squeals of a clarinet in the hands of an eleven-year old desperately trying to make an embouchure, the right tension of lips and mouth in order to produce the purity of the notes of which that instrument is capable. Imagine the terrible effect of those squeals as he attempted to climb the scales, like a demented rodent suffering from the extremes of rat poison ascending and descending a stairway made from barbed wire. Imagine the Professor in his study, fingers poised over the keys of his dusty Underwood typewriter, face distorted in a rictus fury as his latest theory on the ascendancy of the Aryan race was shrieked into ridicule by his misshapen son.

'Out! Out! Get this *verrukte* child out of the house!' His head exeunted the door as if on an extendable neck, his mouth spouting the closest things to imprecations a professor of Sociological Anthropology in mid-Germany in the early part of the twentieth century could possibly sputter.

So Magdalena, the saintly mother of the put-upon child, ushered him out of the house and down to the garden to infuriate the neighbours instead.

Strange to tell: within a year the boy had all but mastered the instrument. In fact his little fingers flew about the keys like fluttering butterfly wings, yet each finger landed precisely and exactly where, with perfect embouchure, the rounded soul of the music lived and breathed. To the extent that admiring neighbours would gather on the other side of the fence in all weathers to marvel at the Andante from Mozart's Clarinet Concerto, 'Played by an angel!' As Frau Heimlich would raptly intone.

Feddy was thrilled to discover that the dots and dashes and curly symbols on the pages of scores sang in his head. He could so easily hear the page - at first, when reading the notations for a single instrument; then duets, trios, quartets, quintets, sextets, septets, octets and then (are there novtets and dectets?) whole orchestrations.. With singers too!

His tutor was so impressed at the progress of this marvel that on days when he was indisposed or unwilling or too lazy to play the boy would take his place in the orchestra. This was (eventually) with the delighted agreement of Herr Meizel the Direktor, who much preferred the presence of a twelve-year old prodigy on the third clarinet than the often drunk Herr Hassler.

It wasn't long before Feddy decided that the clarinet was simply not enough for him and with the aid of various members of the orchestra, mastered first the flute, then the harp and eventually the keyboards too which seemed a minor challenge. Piano, harpsichord, organ. So simple, just press the ivory, no embouchure required. The strings presented a far more complicated set of problems – but Feddy was a prodigy and a genius and had decided that whatever Mozart could do, he could do better.

By the age of eighteen he was conducting the orchestra. Well, the death of Herr Meizels from a severe case of Old Age (he was 90, and had been suffering from Old Age for at least sixty years) had left a considerable gap in the town's cultural life. He had been a much beloved if eccentric landmark there for practically ever. And Feddy seemed to slot into conducting the Orchestra as naturally as a prince succeeds a king. Herr Meizel had been inordinately fond of the strangely-shaped young man and had taken intense delight in his accomplishments, encouraging him in his musical explorations, arranging for lessons in all the different instruments, and giving him his first lessons in conducting the orchestra.

There were those in the audience, and amongst the good citizens of the town, who referred to Feddy cruelly as 'Meizel's monkey'. There is an explanation for this as you would have seen had you witnessed how proudly the ancient man would show off his protégé. 'See what he can do!' The Dirigent would boast, 'Can you imagine! He plays, he sings, he even conducts! Watch!' And they would watch, out of love for this wizened stick of a crumpled Conductor, this always delighted sparkle-eyed giant. Even though they often laughed behind his back it was always with the deepest affection.

And so Feddy became the natural inheritor of the title of Dirigent, even though it took the Burgermeister and the Chancellor of the University and the Faculty five years to award the title. As soon as they realized that the title 'Dirigent Pro Tem' was somewhat redundant, as the entire Orchestra loved their Affe, (pron '*ufffuh*') as they called him. This being German for Monkey.

I forgot to mention why they finally gave him the permanent title.

Much as Feddy loved the music and example of Mozart, he loved Handel more. But even more than Handel, his adoration and heart and soul and his very body was riven with love for the daughter of Herr Hassler, the divine Gertrude.

Poor Gertrude! As the years went by, the rather tubby pigtailed girl developed into an utterly beautiful young woman. The freckled pinkness vanished from her cheeks to be replaced by a serene shade of adorable. Her breasts, which once had the promise of fecund plumminess had developed into perfect melons. Her shape…I can best describe the transformation as from stereotypical Wagnerian proportions to sylph-like Pre-Raphaelite. And annoyingly enough, to add to this perfection, her singing voice can best be described as Approaching Bel Canto Heaven. At least as far as Feddy was concerned.

What had not quite kept up with the wonderful development of her body was, sadly, her mind. Poor Gertrude…the whole academic community would always attach the adjective to the name. Nowadays we would call her educationally subnormal, perhaps. Or the more ignorant would simply call her Stupid. There can be no doubt that many made fun of her, and there were rumours that several of the less moral amongst the young men of the environs took advantage of her gullibility and her longing for affection. Her father was often far too drunk to take proper care of her and this was indeed a source of scandal. And had not the gallant Feddy decided to take somewhat of a role *in loco ebrios parentis*, no doubt the scandal would have become unmanageable.

Scene 1: A Woodland Glade.

An oaken bower, dominated by a large tree under which a baby grand piano luxuriates, its keys a grin in the mouth of an old friend. Beneath the tree, Feddy and Gertrude sit on a blanket, the remains of a picnic scattered about them.

Gertrude: (Somewhat petulant, but playful at the same time) You said there would be wine. I like wine.

Feddy: Your father said you must not drink.

Gertrude: But *he* drinks! Sometime he gives me little sips.

Feddy: Yes I know but I don't like you to drink. You are never to drink. I won't have it when we are married.

Gertrude: Are we getting married?

Feddy: I forgot to tell you. I asked your father yesterday. He said, 'yes please'.

Gertrude: But Feddy, I want to marry someone handsome, like a prince or a soldier.

Feddy: You know I love you. That should be enough.

Gertrude: Yes but how will I know if I love you? Why do you love me?

Feddy: Ever since I was twelve I loved you Gertrude.

Gertrude: But which parts of me do you love Feddy?

Feddy: don't be difficult!

Gertrude: But liebling, tell your little Gerty-Werty. Is it my pert little lips?

Feddy: Yes of course. Those are...very nice.

Gertrude: (playful, teasing. This scene must be played in the spirit of Bottom and the Fairy Queen in Midsummer Night's Dream or Papageno and Papagena in Magic Flute. Because that is the painfully cutesy way Gertrude's small mind works.) (And Feddy is not stupid. He knows damn well if he wants the girl he has to play her like a violin.) And what about my delicious little botsies? (Pushing her tits up with her hands - almost into his face)

Feddy: (Pulls back) they are both very lovely

Gertrude: You are very sweet to me. Though you are a very little man. I would still rather you were Hans! He has such a big -

Feddy: Gertrude you can be so...
Gertrude:...beautiful! I know! So what else do you like about me?
Feddy: Well there's your -
Gertrude: My what, little man?
Feddy: Your -
Gertrude: I know! Stop pretending! It's my voice!
Feddy: (groans)
Gertrude: It's my voice you love! (Sings an arpeggio)
Feddy: (groans) Very nice
Gertrude: (sings) *Where the bee sucks there suck I!* (Buries her face briefly in his crotch) *In a cowslip's bell I lie....(*drapes herself coquettishly about him) you love it when I sing!
Feddy: you have a beautiful voice but (tries to snatch at her head in order to bring it to his crotch again. She writhes free, holding on to her glasses and laughing at him)
Gertrude: Naughty naughty little Feddy! (Leaps up and does a little dance around him)
Feddy: Come back! Come sit here! By me!
Gertrude: (pouting) Naughty! ((Sings – from Handel's Semele. Pun available.) *Where ere you walk/Cool gales shall fan the spade/ trees where you spit* - (Giggles!) Silly boy! What are the words?
Feddy: Ahhhh the divine Handel....
Gertrude: Don't interrupt (sings the second verse with dreadful guesses at the lyrics which she has quite forgotten*) Shall crowd into a glade/ a glay ay ay ay ayde/ where ere you Fed* (giggles)
Feddy: Yes I love your voice
Gertrude; Oh Feddy! (Strokes his head) If you really loved me you would let me sing with the Orchestra.
Feddy: But my dearest...you know you don't always remember the words…
Gertrude: I do, I do! I know all the words! Say you believe me!
Feddy: (Groans) Sometimes…
Gertrude: If you let me sing with the Orchestra I may even...(buries her head for a moment in his crotch) Marry you!
Feddy: Marry me…
Gertrude: I promise!
Feddy: (Grabs her by the head and forces it gleefully toward his crotch. Speedy curtain.)
And so, as often happens in the best Opera Buffo, the hero and the heroine win their heart's joy at a critical cost. In this case Gertrude

surrendered both Hans and Franz in favour of the ugly big-nosed dwarf who could give her what she most desired: a stage, an orchestra, and an adoring public, including, of course, Daddy in the front row. And Feddy, on the other hand, gained not just a wife but an entire Opera.

It seemed like the obvious thing to do. An Opera! To combine the divine singing voice of his adored new wife with his profound love of the music of Handel and the Orchestra - which he had by now moulded into his perfect machine for the making of heavenly sounds. An Opera.- and he would send a message out for a really excellent cast. None but the best to support his Diva!

*

It is too much of a coincidence that Feddy chose Rodelinda. After all, this was probably the result of this letter:

Dear Direktor
It has come to my attention that you are considering a revival of Handel Opera at your University.

As a devoted fan of Handel, I would urge you to consider the excellent Opera Rodelinda. It is one of my favourites, and you will find it very easy to stage, as it requires a small orchestra, a small cast and simple staging.

Of course it is essential to cast the role of Bertarido very carefully. You will need a wonderful voice, a very special voice.

Should you decide to take my advice, I will instruct my bankers to provide for you the sum of 5.000 Marks in order to at least partly cover your costs.

Yours sincerely
Fr M

MEANWHILE...

Like the viruses in my eye which slowly gathered themselves into the illness that filled my lungs and probably killed me, our characters in this grand Opera are coalescing and ultimately there will be eruptions! The winds will blow! Cymbals will clash! Trumpets will sound! The King shall return to his throne! But not yet.

While your attention has been transfixed by me in the middle of Germany, Guido and Gramaschi, along with their new companion Sr

Capodimonte, have completed the run of Tosca at Berne. The notices were lukewarm and downright sniffy for cast and production but not, I assure you for the Shepherd Boy in Act 3.

The Berne Blattet, for example: 'While it was a difficult experience for this reviewer to watch this bunch of fat people screaming at each other in Italian, there were sublime moments. Two in particular: the hilarious resurrection of the heroine at the end which had the audience in fits of laughter as, straight after her melodramatic dive from the battlements of the Castel' Sant Angelo, she bounced straight back up as a result of a faulty mattress; and the genuinely beautiful shepherd boy's haunting song at the beginning of act 3 by Guido della Roccaporca. This boy (or girl?) will go far. ' And so, sad as it may seem, Mayor Opus decided for the moment at least to stop Opera productions at the Opera House and invite the Moulin Rouge back in. Which meant that Sr Capodimonte's ass hit the pavement after only six performances. As did that of Sr Gramaschi and of course that of our hero Guido Del' Roccaporca .

Fortunately for this trio of travelling Operatic minstrels, Sr Capo had heard that somewhere in the middle of Germany, in a minor university town, there was a Musical Direktor in search of a cast for a Handel Opera….

Because for some reason, he had received this:

Handel Hits the Headlines!

Grand Opera comes to Fohlingen

Seldom has our small town been in such a fever. Our young Direktor of the University Orchestra Herr Arschlock has announced that one of Herr Handel's greatest operas, the Rodel Hinder, will be performed in August this year at the Konzerthalle of the University. The excitement in the University and the town is mounting, and only a few people are shouting out, so why not perform the Messiah as did the dearly beloved and much missed Herr, the former Direktor of the orchestra? Why indeed. As they say, everybody loves the Messiah. But such is life.

Scene 2: On a Train

(Train music) Choochoo. Steam blurring the world through windows grimed by fingers, cheeks, tears. Through twenties Germany, broken here and there but mostly there. This is a grimy war-blown country, very brown, still dejected by defeat but the determination to rebuild is stirring. Factories, houses. Green and pleasant lands, smudged by the steam from the engine. Small stations mired in grime and partings. Churches off in distant valleys, the sharp needles of their steeples ripping holes in the sky.

In a compartment a trio of hope and despair. A sweating fattish man, foppishly dressed in his bizarre twenties' Film Director pastiche, a tweed dogtooth jacket, plus-fours and blow me down, I swear puttees. Capodimonte. Opposite him sits the remains of Gramaschi, whose self-esteem and self-confidence have long fled, leaving ta leafless stick from a dead tree, swaying perilously in the wind. And stuck at the window, a boy with a beautiful face and a bizarrely misshapen barrel for a body. Guido, eyes glued to Germany.

It would seem that almost by default Capodimonte was sliding day-by day into the role of Guido's Manager and agent. Gramaschi's role in this had shrunken to next to nothing.

It was a long and complicated train journey from Berne to Fohlingen in 1920. Nowadays, a direct train takes six hours. This is a journey of desperate hope because the trio have little money. If this gamble doesn't work, any more train tickets will bankrupt them.

Gramaschi is already dead, all but physically. His last schnapps bottle has drip-fed itself through the layers of what was once a scintillating mind and dissolved what was so awash with music, a cornucopia of delicious crotchets and quavers and minims swirling in patterns of delight. Leaving only echoes. Across the width of the railway compartment sits the boy he had nurtured, trained, cosseted, loved. That beautiful creature which had now morphed from butterfly into caterpillar, a creature with complete competence in survival. Needing him not at all.

And there sits Guido's new mentor - more manager than mentor perhaps. Ridiculous creature made of pomposity and arrogance.

What is left of the teacher stands, mutters something about toilet and goes outside. Shortly thereafter, Guido follows.

*

I am tempted to say that he echoed Captain Oates' 'I may be some time' but he didn't. He would have if he'd thought of it.

*

Three set out, two arrived. Capodimonte must have wondered what had happened to this spectral creature who had come from Castle Otranto to create the most wonderful voice of the twentieth century. Who had worked his heart out to educate the boy in music, who had spent his nights awake and his days in fear lest his creation should be less than astonishing. He had made magic. But after merely displaying some irritation that the man wasn't there at their destination, he forgot about it.

Guido hardly thought about it at all.

Perhaps I should tell you a story now. It's just that I'm feeling really sad about him right now and will miss him.

A VICTORY FOR VITTORIO

The son of an indentured farm labourer in a tiny town (or overgrown village) called Andrea del' Morto in the district of Groparello in Toscania, Alberto Silvestri grew up in the knowledge that he was massively different from everyone he knew. Except perhaps his father. Certainly in looks. Papa was the most handsome man in the village, probably the province. Perfectly muscled, 6 foot, the embodiment (despite the voluminous moustache) of tall dark and lovesome.

Papa Vittorio Silvestri, farm labourer as he was, was also an accomplished violinist as well as the official Lothario of the district. His violin was the instrument of his passion, the tool which opened the bedroom doors of at least 40% of the lonely, the bereft, the man-hungry, the dreamers.

Mind you his other tool was also famous amongst those in the know. Behind his back, those who knew called him Donkey Delight.

As he grew older, rumours of his daddy's dalliances began to penetrate into Alberto's world of beasts and fields and bees. Of course, most of the rumours were wrong. Way wrong. Way, way wrong.

Mama in the other hand was a dumpy woman in black. Stereotypically shrewish in the way Italian mamas can be, she was the type whose setting was perpetually on autopilot mama mode. Like a black-clad machine she cooked cleaned complained gossiped shouted at her husband and was addicted to very large carrots which she seldom ate.

The match was not one made in heaven, for sure. Rather it was made in the taverna, the result of a despairing conversation between two fathers regarding the apparent lack of interest their son/daughter seemed to have in pairing up and making babies. It seemed like a good idea to put them together, even at the point of a stiletto.

They had sex, didn't enjoy it. Worth a try. And abracadabra, a son. Like magic!

Mama and Papa hardly ever talked amongst themselves when Alberto was around (he was an only child, much spoiled and fussed over) but often at night when father came in drunk, his violin serenading his tottering arrival, he would hear her shrieking at him, he would hear her parade of insults, imprecations, always ending in tears. And the next day, nothing. Papa would be off to the fields at dawn. Mama would make the boy a quick breakfast, then usher him fussily to Signora Castri's house, where this formidable philanthropist widow taught reading, writing and music to twelve of the farm children. The Signora was a creature of the Enlightenment - an intellectual, a lover of classical music and books. Secretly an atheist. Well, she had to attend church on Sundays by law but managed somehow to avoid Confession. Her presence was good enough for the gossipy villagers.

She taught little Alberto to read and love music. He was singing at the piano with the other 11 and playing as well. He learned violin from papa who did not read music but had a fantastic ear. But above all this was where he received the virus, the bacterial infection, the obsession that is Opera. Which reached a crescendo (apologies) when, in front of a confused and bemused group of villagers in the Church Hall, her students presented Purcell's Dido and Aeneas (in Italian!) with Signora accompanying on the piano and Papa Silvestri on the violin, junior in the role of Dido. Well, his voice hadn't broken yet and he was quite a pretty little boy.

For his father this was the greatest night of his life. Not only was his son performing in front of the whole village, but seeing him in full drag! He was SO proud!

I forgot to mention - Vittorio's lovers were predominantly male. I cannot convey the depth of the scandal this could have caused in rural Italy in the nineteenth century.

A powder keg with a fuse.

Vittorio's 'regulars' comprised a select list of men in the local area. Including the village priest and even the Bishop. Let's face it, homosexuality has always been rampant in Italy. It's one of those phenomena which is common knowledge but never spoken about. And should it ever be brought out into the open, several of the shits would be hit by fans. Not that I consider them shits, it's just a pun I enjoy. And so many of the shits would be in clerical garb. Not that they are shits, just hypocrites.

It was the best evening in Junior Silvestri's life too. For once, papa was happy, Mama was happy because Papa was happy, Junior was happy because he'd just starred in an Opera and because papa was happy and mama was happy.

Everybody sing 'Happy We' from my Opera Acis and Galatea! (Certainly now you really should go to YouTube. Time to stop reading and start singing.)

Louder!

It was the last happy day for the Silvestri family for ever.

It was only a matter of time before eventually Vittorio's carefree lifestyle would catch up with him. And her. And him too. And Giovanni, the Bishop of Inferno. And Pietro, the Parish Priest of Andrea Del Morto. I will not divulge surnames without payment.

And the battle it turns out, was for the heart, soul and pert bottom of little Alberto Silvestri.

Ahhhh poor little Alberto. For in the audience that evening for the first performance of Dido and Aeneas, the Bishop sat in the front row as an honoured guest. And he fell hopelessly in love with the beautiful Dido.

As a client of Vittorio Silvestri, he took his opportunity to interrogate the man in the cosy comfort of their holy bed about the delicious fifteen-year old youth who had so prettily taken the role of the leading lady.

'Your son, she is very pretty,' said the Bishop.

'Ahh your Holiness, you are too kind!'

'Nearly as pretty as you, my handsome prince.'

'How sweet you are Holiness.'

As polite as he seemed, Vittorio felt panic and despair rising in him. What a terrible mistake to have invited this pompous queen of the priestly classes, this predator, this cynical twirler of lorgnettes, this bovine obese cleric who possessed neither caution nor any moral consciousness, this thigh-driven thief of youth and, frankly, anything in trousers that could be persuaded, bought or stolen for what he called the privilege of his bedchamber. His catchphrase was 'if you never try you never get', and so he never stopped trying. He lived in the conviction that while every man was not homosexual, there were none who wouldn't try it in the right circumstances. With him.

Alas Vittorio. The last thing he wanted was for his son to have to follow his path. In a secret corner of his heart there was a golden-framed picture of his son in the future as a great Opera star or conductor or violinist, adored by all of Italy and tremendously rich. Of course attached to this picture was one of himself in the magnificent villa supplied by his adoring son, a handsome or beautiful loving sex-creature at his side. Mama did not feature in this fantasy at all.

'*Caro*,' the Bishop playfully tweaked Vittorio's nipple, '*Caro*, you will bring him to visit me, no?'

'Ah Monsignor!' (The Bishop always insisted on his title, even in bed) 'I would love to. But it's impossible.'

'For you? Nothing is impossible.' He applied his bull's teeth to the nipple and nipped.

'Ow! Monsignore, no I would do anything for you, you know that. But the Mama is always watching. She has eyes like a vulture. She never lets him out of her sight. Just imagine what would happen if she knew – '

'You had better not be threatening me *carissimo*.' He leaned over, bit the other nipple. 'Because if you do…' he stretched himself across the vast bushy mound and valley of Vittorio's chest and stomach and nipped a testicle. 'Why, I'll have your balls for breakfast!'

'Ow!'

'And your cock for sausage!'

Look away now, because this part is a little graphic.

Music please.

The Bishop emerges, takes a breath. 'You bring me the pretty boy, yes?'

'Monsignore, I cannot!'

'You are making me angry now!' He rears upward, his walrus-like flubbery body looming over his victim, quite cutting out the light from the candle. 'Making me angry is a biiiiig mistake. You know that.'

Vittorio is genuinely frightened now. He knows that between them there is a contract of mutual benefit which goes, if you screw me, I screw you. Literally and figuratively. Well, being pedantic, just figuratively. There is also the contract of mutual fear – which goes, you expose me, I expose you. Literally and figuratively, for sure. The Bishop would have most to lose. In theory, anyway. But I am sure you know that what they would have regarded as sexual perversion permeated the Church then, as now. Homosexual practices were ingrained in the seminaries, and at every level up to and including the Vatican. Hypocrisy was everywhere, as it is now. Choir boys, for example, as well as boys in the Catholic schools, were considered appropriate targets for predation. And if there ever was a scandal the establishment would rapidly hush it up, perhaps with a reprimand and the promise of many Hail Marys.

Then, as now.

To be expected when you insist that men burdened with balls should be officially forbidden from enjoying their function? All kinds of results, including pedophiles regarding the church as a safe place from which to prey upon their victims.

The Bishop could feel perfectly secure, really. His hunger for young male flesh, his predations, his conquests were regarded by many in the ranks above him in the Church as merely mildly annoyingly charming.

Whereas the poor local dick-puller could be easily disposed of if he represented a threat. He could be silenced with money. Or his tongue pulled out and dumped in a pond. Easily arranged. And the Church, as you know, is everywhere, so there is no escape.

Vittorio knew that he had made the biggest mistake of his life. The last thing he wanted was for his only son to become the plaything of this monster. He decided to resort to pleas.

'I beg you Monsignor…he is too young. He is so innocent!'

'*Innocente son io!*' the Bishop joked. 'So am I, my little farm boy. You are very pretty and you have made something very pretty. And did you know it would be just for me? Oh you tease me!' This with twirling the curly hairs on Vittorio's chest around two fingers and pulling.

'Ow. Monsignor, you know I would do anything for you - !'

'This is such a small thing, caro mio. Such a very small little pretty little *putto*. A cherub, I ask of you. Dido herself, I will make your little cherub rich, happy, he will swim around me, like the little fishes of Tiberius, he will be so happy. And so shall you!'

Here he takes Vittorio's earlobe and pulls his mouth closer to his own toadlike orifice, which had been responsible for the ingestion of anything ingestible which came anywhere near this gargantuan monster. 'I will give you whatever you want. He will move in here with me! He will have everything. The best education, food, money, whatever you want. And for you and his Mama, a hundred lira a month.'

Vittorio pulls away in horror.

'Five hundred.'

Vittorio stands, ready to grab his trousers and run.

'A thousand.'

Vittorio hesitates.

'Five thousand. That's it! You get no more! Five thousand, you can buy a mansion! Never work again! My pretty Papa, what do you say?'

Vittorio feels as if his foot has been caught in a mantrap and the gamekeeper is asking him if he wants it cut off.

'Yes', he mutters.

'Louder, my lovely. I need to remember this moment!'

'Yes.'

'Good! Now come back to bed.'

*

A week later. A man and a boy climb out of a window of the Bishop's Palace and jump. The boy is protesting. He doesn't want to go. But the man, who we realize is his father, is adamant. You will. You will come with me. But I don't want to leave Papa, what about my birds and the dog. I will get you a bird and a dog. But Monsignor! He will cry. I am your Papa. He is not. He will *touch* you! But Papa. Alberto, shut up and jump!

And off they go into the deep depths of Italy in their coach-and four, then in the train, then another train, and on horseback, fleeing the wrath of the Monsignor and the wrath of the Church.

And Mama? I am sorry to report I have no idea. I have the horrible thought that perhaps Monsignor caught her, confined her in a dungeon in the basement of his ancient palace and tortured her for the whereabouts of father and son. Her body probably expelled through an oubliette into somewhere dark and very wet. A little too fanciful and romantic, perhaps. A little too Operatic.

Perhaps not.

But I do know these things: The Bishop accused father and son of having stolen money and jewels, and set the police after them. His fury grew with time. As far as the Church was concerned, they were convinced that Vittorio and Alberto Silvestri were agents of Satan who had wormed their way into the Bishop's affections in order to steal from him and the Holy Church, to destroy Holy Relics, and to bring down all the works of Jesus. For this reason, the two became fugitives for life and it wasn't until the death of Vittorio in mysterious circumstances and Alberto's gaining the sinecure at Castle Schweinstein that the son felt relatively safe. Under the name, you would have guessed, of Gramaschi.

I will have to write the whole story one day. The time between the escape from the castle and the arrival of the tutor at the Castle is rich. No space or time at the moment. I am sure you want me to get on with the story of Guido now.

*

Ebbene! So we are back in the middle of Germany, the University Town of Fohlingen (not its real name) and the arrival at the University Konzerthalle of an impecunious thoroughly unmatched pair of adventurers.

The singer Guido del' Roccaporca , Castrato. Aged now 15 and already almost 6 foot, very broad in the beam and chest. His head, gloriously handsome with his black hair and blue eyes, is rather too small for his body.

With him the flamboyantly dressed Sr Capodimonte, formerly a director and Operatic impresario, now acting as the boy's manager and general factotum. Like his predecessor in this he will begin by thinking he is in control, making all the decisions. And will end up swallowed up and spat out. He doesn't know this yet. Watch.

Remember these two are nearly out of money, which makes their conversation with Feddy extremely nuanced. Listen!

Scene 3 The Office

This is Feddy's 'office'. A small chamber attached to the Box Office of the Konzerthalle, where Feddy is doing the auditions. There is an upright piano squeezed into this small space, and a desk and two chairs. Capo and Guido sit on battered threadbare chairs facing Feddy across his paper-strewn desk.

Feddy: Signor Gramaschi! Kind of you to come so far for my little audition. This must be - uh Guido?

Capo:(shakes the extended hand which frankly makes him cringe and suppress his automatic response, which is to take out his scented handkerchief and wipe his fingers to frantically remove every trace of contact with this ugly dwarf.) Ah yes! I am Signor Capodimonte, Signor Gramaschi was - uh-
Guido: (expressionless) Called away.

Feddy: Oh. I see.
Capo: (sees that explanation is necessary) Oh. But he is the manager no?
Guido: Not anymore!
Feddy: I see! So which role are you auditioning for?
Guido: Bertarido, of course!
Feddy: (with a patronising cough) No no, perhaps you don't know the Opera. I need a mezzo or a contralto for that. A woman you see. Dressing as a man. What we call a Trouser. What voice are you?
Guido: Uh. Alto.
Feddy: Alto? Oh. Well perhaps Anulfo. He is Bertarido's friend. I need someone uh - older, more gravitas as the hero. It depends if you can sing. How old are you?
Capo (interrupting): he's twenty!
Feddy: (disbelieving) Twenty??? I - uh - I don't think the range is right – is he a counter tenor? What voice have you?
Capo: (a note of desperation) Herr - herr - Listen to him. You must hear him sing! I beg you. Just LISTEN to him!
Feddy: (sighs) well, come to the piano then. What will you sing? You need the score? What key?

Guido: I don't need the piano. (He sings *a capella*. Guido sings *'Dove sei, amato bene?'* from *Rodelinda,* which, incidentally, I wrote for the great Castrato Senesino. He delicately attacks the first note, holds it a beat or two longer than written, swells to a crescendo then a flawless diminuendo. His pure crystal voice cuts the air like a chandelier plunging to earth in slow-motion, like the splash of pure freezing water across the face in a warm room, like a blue moon over a black ocean.

(YouTube! If you want to get on with the narrative, listen from 2.33 – that's the part *he* sang)

What did you expect? I didn't really need to write that scene. I just so enjoyed the expressions. There was Feddy, directing his first ever Opera and having to pretend to be completely in control of the situation. Believe me, every aspect of what he wore for the auditions had been agonised over by Feddy with over-enthusiastic contributions from Gertude. The black velvet tailcoat. The frilled shirt with the braces. Not too easy to put together an ensemble like this if you're four foot ten. The gentle blue of the bowtie. The brown boots. (He was painfully aware of how wrong they were! Interesting note: brown boots became a particular trademark of his which he wore for the next thirty years. A pair of his brown boots are in a glass case now, perched above the staircase leading to the Upper Circle of the Metropolitan Opera New York. He called them *mein gluckliche Fusspar*) Let us enjoy that picture.

And also the faces of our two beggars - so determined to seem not to be desperate, so fearful of appearing just the wrong side of grubby, so conscious of the possibility of exuding a miasma of sweat and stale fart. And yet bearing hidden within the throat and chest of the boy, a treasure greater than gold.

And then the moment of revelation! How everything changed in an instant with that aria. Straight away the roles were reversed, from buyer's market to seller's, all in the space of a few bars of *a capella* magic, filling the small room like a storm of tiny shreds of glass. And sealed, when Capodimonte told Feddy, 'in strict confidence' that Guido is a genuine Castrato.

'A Castrato! Oh my goodness young man, my sympathies – how – why –

'Please do not ask!' Capo is adamant.

'But this is – but people will flock to hear – this is – '

'It is not to be spoken!' Capo says. 'It is illegal, besides anything.'

'But – '

Naturally, the role of Bertarido was offered to Guido on a plate like the head of John the Baptist to Salome. Also, when Capo pretended to demur, a good fat fee. And when the demurral was repeated, a place to stay near the campus. As well as a handful of cash in advance.

Being fair, Capo knew how to negotiate. He had, after all survived for twenty years since leaving his family, living from job to job. Conducting, directing, even playing in some productions.

He had spent his war as a cook in the Italian Army. He was as good at cooking as he was at playing the tuba. Useless. In fact he was as useless at both cooking and the tuba as Italy was in deciding which side to be on.

It was in negotiations for supplies for the eternally diminishing Army (diminishing because thousands kept being killed) that Capo learned his skills. Negotiating - that was his thing.

There are three reasons he never made a fortune after the war.

1) His impatience. So often he would walk out of an excellent job or contract simply because it was taking too long to reach a goal. Or another opportunity presented itself. As in Berne.

2) His irascibility. As far as Capo was concerned, other people were what he called 'Cheeseheads'. He would distinguish between the Parmesani (basically, flakes) and the Gruyere or Emmentaler tendency, for example (full of holes) the Gorgonzola (part monster, but riddled with bacteria) and the Camembert (very floppy). Being Italian he naturally dismissed Cheddar contemptuously as 'English cheeses' Capo had an allergy to cheese.

3) His boundless arrogance. He believed implicitly in his own infallibility. Very often, people who assert that they are utterly perfectly and invariably right about everything have a well of insecurity deep inside. Not in Capo's case. Sr Capodimonte believed that everyone else had a deep well of insecurity inside quite justifiably, because they were always wrong.

These 3 character flaws will feature alarmingly as our story progresses.

Scene 4: The Gasthaus

Unfortunately for our heroes, the 'University accommodation' offered was in the Gasthaus zur Schwuhl, the kingdom of the redoubtable Frau Sach. This being the Summer Break, fortunately for the pair, there were no students.

The beds were made of iron tubes and a horsehair mattress flopped on each like a dead donkey. A huge voluminous duvet lay on each, stained with the mysterious effluvia students exude. Through the high windows on their left, dust-spattered sunbeams, reminiscent of light.

Guido: There is no AIR! I cannot breathe! (He flings his canvass holdall onto a bed and paces, irritated, hot, frustrated. I need a bath!

Capo: These peasants never bathe. Pure Limburger. I will ask the woman.

(He turns to exit almost knocks Frau Sach over. She is carrying clean sheets and a pewter jug and basin for ablutions.)

Frau Sack: forsicht! You almost knocked me down!

Capo: Excuse me, Frau.

(She busies herself laying out sheets, towels. Puts the jug and basin on a side table.)

Capo: We need a bath

Frau: (snorts) I can tell that! I smell it!

Capo: And where would you say we can bathe?

Frau S: (She points to the basin and ewer) your bath! You will keep this floor free of splash. *Klar*?

Capo (is getting annoyed) Surely you have a bath? Can you not heat some water?

This is what is going through the good Frau's mind: *how rude! None of my kleinschen - her pet name for her student lodgers - would dare to speak to her like that! But these two, it was made clear to her, are guests of the University and have to be treated with respect! But why? Look at them! A pinhead and a homosexual. Or artist. Anyway someone whose view of himself is as if he was an angel itself or God or an apostle at least! Normally she would have said 'You jumped-up catastrophe from the slums of hell! So you want a bath do you? For you I will put the fire right under your arsch!*

Serves you right, Frau Sach, for your nasty evil thoughts that within days you will be frantically scrubbing blood as dark as your heart from the floor, from the sheets, from the bed.

ACT 7

Einführung
RODELINDA BY G F HANDEL

The Draft Cast List:

Rodelinda, *Queen of Lombardy*	Gertrude Hassler, Soprano
Bertarido, *usurped King of Lombardy*	Guido della Roccaporca , Alto
Grimoaldo, *Duke of Benevento, Bertarido's usurper*	Franz von Buhlow, tenor
Eduige, *Bertarido's sister, betrothed to Grimoaldo*	Beatrix Müller, Contralto
Unulfo, *Bertarido's friend and counselor*	Lucia del'Isola, Alto
Garibaldo, *Grimoaldo's counsellor, duke of Turin*	Hans von von Bülow , Bass
Flavio, *Rodelinda's son*	silent

And there they are, finally, the whole cast decided after three weeks of auditions, many displays of bravura, tears, confrontations, and a duel.

Hans and Franz von Bülow you may remember as Gertrude's rejected suitors, before she decided to throw her lot and her botsies at the lucky Feddy. We must be in no doubt that: 1) They still adored the girl; 2) They hated Feddy with the contempt and fury only the Adel (the German aristocracy) could have for the 'peasant' who had stolen their plaything from them.

Tragically, both brothers, who were students at the University and keen singers would kill for the honour of deflowering their favourite virgin. So Franz killed Hans in a duel. Hans and Franz. Franz and Hans. Always together. Together in everything. A city of two. A Duetto of perfect harmony. Completing each-other's sentences. Parts of the same hole. And that hole was the mouth of the voracious Gertrude Hassler

This is a picture of three duelists at the University at the time. Neither is Franz or Hans, I think, as these are far younger.

Four years ago, they were only boys, these brothers, new to the eruptions of pimples and boy explosions of sexuality when they fell – so they thought – in love. How can one expect them to have some self-control when they are rivals for the affections of a girl? Perhaps you remember the intensity of your first love. I remember mine….no, I intend to say nothing about that! Bear in mind: Gertrude had introduced these brothers to far more enjoyable penis-play than the masturbation – sometimes mutual – they had been experimenting with for years.

In my experience when there are three in some kind of intense relationship, someone gets hurt. Or killed. I learned this from so many libretti. Stupid boys should have studied the works of Metastasio rather than Goethe. And so eventually their cosy co-conspiracy to share young Gertrude became a fervid rivalry to be the first to penetrate that other opening, that gate to exquisite joy, the one they continually heard about from their more raucous companions at the University – that opening that made the pleasures of mouth and tongue entirely second-grade. The one opening that on no account Gertrude would allow any man to enter.

'Who shall be first?' quoth Franz. Whose tongue, whose soul, whose schwantz?' The boys are walking arm-in arm down Schnucki-allee, in a daze of post-coital fraternal camaraderie.

His brother laughs. 'Why, my silly penis-brain, it could only be me! I am the oldest –'

'By mere minutes! And I, dear one –' he pinches Hans' cheek painfully 'am the most handsome and my –'

'Schwantz -head! Is the same size –'

'No it is not! I am much bigger than you!'

'Liar! Come – get it out – '

'No! You are crazy!'

'Come on! Over here – ' he drags his brother into a doorway. 'No-one is around. Take it out!'

'No! You've seen it before many times. You know – '

'Come on! Let's measure them'

'You're crazy.'

'Come on!'

'And then! And then whoever's is the greatest gets to go in first! Agree!'

'Oh very well agree. Now take it out. Here's mine.'

And so the two loving brothers whip out their equipment and try to measure each-other's against a piece of string. This is as uncomfortable for me to write as it is for you to read, but it is essential for an understanding of what happened next.

Yes, of course they realised that it would be more accurate to measure each-other's if they were erect, and so each assisted his brother until, inevitably, Frau Emmerich, wife of the Pastor opened the door from the inside of the doorway in which they had been so scandalously lurking and exploded with indignation which must, regrettably, actually labelled righteous.

There were appropriate consequences, naturally. The only thing that saved the boys from complete shame, luckily for them, was Frau Emmerich's refusal to explain precisely what they had been up to when she opened the door. 'Sodom! Gomorrah! Wickedness!' was all she would say and so their venerable father, Herr von Bülow, [JE1] [JE2] assumed that whatever it was, Frau Emmerich would have been exaggerating. Boys will be *junge*. Ho ho ho. Of course, Frau, I will whip them and keep them from Church for a month. What a punishment.

The escalation from the shame of the Emmerich incident to utter hatred was rapid and inevitable. Both boys felt terrible, deep shame and guilt, each blamed the other. Then there was their jealousy over Gertrude. And when finally they were sent back to University, each shared their own lies about the events with their friends. The lies grew and grew. The antipathy likewise. Until there was only one possible solution according to their contemporaries: A duel[JE3] .

A MENSUR FOR A MÄDCHEN

The formal duel (or Mensur) in a German University begins with the Insult. And so Franz, egged on by his new best friend Karl, confronts Hans, his identical brother. To the delight of all the students there present in the quadrangle, he says two words. It is an unforgiveable insult which can only be resolved with blood. '*Dummer Junge*!' A translation in context would be something like 'dumbo', 'idiot', 'stupid boy'. And the formal response is the challenge to a duel.

The rules and rituals of duels have evolved a great deal amongst German students since hundreds of years ago when they were always to the death. By this time many have become mere tokenism. How dull! In my day there was much more blood I assure you! But these callow students with their melodramatic simulacra of great passion, these pimpled boys will accept a single drop of blood as a victory.

Both Hans and Franz are secretly very grateful for this gentlemanly way of resolving their new-found brotherly antipathy. Both want to get back to their old ways – two halves of a twin whole. Companions in everything – everything that is apart from the artistry of dear Gertrude. Fine! The winner, the man who draws the first blood

– will not only have exclusive access to her (her opinion notwithstanding) but will universally be acknowledged as having the biggest *schwantz.*

I mean, no-one ever *dies* in a duel nowadays! A flick and a prick, the Pariser (the sword often used – an epee with a sharp point -) would scratch. A drop of boy-blood would pop onto the surface of a tiny lesion on a cheek. Honour satisfied. Possession of the girl established. Brothers back in arms.

*

And so, on a rainy afternoon in April two identical young men, identically dressed, like facing mirrors face each-other. We are in the Gymnasium, the Sports Hall of the University. It smells of sweat and leather. The parallel bars are stained and grubby. The wooden floor shines with the resentful glow of resentful forced student labour, cleaned by punished students with towels and their knees. Around them, the studentenverbindung, the student body of the First Year. Behind each of the Paukanten – the duellists - stands a youth designated as a physician, although neither had completed their medical studies.

Picture Hans and Franz then, Dressed in their duelling kit: spectacles of iron, not masks. This is to allow the opponent's blade access to the cheek- practically the only place open enough to receive the cut which would end the match. Each wears a padded jacket, each holding their thin razor-sharp duelling sword. Left hands behind their backs, right in a leather gauntlet.

I can't tell them apart.

And when, seconds after the signal is given to commence duelling, the point of a sword pricks its way into the most vulnerable part of a padded jacket, slips like a phantom into a lung, slips straight out – with a laugh from both men, a relieved laugh even though it would be better if the bloodletting had been from the face, this finishes it. In seconds. Hurrah for the drop of blood….

Who won? All the young men ask, disappointed it was so quick and yet relieved. Hurrah. Franz or Hans? Who

Who is it slowly stopping laughing and sitting suddenly, coughing.

Letting out a speck of blood from his mouth and saying, 'hey Franz–'

Coughing, so that a light spray of blood spitters over his white padded jacket

'Look!' he says. Proudly. 'Blood!'
But he bows over, kowtowing
And must lie down.
The physician runs to him
'*Scheisse! Lungenfuchser*! His lung!'

*

Herr von Bülow, the boys' father was determined to hush up the entire episode. If he mourned, only in public. He could never feel or understand the great chasm in the heart of the surviving twin. Herr von Bülow, a minor official in the Weimar Republic, was a powerful man in the province and an influential member of the Assembly. He feared nothing in life. Except his wife, his sons, and the loss of his reputation. He had no patience with self-pity or regret.

Besides, von Bülow had been a participant in a duel in 1880 at the same university, killing his opponent for the supposed affection of a prostitute. His own father suppressed that scandal, as he suppressed this one. With an appropriate payment and a quick funeral, of course. Like father like son. And to be honest, the Herr never liked Hans. Too smart, too arrogant, too argumentative. Too beloved of his mother.

*

Franz was perfect for the role of villain. Tall, 6ft 3', heavy-built, mutton-chop whiskers, balding at the age of 25, looked forty. Remember: still in love with Gertrude, still despising Feddy. Now you need to think about what he would have thought of Guido!

A clue: being rather provincial, completely ignorant about Opera and the history thereof (despite being a powerful and accurate Tenor, more used to singing in church or belting out drinking songs), he would have been described in these modern times as intensely homophobic, bigoted, tending toward Fascism. You wouldn't have liked him. Bumptiously abrasive, always combative, Franz could have been the model for the original agent provocateur.

Scene 1: The Bierkeller *Gute Reise*, a student drinking haunt near the University.

'You've never seen anything like it!' Franz spat a thin rain of beer into the air. Here, in this sweaty-paneled (the panels seemed to run with sweat. Or beer. Or perhaps it was simply a sweaty seeping of damp from the once free-flowing *Forellenbach*, which had once jumped with trout and now lay dead beneath the rotting wooden floor of the ancient building) the male students from the University spend their statutory Carousing Years bemoaning the fickleness of women, the stupidity of their professors, the intractability of Goethe or Schiller, the irrelevance of the Impressionists, why Kant got it wrong, and so on. The panoply of the pomposity of all-knowing students all over the world. And as their drug of choice, usually alcohol, fuzzed their brains inevitably there would be strutting, boasting, fighting, even sometimes, even, weeping. But only about girls.

Franz' voice was always the loudest for simple reasons: not only did he have the throat of a bull and a chest to match (hence the power of his singing) but in addition he was always right. Obviously. And everyone else was wrong. Because of course they were his intellectual inferiors, milksops, far too 'humanitarian' to survive in the real world.

His standard techniques in winning every argument were these, in case you ever want to use them; speak louder than the opposer; interrupt within the first five words of his argument; leap from topic to topic, argument to argument as soon as you suspect you may be losing and if in doubt challenge him to a duel. Hans really should have known better.

'You've never seen anything like it' he repeated. 'This strange fellow, head like a pin, body like a barrel, sings like a girl!'

'Like a girl you say?' Karl chortled. Karl was one of Franz' acolytes, always there to support his friend, always ready with obsequious praise and apparently riddled with a desire to please. 'He probably needs a good beating.'

'Or a good banging!' August inserted.

'Banging or beating? Banging or beating?' Bashing their tankards on their tables in rhythm, the *Brüderschaft* (Band of Brothers – their name for their group of hard drinking hard fighting students) took up the chant.

'We'll take a vote!' Franz announced, standing. 'We debate! Right now! So, I stand for the beat, Karl stands for the bang.'

Formal debates in the style of the Oxford Union are a traditional part of Fohlingen student life. In the Bierkeller, however, these debates follow their own bizarre rules.

'Chairman!' Franz takes a bottle in hand, lays it on its side and spins it energetically. Eventually it points to little Katsoumi Tabatabaee, the Persian student whose German is not of the best quality. 'Chair man! Chair Man! Chair Man!' the room chants, until a chair has been hoisted onto the table top and the small bespectacled very confused foreigner placed ceremoniously on it.

'Wherefore must I do?' he asks anxiously.

'Chair the meeting!' Franz laughs.

'How for?'

'Drink! Chair!' Franz says, passing him up a foaming stein. 'You are selected! By divine providence! Your decision is law!'

Poor Katsoumi is unused to drinking. In fact in Persia where he grew up, his father had been a drunkard (wine, exclusively) as well as being Prime Minister, which had driven the son into a period of religious abstinence and a prudish distaste for drink. This was his first visit to the bierkeller, in an innocent desire to make friends.

'I will now propose the motion. Silence!' Franz waits for order. Then he begins. 'The motion I am proposing Mr Chairman is, 'This house declares that as a punishment to the Jewish dwarf for stealing his girlfriend, the freak known as Guido shall be soundly beaten, so that his bizarre kind shall never procreate or have the opportunity to ever play Bertarido again'.'

I need to interject a point of fact here. If I was there, I would have made a Point of Order. Feddy is not nor has ever been Jewish. Later, in his new life over the seas he would take advantage of his apparently Jewish appearance in the minds of those who knew little of Jews. In the stifling ignorant atmosphere of this University town which had never knowingly seen a Jew, it was easy to attach labels to people one didn't understand or like. Especially when the slow insidious growth of Anti-Semitism had begun to infect even this absurd provincial outpost.

'I will now explain my reasons that you my dear colleagues and brothers should vote for the motion: Firstly, know that the *boser Zwerg* '

'Böse Böse!' the brothers chant. (pronounce it like buh zuh) (It means evil)

'Is a thief and a liar. Also a murderer!'

'Ohhhhh!' they sigh melodramatically.

'A thief of love and a pretender who has stolen the heart of the beautiful German maiden Gertrude from me and my brother, stolen her away by promising her a life of fame and fortune in the Opera, a life he can never deliver!'

'Fame! Shame! Fame! Shame!'

'And THEN this creature from the very depths of the forest, this beast of evil, this stench of the entrails of hell.....kills my brother! My beloved brother! The one with the spectacles!'

'Point of order Mr Chairman!' Karl interjects. 'In fact – point of fact!'

'Ruling required Mr Chairman' Franz silences the room imperiously.

'Ru ling! Ru ling! Ru ling!'

Actually the German sounds better: '*Ent schei dung! Ent schei dung! Ent schei dung*!' As it has three syllables.

'What must I do? Katsoumi whispers to Franz.

'Tell him to go away'

'Go! Way!' Katsoumi rules.

Karl (Misunderstanding): Thank you. Point of fact! YOU sliced your brother! You sliced him diced him and served him for breakfast!
Franz: An *Affaire d'Honneur*!
Karl: (Contemptuously) for a role in an Opera???
Franz: For a girl!
Karl: A married woman!
Franz: Still a girl! Marrying a Jewish dwarf!

Karl: (goes face-to face with Franz) My mother was Jewish you swine!

Franz: (slaps him across the face with a white glove) *You* swine!

Karl: *Swine! (*slaps him back with a white glove)

Franz: Swine!

Karl: Challenge accepted!

Franz: Weapons?

Students (chant): Weapons! Weapons! Weapons!

Franz: (Commands) Silence!

(With a dark G Minor chord of strings and woodwind, a pregnant silence descends on the room.)

(We fear for both of them. So do they. Franz has dealt death in the past. Karl decides to live.)

Karl: *Wurst!*

Franz (Secretly disappointed): *Kartoffeln!*

Karl: Bring the weapons!

(Several students rush to the combatants with plates of sausage and mash. A furious food fight between Karl and Franz ensues, with the combatants slapping, throwing, attempting to insert foodstuff into each other, to the wild drunken encouragement of the students. Music here needs to be in the Rossini style. Until all are thoroughly exhausted and the two rivals are in a Siamese-twinned heap on the floor.)

Franz: (blurts) Your mother was not really Jewish was she?

Karl: Yes she is, actually.

Franz: I don't like Jews.

Karl: I know. That is a problem for you!

Franz: I love you anyway!.

Karl: I love you also.

(They embrace blokily)

A student: Vote!

Students chant: Vote! Vote! Vote:
It is not necessary for me to relate that this drunken bunch of the

Fohlngen elite youth voted unanimously for extreme measures to be taken: not just against poor Feddy, not only against poor Guido, but against the whole damn Opera.

A Crisis for Katsoumi

Katsoumi Tabatabee was the son of the Persian revolutionary Mohammad Tabatabee, who became obsessed with overturning the Monarchy when some sugar merchants were punished by having their feet beaten for refusing to lower their prices. For ten years, until the final establishment of the *Majlis*, the Persian parliament, this genuinely liberal man fought for a form of democracy in a country riddled with poverty and privilege.

And as an advocate of Western Democracy, Big Daddy ensured that his boy children were taught languages, mathematics, politics and science at Teheran's famous International School. He was far too busy attending meetings, leading demonstrations and writing articles in newspapers to do other than occasionally barking at them in the few hours he spent at home.

Being his son was hard cheese. Or soft cheese. Panir, as they call it. Soft and crumbly, full of holes and in poor Tabby Kat's case (the name was given to him by Roland Grieve, the son of the British Consul) full of worms. For much of the boy's schooling at the International School in Tehran, the name chased him around the quadrangle, sought him out in notes sneaked into his pocket, even followed him in whispers to the one place he should have felt safe, the toilet block. In class, a plaintive *miaow* would trickle out of a mouth, waft like a barely discernible scent over to the cringing boy where he would feel suffocated by it and desperate to escape.

As a boy there can be no doubt Katsoumi was somewhat feline. As slim and svelte as a starved panther, he didn't so much move as slink. Partly, this was learned as an attempt to remain invisible, to blend into the dappled shadows of the tree-lined quadrangle. Mostly it was an attempt to escape the shabby overwhelming reality of his victimhood.

Roland was his tormentor-in chief. Tall for his age, Roland had the nervous energy of a rabid dog and the looks of a Borzoi. Always dressed elegantly and impeccably, he would have been regarded as effete by the other boys if he hadn't always been so very manic. So much so, in fact, that his father hadn't followed the usual practice of

British Diplomats abroad and sent the boy to an exclusive Public School as a boarder. 'I want him by me! You never know what the blighter will do next!' he would say if you were to ask. Besides, the International School in Tehran was an excellent educational establishment which based its curriculum and ethos on the Public Schools of England. The Grand Master (too grand to be called High Master or Headmaster) had once been a Deputy at St Paul's in London. The boys there were not just the sons of diplomats, but princes and sons of the aristocratic elite.

The son of a cleric and revolutionary would never feel comfortable here in the very throat of the Establishment, and Roland was certainly going to make him know it.

For his part, papa Tabatabee, if you were to ask this: 'Tell me papa T, how can you have your son educated at such an establishment where the establishment of the establishment learn how to oppress the people?' he would reply, after a soulful swig from a bottle of Chateuneuf, 'Know thy enemy! The boy will learn how they think! What they think! And will know how to undermine them, right?' Or perhaps, wrong.

When Katsoumi came home bruised, or muddy, or even once with a black eye, would Papa regret sending him there? Or even ask how it happened? Mama would, sometimes, but would Papa listen to her? Or would he just say, 'The boy must toughen up! These are bad people. I am abused every day! Do I cry about it? Until there is a democratic parliament in this country…' (Swig swig) Yes he would. And then launch into a rant on politics and freedom and the great legacy for the Persian peoples and Mama would shut her ears and long for a sweet swift death. Then he would find Katsoumi and say '*Khak too Saret!*' Idiot. Shame on you. And go off to a meeting.

As he grew up in all this misery, Katsoumi would take refuge in reading history. Yes, including Herodotus and Xenophon – in this, he was so similar to Guido. But what interested him most was the glimpse these writers afforded into ancient Persia. Into the Persian Empire before Mohamed, before Christ or the Sassanids. The great kings Cyrus, Darius, Xerxes. Yet there were no modern writers who had satisfactorily – and more pertinent, unbiasedly researched and recorded the history of what was once the greatest empire in the world.

I am so fascinated by Persian history I wrote the music for two Operas about ancient Persia. When I wrote the music for Serse (Xerxes), and Siroe if only I had Google then I could tell those librettists what ignorant idiots they are. (Very well I admit I adapted the libretto of Serse myself. It was so humourless I had to. This is a secret. No-one liked it at first.)

Archaeological discoveries were happening all the time. Cuneiform, the ancient script of the lands between the Tigris and the Euphrates, had been deciphered 50 years ago. But where were the translations? Where had all the clay tablets been gathered and used as source material for a real history of these ancient lands?

All he wanted to do with his life was to become the greatest historian in Persia, and to produce volumes of history based on fact and research. But first he needed to kill Roland.

The desire started as a sparklet of light in his dark world as he lay weeping on his bed, blood and sand spattering the milk-white pillow. The encounter with Roland after school had been ugly.

How to kill him.

The Persian princes at the ancient court were taught to ride, shoot a straight arrow, and tell the truth.

He would shoot him with an arrow! He could lurk unseen behind a wall or a bush, bow and arrow ready, whoosh! Then vanish!

There was a peremptory knock at the door. Enter Muhamad Tabatabee, the father himself.

Dad: Boy! Get up! Why aren't you studying!

Son: I was reading –

Dad: What is this. (Whips a book off the bed) Thucydides? What will that tell you. I told you read Plato. Did you pray this afternoon?

Son: (Lying) Yes.

Dad: Wash your face! You look dirty. By God, you are… (removes a package from the bag he's carrying)…it's time for you to be a man. A man! Do you know where I was this last week?

Son: No father.

Dad: Indonesia. For a meeting with the most powerful people in the world. I brought you a present. Stand straight!

Son: ? (Dad hardly ever brought presents. This was absolutely out of character.)

(Muhamad Tabatabee unwraps the Kris, nestled in its decorated leather scabbard. Drops the wrapping paper onto the floor.)

Dad: Do you know what this is? (Slowly, he withdraws the knife from the scabbard. The blade glows. He turns it this way and that, so that a sparkle of lethal light jumps from the zigzag of the blade across walls, floor and ceiling. The boy gasps.)

Son: (Awed) It's a knife.

Father: When a boy is grown in Persia his father gives him a sword to defend his Faith, to defend his country. You are fourteen, so you get a knife. It will save you from your nemesis. The sword comes later.

(He returns the knife to the sheath and then with both hands, passes it ceremoniously to his son. There is a tear in the Father's eye.)

Son: Thank you Father. Thank you God.

Here is a strange thing. Uncle Ardashir. Who Mummy called Babak, which means Little Father. When Muhamad was away, he would summon his younger brother from Esfahan to stand *in loco parentis*, to look after and protect the family. Short, fat and frantic, Babak was one of those small men who in their own minds are huge. The source of all knowledge, the fountain of wisdom, and with an endless supply of advice for little ones And love too, it must be said. Many of his boasts were lies. Or exaggerations..

And so, when he looked out of a window at midnight and saw Katsoumi leaping about panther-like, making sweeps, swoops and stabs with his knife in the courtyard, he had to do something.

Donning a silk bathrobe he went downstairs and watched for a while until the boy, sensing his presence, stopped, sheathed the dagger, and said 'Uncle.'

'Boy…so tell me' – he motioned for the youth to sit next to him on the doorstep. 'Who are you killing?'

Katsoumi wants to shower, go to bed. But he obeys and seats himself next to his corpulent relative.

'Nobody.' He says.

'What did you tell me. The Prince always tells the truth!'

'Oh.'

'So tell me. Get your breath.'

Katsoumi tells him. He is deeply ashamed to admit being bullied, but he has to tell somebody! He recounts the insults, the injuries, the taunts. Everything. And he begs Babak not to tell anyone. Anyone! And when he's told all, the tears flow.

'Now now now…' Uncle enfolds him in a bear-hug. 'you must not be ashamed! I could tell you a story about your father – did you know he was treated like a pariah at school? He went to a religious school, a Madrassar in the south. Terrible time! Because he read so much Western philosophers, Persian poetry, political theory, and even novels, they called him Kufar! The Kufar! And that is why he is such a brilliant scholar of the Q'ran. He is a Hafiz, you know that! He had to outlearn them, to show them he was no Kufar!'

'Katsoumi laughed. 'Are you serious Uncle!?'

'Oh yes. That's why I went to the Army. I didn't want to go through the torments at the Madrassar. Oh Yes.'

'You were in the army many years Uncle?'

'Sixteen years my boy. I left as a Major.' (A Captain.)

'Uncle....did they teach you knife fighting?'

'Yes boy.' (Well, no. But he did use other weapons. Until they put him in the Medical Corps.) 'They taught me to fight with the knife, the sword, the gun. I was once part of the Royal Guard. We had to protect the King.'

'Uncle......'

'On one condition! You will NEVER use the skills I teach you –'

'Uncle! What's the point of that? –'

'And above all, you will NEVER kill, unless you are defending your life or the life of another!'

'I have to kill him. I have to!'

'Our way is the way of Honour, my boy. Once you have these skills, trust me, nobody will ever attack you. They will see your strength. They will respect you. And that way you will not follow Shaitan. You will follow Allah, like your father and like me.'

'No more tears little one. I will tell you what I will do for you! Listen to me.'

'What.'

'I will get your father to take you out of that school. It is time for you to go to a proper high school anyway. There is a wonderful school in Esfahan, where this family comes from. My house is big. You will have a room. You will gain your certificates. Then you will go to University in another country. You will never see that – what's his name – Roland again in your life. And I will teach you to fight with knife, with sword, with stick. It is time for me to go back to Esfahan anyway.'

And that's what happened. As much as Babak was portly, he could move with immense power and speed, he knew every trick of combat with weapons. And in wrestling, he was unbeatable. Katsoumi's time in Esfahan was golden. He was almost happy.

The same cannot be said for Roland. He died, stabbed to death in an alley, a year later. No, Katsoumi was not responsible. Perhaps poetic justice. Perhaps a debt paid to a Major. Or rather, a Captain.

Babak did teach Katsoumi a version of knife fighting. Mostly from his imagination, and a useful book called 'Knife Fighting for Beginners', probably.

Scene 2: First Rehearsals

The rehearsals for Rodelinda began on a sweltering July day, as the swallows swooped in a cloudless sky and flowers thrust their heads into the musky heat begging for bees. Outside the Konzerthalle, every living thing reveled in the glorious summer except, of course, for humans.

Inside, happy termites munched on the oak floorboards. Well wouldn't you be happy if you lived your entire life surrounded by your favourite food? I suppose cows feel much the same way, but the difference is, termites are seldom turned into food themselves.

The unhappy humans sat on chairs on the stage in a circle. Next to Feddy on his right, his newest ally and friend, Sr Capodimonte, who had agreed to be Stage Director. To Feddy's left, his wife-to be Gertrude (Rodelinda). Next to Capo, Guido (Bertarido). Franz (Grimoaldo) sat next to Gertrude.

The others, going clockwise: Eduige, Bertarido's sister in the story, to be played by Beatrix Müller, who was also the pianist for rehearsals. A woman in her late fifties, Fr Müller was a blowsy dame, very much the stanchion and bulwark of music at the university for at least thirty years. Always at the side of the late Direktor, she had adopted Feddy immediately on first meeting when he had sat in the orchestra and tootled his way through the slow movement of Mozart's Clarinet Concerto. 'Such a lovely boy!' she had squealed, 'Such timbre!'

As she was his greatest fan, Feddy had felt morally obliged to give the role of a simpering young woman to this obese Hausfrau. Besides which she had contributed marks in the sum of a number plus too many zeros to fit in here, toward the production.

Next to her: the mute role of Flavio, Rodelinda and Bertarido's son, ended up with little Lisa Müller, the 12-year old daughter of Frau Müller. Beatrix Müller adored her daughter like some single women adore their pussycat. She stroked, she coo-cooed, she pampered and fussed. Lisa hated this. She felt stifled, smothered, drowned in pink and fluffy love. Not surprising, then, that she craved an opportunity to escape.

Bertarido's best friend Unulfo ended up a trouser role. The buxom lesbian Lucia dell'isola, an Italian student sent to the German University by her Mussolini-supporting parents in the belief that eventually he would be Prime Minister of Italy and Italy and Germany would join to form the New Roman Empire. They wanted their daughter to be right at the heart of the action.

Garibaldo, Grimoaldo the baddie's sidekick was given to Karl Schultz, Franz von Bülow's sidekick. As out there, so in here.

So much for the singers. The Orchestra would rehearse separately for the first three weeks; Feddy's plan was to ensure the singers had the singing and the acting in place before mounting the whole thing within the orchestration.

Feddy: And so welcome to my cast. I present you to me, your Music Direktor, repetiteur and Conductor. We are very fortunate to have also Signor Capodimonte as another Regisseur, the son of the famous Director at La Scala, who has himself directed stunning performances from – from –

Capo: Napoli

Feddy: To – to –

Capo: Berne

Feddy: And many places between! Your two maestros! (bows)

Capo is at his most flamboyant. He wears a red velvet jacket over striped jodhpurs, tucked into flaming red boots. He has a pink lace cravat at his throat, and in appearance resembles a ringmaster from the previous century.

When he first entered the stage and sat down, the giggles and nudging between Franz and Karl became close to embarrassing. And now every time Capo says anything the two exchange glances which causes the laughter trapped in their bodies almost to choke them.

Capo: (*Sotto voce*, whispers to Feddy) Can you please tell those boys to be silent? Where did you get them, the zoo?

Feddy: Here also we have the very famous Guido della Roccaporca straight from a starring role at the Berne Opera, our wonderful discovery to play the hero, Bertarido! (He exaggeratedly applauds, some of the others join in.) Voice of an angel!

Guido: (Stands, bows, sits) Thank you Maestro.

Fresh outbreaks of giggling follow from Franz and Karl. This is the first time Karl has seen Guido, and the boy looks to him like a complete freak. Guido flinches as he feels the ridicule, mixed with sarcasm and contempt.

Capo: (Aside) MY wonderful discovery.

Feddy: And for our title role of Rodelinda, wife of Bertarido I am so very proud to present to you my delightful wife-to be, the very lovely Gertrude Hassler! (His applause starts at chest level and rises to well above his head. The others half-heartedly join in,) Gertrude is the wonderful wife of our hero who refuses to believe him dead. What a wonderful woman!

Gertrude: (Simpers unconvincingly) Oh Feddy, I know you will be proud of me!

Feddy: I already am my dearest one.

(Franz glares at Feddy, his hatred bursting through an attempt to keep a neutral expression.)

Feddy: Which brings me to our villain, our Grimoaldo, Herr Franz von Bülow, whose wonderful baritone has woken up so many people in church. It is his job to usurp the throne and pursue the wife of poor Bertarido.

Karl applauds enthusiastically. Some of the others join in. Guido glares at him, expressionless.

Dutifully, Feddy introduces Lucia as Bertarido's best friend, Unulfo, Karl as Garibaldo the villain's counsellor and Lisa as little Flavio.

Feddy: And so! That is our cast, our little family. Believe me we are a family, and we will together make this beautiful Opera. So now – (reaches for a box by his seat) The great moment! Your parts! (With due ceremony he hands the cast their parts.)

As the parts are handed out, our cast have the opportunity to allow themselves to study their fellow cast members. Here is one example: Guido and Gertrude.

Guido fell hopelessly in love – or rather, in desire – with the buxom Gertrude. Guido has very little understanding of that act between men and women in which one impales the other – usually of course, the man impales the woman. Guido had witnessed this act way back in the Baron's castle when he saw the boy Janek impaling the servant girl in a way which made him angry, as the woman hadn't seemed to enjoy the experience in the least. This had, as related, resulted in the mysterious death of the youth as he tried the same trick on Guido. Guido realized he should be called the Rapist. And now as Guido studied the maiden sitting so very near to him, there was no controlling his heart. Or his loins.

CURTAIN

The Opera was two months away which sounds like quite a long time. It is, after all, about sixty days, which is 60 x 24 hours, and you can work out how many minutes and seconds that is for yourself. I assure you Feddy knew the number. Which is 1,440 hours. Which is 86,400 minutes. Which equals 5,184,000 seconds. Each of which Feddy was determined to make count.

Poor Feddy! He was, after all, cast in the role of dictator upon whom the entire state depended. And remember, he had never directed an Opera before. Certainly Capo was a help. Also, a major hindrance. To describe their relationship as prickly would be to underestimate hedgehogs. To assert that there was a clash between their temperaments would be to misunderstand the sound of cymbals in a war.

It didn't start as a war. Initially, Feddy was impressed by the gravitas and showmanship of the Italian. His flamboyant clothes, the moustache which resembled a writhing, living pet which had attached itself to the upper lip of the Maestro like an hirsute leech. The incredible jodhpurs with their stains and fustian stench. Were you to ask Feddy to describe the man he would certainly add a whip to the aforegoing description, even though we know he never carried one.

They say it is not good to have two women in a kitchen. The same applies to two directors of an Opera, both coveting the title of 'Maestro'.

The first days were more-or less without serious incidents. This was the phony war period when Capo would watch and listen while Feddy took each member of the cast through their lines, accompanied by Fr Müller on the piano. The official – and agreed remits of the two Directors was, Feddy: music; Capo: Stage. However as we know, Capo had quite some experience at both, and for the first few days he had to bite his tongue, purse his lips and cross his legs. Every now and then words or sentences or phrases would escape the prison of his lips. And as those seconds flew, the number of words and sentences and phrases grew. In direct proportion, Feddy's irritation grew too.

Scene 3: More rehearsing

Feddy quite rightly decided to rehearse the Opera scene by scene, from the beginning, then select the most difficult parts and do them again again and again. At the beginning of each scene which was being rehearsed for the first time, Feddy would do what he called his 'Plot Check', in which he would explain exactly where the scene fits into the plot. I have no idea why. Yes, the plot is complicated, but so is life! I preferred to leave understanding the plot to the librettist.

Which is a joke. Which librettist can you name who got the plot? (Maybe Giulio Cesare. Discuss.)

Anyway if ever you are confused nowadays, you just ask Mr Wiki.

I will humour the little man. I will quote his Plot Check,

Plot Check 1:
Rodelinda by GF Handel plot by Haym after Salvi after Corneille. No wonder it's complicated!

Rodelinda Act 1 Scene 1

'This Opera starts sadly my dear friends. Rodelinda thinks her husband the king Bertarido was killed in battle. The disgusting usurper Grimoaldo – (Franz) wants to marry her. She says no, after all he's engaged to Eduige – Frau Müller – who is the deposed Bertarido's sister. So she kicks him out. Then we meet Garibaldo the two-timing Counsellor (Hans) who says he loves Eduige -= but he's only really saying it because he wants the throne for himself. All clear?'

'Hah!' Frans' face does not hide his bafflement. 'I have no idea whatsoever. This one loves that one but that one loves someone else and in the end it's all about who gets the throne. And the woman?'

'Precisely right!' Feddy says. 'That's exactly what most Baroque operas are about. Just understand – you are the Bad One. Guido here is the Good One. Gertrude is the Faithful One. The rest of them are just there to make sure there's a happy ending. Now on to the music!'

The Little Man could not be more wrong! My operas all have drama, stories, real characters with hearts – if only I could kick him!

*

Rehearsals started with Rodelinda's very first aria, *L'empio rigor del fato* (YouTube…)

'It's about the wickedness of fate, darling', Feddy says as his beloved Gertrude stands next to the piano, waiting for Fr Müller to play the intro. 'Now sing for us.'

So simpering Gertrude places the music on the stand, turns sweetly to the page, and begins. '*L'empio rigor del fato*….'

Watch their faces, Feddy and Capo. On Feddy's, his love for this luscious example of German womanhood, a creature Wagner would have loved to cast as Brunhilda, this perfect parody of Pre-Raphaelite perfection simpers her way through an aria which is supposed to be a railing against cruel fate. For Feddy, the performance is lush. He is so thrilled that she manages to get through the whole thing, more-or less on the notes. This for him is a huge relief and progress indeed.

As we watch Capo's face we see something rather different. Frustration, confusion, then comprehension perhaps, if the writhing of the moustache is anything to go by. He too is thinking of the wickedness of fate in forcing him to accept Gertrude in the title role!

'Bravo!' Feddy claps when the thing is finished.

'Thank you! Thank you!' Gertrude soaks up his adulation, looks over at Capo in his chair and sees no confirmation.

'You see why I have chosen her Maestro!' Feddy says.

'Yes I suppose so Maestro.' Capo replies.

At this stage both our Directors are still addressing each-other as Maestro, to show mutual respect and understanding.

But the word 'suppose' hangs in the air. Feddy decides to attempt to snatch at it. 'Gertrude will win the hearts, all of them, won't she Maestro.' Partly addressed to Gertrude, to boost her confidence.

'She is very – heartfelt Maestro'. Capo replies.

'Oh yes! What a good point Maestro.'

'Only – '

'Please! Please! Any suggestions are gratefully received!' Feddy gushes.

'Just perhaps, we can have a little more – '

'You didn't like it?' Gertrude asks

'Yes yes of course I liked it. Just Remember – '

'What? I remember the lines well!'

'You are upset. You are complaining about Fate. Perhaps a little less – '

'Less what!'

'Less what!'

'Less what Maestro? Please Gertrude – '

'Maybe a little less – beautiful. More – angry.'

'Angry?' Gertrude is getting tearful. 'But this is only the first time! I was singing it for the notes, not the expression!'

'She will of course put the acting in Maestro. I will coach her.' Feddy is alarmed, feels this rehearsal slipping away from him.

'I can act! You know I can act! Why are you being so nasty!'

'Yes yes I know – '

'I don't have to take this from my husband-to be! You can stuff your bloody Opera!' At which she throws the part high into the air where it exercises an excellent loop-the loop and lands, open and unreachable, on a stayrope.

Exit Gertrude, in tears.

Capo shakes his head. He is slightly amused. 'Very melodramatic Maestro,' he says. 'At least it shows she has spirit.'

Feddy sighs. 'She certainly has that, Maestro,' he says.

Watching from the wings our Guido waits like a spider, eyes glued to the head of his prey with its shining gold, her pink cheeks streaked with tears. And when she flees, Guido follows.

He catches up with her in the street,

The midday streets are streaked wet. The sky is wet too, and our soon-to be united pair are being soaked through.

'Fräulein! Fräulein!' He shouts and eventually, as she stumbles clickety-clack over the wet cobbles, she hears and turns.

'*Liebe Gott*! What do YOU want!'

'I saw that. I watched your performance! You were - divine'

'Divine?' She stares at this grotesque youth, who, even at the age of sixteen, towers over her. The beautiful face in his tiny head is glowing with adoration which she can see is utterly sincere. 'You think so?'

The rain, desperate to be noticed, intensifies its attack.

'Fräulein believe me! I have seen so many fine sopranos - all over Europe! And none so - so coloratura, so elegant in bel canto!'

Ah you charming liar. You haven't spoken even one moment of truth since you stepped into the rain. You are taking a huge gamble, dear man. For a start, does this German provincial know the first thing about bel canto, coloratura? And she hasn't said a word to you since first you met...

'Bel canto!'

'You pronounce Italian so well. I could tell from your singing! You speak Italiano?'

'Oh signor! A little - enough for Opera - '

'Never enough Italiano! I speak only a little German - '

'You speak so well!'

Dear liar, brought up in Germany, you speak it as well as any native. Stop putting on that accent!

'You are very kind… Perhaps we can find some shelter?'

Having gained each-other's permission, the pair find the overhang of a medieval building to lurk under together. All around them the summer storm whooshes.

'Do you think you could teach me Italian signor?' Gertrude asks breathlessly.

'I would be so honoured and delighted!' Guido is overacting sickeningly at this point. He is speaking German with an absurdly exaggerated Italian accent. Seriously, while he is the greatest singer who ever lived (perhaps) as an actor, he's rubbish.

Gertrude laughs. I hope she is not as stupid as he thinks she is. 'And in return, I will teach you German!'

'It would make me very happy.' Guido says.

'I could even help you with this!' she says, grasping the tent pole which is attempting an escape through the young man's trousers.

'Really?' Guido asks as he unbuttons his flies.

Scene 3: MORE SEX

Protected by the overhang of the medieval building from both rain and prying eyes, a sex act is taking place. I forgot to mention that Gertrude's skill in this particular sex act is beyond compare. I mean what is formally called *fellatio*, less formally, a blow job. This is a skill she has worked on perfecting since the age of twelve, when she developed the skills and artistry of her lips, tongue and palate for her father's gratification, under his tutelage.

I'm afraid so. That upright burger and staunch bastion of his community was, in the privacy of his own home, a disgusting drunken pervert with a sexual obsession about his own daughter. How did he initiate this perversion? He persuaded the adoring, self-obsessed little girl that there was one sure and secret way for her to forever keep her complexion smooth and free of wrinkles: and that was by the application of that precious substance whose only sure source was the penis of a man.

As she was growing up Gertrude learned that her mouth was a golden route to gratification for men, and she wasn't slow in offering them the benefit of her expertise in exchange for the essence of youth, as it was called by her father. Hence, Hanz and Franz, the two brothers, were her slaves and entirely at her beck and call as they were discovering what sex is, and how it works. And she, after each act of fellatio, would lave her face with the essence of man and leave it there to dry. If asked about the mysterious incrustations about her cheeks she would say, as instructed by her father, that she used the white of eggs to keep her complexion.

Her fame spread throughout the young men of the town and she never lacked, therefore, all the fripperies of growing womanhood – from chocolates and *kuche* to pretty ribbons and even dresses. And of course, her beauty secret which she would never share with anyone because her daddy had told her that should she do this, the secret of eternal youth would be lost to her forever.

She remained, by the way, a virgin. Both she and her father, being somewhat of a religious bent, would resist furiously any attempts to take her maidenhood away before she married.

Had she made this clear to Hans and Franz, this history would have been completely different.

So here we have the sex act, Gertrude once more in pursuit of that which she believed was essential to the maintenance of her youth. From Guido, who could not possibly produce it.

It went on.

And on.

And also, on.

The rain it raineth.

Water cascades down the building, a waterfall protecting them from the eyes of any who would be foolish enough to venture out in this monsoon-like downpour.

And on.

Perhaps while this couple continue to indulge in this rather pointless non-conjugal act, I should keep you entertained with a story. I will tell you more about Gertrude's father, who you may have felt a little indulgent towards but now I've told you what a pig he was I'm sure you hate him.

It may make us feel better to know that when the events recounted here were taking place, Herr Hassler the clarinetist was suffering very badly from the effects of years of excess drink as well as a rather bad case of prostate cancer. A tumour the size of a golf ball was gradually eating out his fundament. He didn't know about this yet. I only know because I know almost everything about everybody in this story.

Annoyingly he was still alive. Although by now he had had the visit that would change his life.

And on. (She is still trying to milk her conquest. We'll get back to them.)

A VISIT FROM A VIRGIN

Herr Hassler lies on straw. Next to him, a pool of vomit. Under his arm the bottle of part-consumed Schnapps. His clarinet in a case at his side. He looks like a Victorian Realist painting produced by the Salvation Army to show the evils of the demon drink. There is nothing about this picture that is in the slightest bit not stereotypical or clichéd.

Something makes him open his eyes to a blinding light. The stable door has opened, and in the harsh light of midday the silhouette of a young woman stands out. He first tries to shield the eyes with his hands, but eventually he peeks through his fingers until he can see the girl staring at his pathetic figure.

'Holy Mary Mother of God!' he exclaims. He means it as an imprecation or a heartfelt gee thanks god for sending me some juicy fruit to pluck! She takes it as a compliment.

'Thank you,' she says. 'So tell me, what are you doing here in these stables?'

The girl Is in her late teens, slim, extraordinarily pretty in a demure dimpled dark-haired way. 'Oh I see', she says. 'Drunk. You look silly.'

'Why? My hair? I brushed yesterday'. He laughs. He is Indeed very drunk and very silly.

(*Meanwhile*: Gertrude's head bobs up, down, up, down on Guido's crotch. His face is seraphic. She is tired. Has to stop now and then for a rest.)

'I'm Dogmar Hassler. How do you do.' He holds out a hand to be shaken.

She accepts the proffered hand and gives it a demure squeeze..

He uses it to gently pull her down next to him. 'Come and sit with me for a little, *gnädige Mädchen*' he says. 'Keep me company!

What is your name?'

She pulls away and sits on a low wall a few feet from him. 'Mary,' she says 'What is that?' she asks, gesturing toward the clarinet in its case.

'That is a clarinet, my lovely. What they play in the orchestra. What they play also in jazz clubs in New Orleans. Do you like jazz?'

'I think so,' she says. 'Can I see?'

'My clarinet? Why not.' He opens the case, takes out and carefully assembles the instrument. He removes a new reed from a small box, licks it lasciviously, his eyes hard on her. 'First, ' he says, 'the reed.'

'Very nice. And then?'

'Look what I do now' he says. Look!' He attaches the reed, and then begins to lick the mouthpiece suggestively. 'You have to love your instrument....you have to make love with your instrument...' He blows an arpeggio. Then toodles a jazz tune 'This is the style of Frank Teschemacher in America. Do you like that? Or maybe this – ' He plays a passage from the Mozart Clarinet Concerto.

She is entranced,

'Could I learn?' she asks shyly.

'Ah, ' he says, 'But before you can play clarinet you must learn *embouchure*.'

'What is that *embouchure*?'

'How to use your lips, your mouth.'

'This is how you practice' he says as he unbuttons his flies.

Have you ever seen utter disgust on the face of a vision?

'Is this how you do it?' she asks.

'Yes, this is how you learn,' he says.

'I mean, is this how you seduce children?'

'Seduce – '

'Children!' The Virgin Mary is now utterly suffused with light. In an instant she grows, a golden fiery ball of total fury. 'Hell,' it growls, 'is too good for you!'

The Virgin Mary must have had a day off or something. Being a Virgin is no doubt quite boring for some. This may be the explanation for her visiting this reprobate of a musician in the stables of the University where he had taken refuge with a large bottle of Schnapps. Or is it possible she hangs around stables in search of an explanation? Or if, in the minds of some, there is such a thing as natural justice, as Karma, as baddies always getting their just desserts, perhaps this is what happened. It is certainly the tale told by Herr Hassler to the Provost, Reverend Martin in the Confessional. He described the experience as a visitation by the Virgin Mary to rescue him from sin. He may have been lying. What the hell. I can't know everything!

Yet he believed intensely that the Virgin visited him in the stable and had cursed him with what he called 'Arsehole cancer' and the only way he could save himself was by giving up drink and never again having any kind of sex. Strangely enough he held to this resolve until he died nine months later.

Meanwhile his daughter was desperately attempting to offload the nuts of young Guido Senestino, who didn't have any.

Scene 4: SEX CONTINUED

...and continued

...and continued

Even the redoubtable Gertrude has to give up eventually. After all there is no juice in an empty jug. She had tried her very best. She had used every trick of tongue, every flick of lips, every tease of teeth and tickle of fingers. She had done her damnedest. And when she finally admitted defeat after a full twenty minutes or so, and scanned his face, she was irritated to see there the purest ecstasy, the deepest joy.

'Don't stop!' he begs.

'Do you like this my liebling?' she asks.

'It's beautiful! Do some more!'

'I am...tired...'

'Please! Do more!'

What a heroine. Wagner would have been so proud of her. She takes a deep breath and down again her blonde head goes!

SEX CONTINUED

Repeat until coda.
Damn there is no coda.
Chorus: 'I am tired'
Chorus: 'Don't stop!'
Chorus: 'I'm tired'
Chorus: 'I am tired'
Chorus: 'Don't stop!'
Chorus: 'I'm tired'
Chorus: 'I am tired'

Chorus: 'Don't stop!'

Chorus: 'I'm tired'

Et seq.....

Gertrude has to admit defeat eventually and perhaps Guido wanted it to stop too, nice as it was. The teeth had begun to be a little scratchy. The foreskin began to feel as if, were she to continue, it would perish like old rubber. He had never had it touched by anyone other than himself before and while he had experienced erections, frequently, he hadn't obviously experienced the cathartic release of ejaculation. Like most teenagers he walked about with an erection quite often. It was nice enough for him to know it would be nicer plunged into a woman. And here was a woman willing to at least offer one of her orifices.

Perhaps, he thought, if he played his cards right, she may offer another.

Perhaps she would like it too? Unlike the maid in the castle, so long ago now.

'Does his mean we are lovers now?' Guido asked shyly.

'Don't be silly! I am an engaged woman! Besides, I am also a virgin.'

'A virgin?' Guido is not entirely clear about the definition of virgin. He always thought that if any of the openings in a woman admitted a penis, the woman was no longer *intacta*. 'But we've just – '

'So tell me, have you been between my legs?'

'No – at least not yet –'

'So if you haven't been in there, I am still a virgin. My father told me this. We are Catholics you see.'

'So am I!' Guido declares boldly. 'I have never entered a woman!'

'Besides, you did not spill your cream. Tell me Guido, why did you not spill your cream?'

'I,' says Guido matter-of factly, 'I am Castrato. I have no cream.'

She doesn't know what to make of this information. Her experiences of nineteen years have not prepared her for this. 'I don't understand' she says.

*

The rain has stopped at last. A glimmer of summer sun struggles bravely through the sodden wet-sheep clouds. The cobbled streets are still awash, and there is a hint of evening about the tired University buildings. Further up the street the Bierkeller beckons, as lectures eject students their brains stifled with Aristotle and Goethe into the fresh air.

Guido buttons his flies. Gertrude wipes her mouth. 'But I *need* cream…' she moans half to herself. Her beauty-fluid, her insurance against growing old.

The pair swish and skitter up the puddled street. Guido feels as if he should reach for her hand, but as their fingers brush she pulls away. Gertrude is confused. She has never met a Castrato. (Nor will she ever meet another.) He has, indeed a beautiful face. His voice shivers her timbers, even his speaking voice has a resonance. It feels as if somehow it sinks beneath her skin, massages every cell of her body, permeates her, wraps around the heart. She has never felt this way about anybody. Which way?

And no cream! No cream after what felt like hours.

Boys in their university cloaks are ahead, heading their way. A brood of boys, a band of boys, a *Brüderschaft* of boy-men, crackling with laughter and testosterone. There are probably eight of them, led by Karl Boehme, who we met at the Bierkeller Gute Reise. Included in this coterie are Katsoumi Tabatabee, who has discovered that in order to avoid being beaten on a regular basis he has to at least pretend to conform; Ferrando Alighieri, an Italian Fascist; Bernard Fleischman the boxer, and some others I don't know. This is a bad mixture. Franz von Buhlow is not in the crowd. He has gone to a rehearsal.

Karl signals a stop as soon as he sees the couple heading towards them. 'Halt!' he commands. 'I spy strangers!'

'It's him! It's the one with the pin head!' Fleischman says. 'The one who we were told – '

'Sooooo,' Karl addresses Guido. 'SO! Herr freak! This is the one,' he explains, 'Sings like a girl!' His voice sugars. 'And where are you going with this beautiful German maiden?'

Guido's only experience of being attacked thus far has been from Capodimonte. He is curious. He wants to know what this means.

'Good afternoon,' he says.

'He says good afternoon! Do we agree boys?' he turns for confirmation to his coterie. 'Is it a good afternoon for Herr Freak here?'

'Please let us past,' Gertrude pleads. 'We just want to get to the Konzerthalle.'

'Young girl this is nothing to do with you,' Karl says. 'I suggest you go away.'

'Leave him alone! I will report you – '

'Go away! You, leave! We will not hurt a woman!'

Gertrude is surrounded and pushed off down an alley. She runs to seek help.

Scene 5: The Konzerthalle, evening, Feddy's office.

Rehearsals have finished for the day. While Guido faces what looks like Nemesis, important events are happening back at the Konzerthalle. You see, the Police have arrived. Specifically Polizeiobermeister Adalbert Weber from the Fohlingen police station with a briefcase full of photographs, recently arrived from Frankfurt.

The tiny office is crammed to the brim with its three occupants: Signor Capodimonte, Herr Feddy Arschlock and Polizeiobermeister Weber. The lack of space is not so much due to the small size of the room, but to the large size, literally and metaphorically, of the three gentlemen.

Capo is one side of the desk. Facing him, his satchel open, the policeman. Feddy stands awkwardly in a corner.

'You were seen on the Berne-Frankfurt train with this man, Signor. Do you recognise him?' The Polizeiobermeister has taken a photograph from his satchel, which he thrusts onto the desktop.

'The picture is very distorted.'

'No, Mein Herr, it is the face and body that is distorted! Can you say why the body is distorted?'

'That poor poor man….'

'Who is that poor man, can you say?'

This could be Commedia dell' Arte, this could be Opera Buffo, this could be played for laughs. But it isn't. So it couldn't. Because the horribly distorted face in the black-and white pictures is undeniably that of Alberto Gramaschi.

'He is Alberto Gramaschi. Italian, like me. Music tutor.'

'Ah!' The policeman allows a confirmatory breath to burst out between them. 'So it says on his passport. Now will you tell me, what were you doing with this man?'

'We were travelling together.'

'On the train yes? You were seen with him on the train. The conductor identifies you. Why did you kill him Signor?'

'Kill him? I did not kill him!'

'He was found at the side of the railway, fallen out of the

train...'

'Povero! Quell' horror!'

'Can you tell me what happened? Why did you kill him?'

'I did not! He walked out! He was depressed. He must have thrown himself – '

'He was *thrown!* Why did you kill him?'

'I would never kill someone! I am an artist! I am an entrepreneur! I am a director!'

'Now tell me mein herr, who was this pretty boy you were both together with?'

'Pretty boy?'

The policeman cannot control the sneer which makes his puffy face even more choleric than it first appeared.

Polizeiobermeister Adalbert Weber is not, it must be admitted, much of a pretty sight himself. His uniform, designed to make any man a fine figure of a man had signally failed in his case. The lawn-green tunic, which should have been nattily waisted and belted had been utterly defeated by rolls of oily fat and decorated with the stains of recent food. The jackboots too were scuffed and grubby. All of which made the policeman even more menacing.

There is no more unsettling sight than a provincial policeman nearing retirement, who has never apprehended any criminal more dangerous than a drunk in his whole career. Who now needs to prove himself and doesn't have the slightest idea how to proceed.

I'm reminded: yes, he has occasionally been asked to investigate the results of a duel, and there are duels in a University town. As, for example, in the case of Franz and his brother Hans. In these cases he invariably records a Suicide. After all it is potentially suicidal to enter into a duel, right? No blame or you spoil the game.

'The pretty boy you were both in the train with. Huh?'

'I don't understand – '

'You understand good! You speak good German. Now tell me! The boy was your – how you say – your play boy? Huh? Tell me.'

It is not easy for a flamboyant Italian dressed like a comedy stereotype of an American film director, or, if you prefer, an Italian Opera Director of the twenties to convince a small-town German policeman that he is not homosexual, not a 'degenerate', not someone likely to be travelling with a captive boychick.

'No! The boy is my – my – I am his manager. He is a singer.'

'Ah! A singer is he! Where are his parents? Have you stolen this boy? What did this – Gramaschi have to do with this?'

'He was the – the tutor. The teacher. He taught the boy music.'

'So why did you kill him!'

'What evidence do you have Herr Police? I had no reason to kill him!'

'No reason you say? How do I know that? Was it jealousy? Where is this boy? I must talk with him!'

'He's back at the Gasthaus I suppose. He will come for rehearsal tomorrow.'

'I must talk with him. In the meanwhile Mein Herr signor you will stay here in this town and do not consider leaving. If you do so you will be arrested. I will come back tomorrow, never fear.' With some considerable effort the Polizeiobermeister heaves himself out of his chair like a blob of jelly would heave itself out of a jelly mould if it was sentient. And a policeman.

Exit Weber.

Feddy: What happened with this Gramaschi? I remember, I was expecting him with you and the boy.

Capo: This is crazy! I have no idea what happened! The man was disturbed, always disturbed. He must have jumped from the train. We just thought he had walked out on us. I asked Guido, he said the man left, that was it, not to ask again. So I didn't.

Enter Gertrude, L. She is terribly distraught, hair and dress all in disarray, frightened out of her wits.

Gertrude: Where is he? Where has he gone?

Feddy: Who?

Gertrude: The policeman! I was told he was here! Please Feddy…

Feddy: He was. He left.

Gertrude: It's Guido! He – he's being attacked!

Feddy: Attacked?

Capo: Attacked?

Gertrude: Attacked! By the University!

Feddy: What? By the *whole* University?

Capo: Explain yourself!

Gertrude: By those – those students! They will kill him!

Feddy: Ach no! I will have to find another Bertarido now. And who – that angel voice! Dammit. I will never find such a voice – where is my pistol?

Gertrude: Your pistol! You have a pistol?

Capo: You have a pistol?

Feddy: The Luger. Wait. (He scrabbles in the drawer of the desk and pulls out a rusty prop gun he discovered backstage)

Gertrude: Leave that! Just get the policeman! Do you have the telephone?

Feddy: There is a telephone in the box office.

Capo: Go and telephone the policeman and tell him to go there!

Feddy: Tell him to go where?

Capo: There! There, idiot! Where must he go. Tell him woman.

Gertrude: Pflaumenstrasse! Toward the bierkeller.

Capo: Show me where. Take me there woman! You (pushes Feddy out of the office) go telephone!

Exeunt omnes.

Silence descends on the little office. We can take this opportunity to enjoy the shabby disarray of this messy room. Smell the cigarette smoke. Wish the desk could be re-leathered, it would do well in an antique shop in the nineteen eighties if it lasts that long. The two chairs certainly have little hope of lasting into the next decade, both have been sat to near smithereens. The beaten piano shows a gap-toothed ivory grin.

Minutes pass. The clock ticks. I forget if there was a clock.

Enter Guido. He is somewhat disheveled and there is a bright splash of blood on his hands and some on his coat. He is relieved to find no-one here. He goes over to a small washstand and washes his hands. He notices the blood on his coat and tries to remove it with a damp cloth.

We notice that his face is seraphic. His face is a mask, almost a rictus grin.

He removes his beloved *tanto*, the long Samurai dagger, sharp as paper, its edge diamond hard, obsidian sharp, from the folds of his coat.

As he wipes the knife with the damp cloth, followed by a dry cotton handkerchief from his pocket, we realize the reverence he has for this blade.

It is a truly noble blade, five hundred years old. Who knows what blood it liberated from oriental bodies before it was bought in Japan by the Baron and placed at rest in his library where a lonely restless boy found it and loved it. Where he, absorbed in the Japanese lore he discovered on those shelves, cleaned it and practiced with it and had his dreams of revenge and romance.

We do know what blood that blade has liberated since this boy took the weapon as his only true companion, his only trusted friend.

First there was the boy in the stable was there not.

And then Henriette Maria of course. There never was a 'Q'. Clever Guido wrote the note to confuse the easily confused police.

Next, I am convinced, the noble Gramaschi, whose throat he slit before pushing him from the train. Stupid police! Because of the wreckage the tracks and the ground and many sharp stones had made of the body, the slit throat escaped their notice.

(It is possible, bearing in mind the story of the father and the escape from – where was it – in Italy – that it was a Church Hit Squad. I doubt it after so long. Research required.)

And now young Karl Boehme lies on rain-sodden cobbles surrounded by his drinking friends, blood pumping out of his chest.

What a mess.

And only I know the whole story.

Scene 4 continued

Let's go back two hours, to that scene in the street. We left Guido facing a posse of students, all fired up by the rhetoric of Karl Boehme, by their own xenophobia, possibly from reading too much Nietsche, definitely influenced by the still nascent but growing Nazis. Not yet drunk, but very much wanting to be. Too much testosterone in one narrow cobbled roadway.

'I know you,' Guido says. 'You are playing Garibaldo, no? In the Opera?'

Karl is not quite sure how to proceed. 'I think you will find,' he hisses, 'I am your nemesis. Not just in the Opera…'

'Perhaps, mein herr, you haven't understood the plot. I think you'll find, in Act three – '

'What are you talking about! I haven't read that far.'

'Yes indeed, it seems I kill you.'

'You kill me!' Poor Karl is sparking with electrifying testosterone and delight. 'No chance! I am a master of fencing!'

'I am impressed, herr. It's not me says I can kill you, it's Handel. Bertarido kills Garibaldo. I will show you the libretto -'

'What does he know,' this stupid young man spouts. Ah, the bravado of the young! The boastful boy who would open his own chest to the knife of a killer for the sake of his male ego. 'I say I could beat you with epee or scimitar, any day of the week!'

'Not in *this* Opera!' Guido laughs.

'You are insulting my swordsmanship!'

'Duel! Duel! Duel!' the boys are chanting. 'Duel! Duel! Duel!'

'I will not fight with you,' Guido says. 'We are colleagues in Opera.'

'Then I will fight with *you*!' Karl steps forward, removes his white glove and ritually slaps Guido across the face.

Guido is delighted. It is as if he has been given a boon. He has read about duels. He knows how they go.

'Very well,' he smiles. I want you to look at his face, to see the smile of this killer. It is a terrifying face right now, the thin beautiful lips like bleeding slashes. Between them the sharp sparkle of a glimpse of teeth. They are not filed sharp, but could so easily seem to be. 'I thank you! When shall we do this duel?'

Karl: 'Choose your weapons!!' Perhaps the deluded student is hoping Guido will say Kartoffeln.

Guido says, 'I choose my knife!'

Karl wants to cross swords. 'Peasant! Knives are for the lower classes! Untermenschen! Choose sabre!'

'Not this knife! This is a Samurai knife!' Guido's historic Tanto nestled at his side like an artificial artery, there to convey blood to his empty heart. It is thirsty.

'Karl', Fleischmann tugs at his sleeve and whispers confidentially 'he has the right to choose the weapon. You made the challenge.'

'Very well!'

'I get to choose place and time then' Karl says, snatching the initiative.

'Here! Now!' Says Guido. He is impatient to get back to Gertrude. His penis is ponderously erect.

'I choose here. I choose now!' Guido announces and the Tanto's sharkskin silk-wound hilt nestles in his hand like a penis. The saya (scabbard) expels the blade. The sun is almost set. Reflected in the blade it has its last look at the day.

As does poor Karl. 'A knife! Does someone have a knife! Quickly!' His fear shows.

'I am waiting...' says Guido. His grin drips blood.

'Here. Here!' Luckily for somebody or something for some reason Tabatabee carries a knife. It is an Indonesian Kris his father gave him as a souvenir. It is a tourist thing, made to flush money from visitors to Indonesia.

HALF TIME

We are approximately half way through this tale which is a tragic Opera and as such, it is a farce as well, like our poor existences. I think we both need to draw a breath here and think about something other than the sharp, cold shards of life like shattered glass. Which sometimes dwells in my pockets. Or beneath my bare feet. I cannot. I need to introduce you properly to two of the props in this story.

I have two knives before me on my desk. The one, an Indonesian Kris, its silvered surface looking worn, rust lines showing through. The blade is sinuous, serpentine, about ten inches long with some indecipherable engravings.

The hilt seems to be mother-of pearl covered, bound to the tang with brass wire. I don't know the maker, although the mysterious engraving on the blade might reveal that secret. Or maybe it just says Good Luck or fuck you stupid tourist buying this.

The blood it has taken is embedded within the atoms of the steel, blood of three distinct people. I only know definitely of one of them.

The other is Guido's famous Tanto. I know who made that, because when Guido stole it from the Baron's library there was a handwritten description from the Bremen dealer in the case. It reads 'Large Tanto signed Soshu No Ju Akihiro (Koto period) c 1397'. Now *that's* old.

Within and amongst the steel atoms of the blade there must be a trace of the blood of Karl Boehme.

These noble blades now rest, spent, on my table. After the Duel neither had yet had its fill of blood.

Interval over. I hope you are refreshed.

*

A KNIFE FIGHT

Do not have great expectations of this description. So swift! Over before I have time to sprinkle sand on my wet words, before blood trickles around the cobbles, cosseting the stones.

You can surely imagine Guido's fighting stance – that of the samurai knife man. As against that of Karl, who has never fought with a knife. His stance is that of a swordsman. Pity the kris has about a third the reach of a rapier. Need I mention Karl holds the knife blade pointing upward and to the front, like all amateurs. Whereas Guido holds the hilt out, blade downward, edge up, for slashing rather than stabbing as advised in the Book of Five Rings, the Samurai manual he had read in his youth.

As soon as Karl dashes forward like the fool he was, Guido side-steps and the student is slashed across the stomach, then across his chest, then lightly on the neck, before he sinks to his knees into a miasma of pain and blood.

The Kris has none of Guido's blood within the atoms of its steel.

Scene 6: Adalbert

The action now takes place on several levels of the stage at the same time. On ground/stage level we see Guido in the office seated at the desk. He is utterly absorbed in what he's doing. With a clean white cloth he is wiping the blade of the tanto, which he has dismantled into its parts. From a pocket he extracts a small container of talcum powder. Carefully he dusts the cloth with the powder then, working up the blade, he pats the powder onto the surface both sides.

The music here is probably a string quartet, playing adagio ponderoso if there is such a thing.

Satisfied with his powdering, he uses yet another cloth to remove the powder with firm, strong strokes.

The blade is now clean, as sharp and shiny as a moonbeam.

Guido holds it to the light, turning and turning the blade very slowly, entranced by the complexities of this incredible construction of steels.

A true Japanese sword or knife blade is no uniform whiteness of steel, oh no. The cutting edge, for example, the *hamon,* is quite visibly different metal to the rest of the blade and the join, in the case of our Tanto, resembles banks of clouds all the way from hilt to tip. And even the surface of the body of the blade is a complication of whorls and squiggles, rather like a burr wood, showing how many twists and turns of steel the master swordsmith incorporated in his magical process of producing a killer work of art.

Guido is immersed, absorbed, entranced.

Eventually, he extracts a phial of Choji oil from his pocket, reverently places a few drops on the cloth with which he oils the blade.

It is possible he sings an aria while he is at this work. Up to you.

On another level we see the Brüderschaft standing in a stunned awed crowd around the body of their friend. Enter Franz. It takes a minute for him to understand what he is seeing.

'What happened? Karl. Karl!'

'It was a duel Franz.' Fleischmann explains.

'With knife' Tabatabee chips in.

'Karl!!!'

'With that monster' Fleischmann adds.

'The monster?' Franz can hardly speak. 'That Guido? He did this?'

Enter Capo and Feddy. Feddy draws the rusty Luger out of his pocket and waves it about.

'What has happened here?' He asks.

'A duel Professor.' Fleischmann calls all University employees professor, just in case.

'A duel?'

Enter Gertrude, distraught. 'Where is he? Did you kill him?'

With so many question marks hanging in the air we could make sky hooks. So let's add another one:

Enter Polizeiobermeister Adalbert Weber, bursting with a bustle of pomposity. He looks rather like a battleship turning up at a turkey shoot. 'What is happening here?' he demands. 'I demand an explanation!' he demands.

CHORUS of CONFUSION

While the chorus continues, another moment for reflection.

I should be ashamed of myself. The death of a beautiful young man full of promise is no laughing matter. After all, had Karl not died I am certain he would have climbed high on the rungs of the SA, perhaps even the SS. Imagine Karl, proud in his sparkling uniform of black and crossbones, standing hips outthrust to greet the new arrivals at a concentration camp. How ruthlessly he would have risen to Kamp Kommandant, how efficiently he would have organized the distribution of the Zyklon B and the disposal of the bodies! How he would have screamed in terror as the noose was placed around his neck at Nuremberg!

Never mind. Just because Karl is dead, there are thousands of others more than capable of filling such shoes and it is probable that the number of murder victims after the war was not substantially changed because of Karl's death. Karma acts to fill a void.

But let us not forget that Karl had a mother, a sister and a girl who wanted him naked between her legs. His father had died on the last day of the War, owing to being drunk and driving his truck straight into a horse. His sister, I need to mention, loved him very much and will mourn with all her heart. As for Frau Schultz his mother, she has dementia and will assume he is at the war and will be home soon. Let's not worry about her. (Perhaps she was Jewish as he said! In which case ignore guesswork above.)

Possibly we should be worrying about Guido, as this chorus of confusion mounts in intensity, goes around a little and falls into, eventually, some sort of resolution.

We also need to worry about Franz because he really loved Karl. Not just the way brothers-in-booze, banter and college-type fraternity love each other. It was deeper and darker than that

After all, Franz had certainly had some sort of crush on Gertrude. Yet my suspicion is aroused by how quickly he seemed to have gotten over it. Certainly she was magic with her mouth and there's no doubt Franz and his late lamented brother thoroughly enjoyed her oral attentions. Yet remember there had been no actual, serious penetrative sex. Gertrude would not allow that.

Karl was no virgin for sure! But we will never know whether he was an active homosexual. Imagine how tragic it would be if all along Karl did feel the same way, but for fear of the ridicule of the Brüderschaft, never acted on it. So here is a possible Greek tragedy. Two so much in love, never declaring because of the prejudices and preconceptions of others, one doomed to die and the remaining lover doomed to forever be seeking revenge, through eternities…

Here on the cobbled street Franz with broken heart kneels sobbing at the side of Karl Schultz. The policeman takes notes and interviews witnesses. A hysterical Gertrude is being heartily slapped across the face by her husband-to be who is wondering how easy it could be to get tired of this woman. The Brüderschaft look on, a tableau of men trying to look manly and concerned at the same time.

Capo is the only man there capable of deciding what to do. So he leaves, heading up the street back toward the Konzerthalle.

He finds Guido just where he expected to find him: in Feddy's tiny office, hunched over his knife.

Scene 7: Feddy's Office

'Quickly! We must go!'

Guido looks up, mildly startled. He looks like a predatory vulture, vaguely disturbed by the arrival of a sparrow.

'Why so?'

'They will arrest you. They will hang you. Or shoot you. Or whatever they do in Germany. You fool!'

'Who do you dare to call a fool?' This is said quietly, with menace. Guido has changed since this murder. He seems far more sure of himself– he is still basking in the afterglow of the killing. Like a boa constrictor digesting prey. 'I am not leaving here'

For probably the first time in his life Signor Capo feels fear.

'Calm down Maestro' this last word with a scintilla of contempt. 'It was a duel. An affair of honour. '

'If you say so. A duel. But tell me – '

'Yes. Tell you what.'

'What happened to the other one? The Gramaschi. That was you wasn't it.'

'Exactly what was me, maestro? What?'

Capo feels fear rising in him as he begins to realize: this strange creature, this corrupted and disfigured boy-man may have killed two people. And he is alone with him, in a small room, no-one else anywhere near. And the boy is coddling and cosseting the blade of a terrible weapon.

He prevaricates. He decides. 'You killed him. You killed your beloved tutor! My God!' It all fits together. Capo is facing a cobra.

'Yes Maestro, I did.' Guido is calm, his voice low and deeply controlled. 'it was necessary. I had finished with him.'

'You had – finished?' Capo finds himself beginning to shake. 'Finished?'

'He could do no more for me Maestro.' Guido's blue eyes have too much depth for Capo not to fall in.

'You pushed him from the train?' Capo whispers the question.

'First I slit him. I didn't want him to suffer.'

He stares down at the knife in the boy's hand.

'Kind of you,' he mutters.

'I did it for you.' Guido states this as if it is too obvious to say.

'For me.'

'Of course Maestro! You are the genius, you are the great Director. Why would you want that old man with his small knowledge and experience to interfere with this great project we are embarked upon?'

'Project?'

'Our project. To make me the greatest and most famous singer in the world! You understand my potential. You saw how they loved me in Berne. You know what I can do.' There is no uncertainty or hesitancy in his voice. He is utterly convinced as to the truth of what he is saying. 'And when we have conquered these provincials, when we have made this Rodelinda the greatest since 1725, we will take the Baroque back into all the greatest Opera houses of the world. When they hear my voice, all the producers at La Scala or Covent Garden or wherever will fall over themselves to bring Handel into their houses. And without me, Handel is nothing any more. And without you. I am nothing. Do you understand?'

'I think I do.'

Poor fool.

'And so we will do this. We will make this Opera beyond magnificent.'

There is a pause here for some dramatic music, as Capo's mind is whipped and torn and flung about like a mouse in the jaws of a cat.

Eventually he says 'You've just killed Garibaldo.'

'Yes, he tried to stand against me, stupid boy. They will find another Garibaldo. It's not a difficult role.'

'It's a nuisance.'

'Just tell him – the dwarf man – find us a Garibaldo. There are plenty of Garibaldos in this University! He doesn't have to be good. That boy was good. Bass-baritone, Too good. Find someone just passable. Understand?'

Exit Capo, his expression unreadable.

Scene 8: The stage of the Konzerthalle. The next day.

The cast of the Opera Rodelinda – minus, of course, Karl Schultz whose mortal remains are awaiting collection from the morgue by his family – sit on folding chairs on the stage facing the auditorium. Feddy sits stage left, Capo stage right. They are like the bread between which the meat of the sandwich festers.

They are waiting.

Between and amongst them like bacteria or worms, their thoughts mutter. Of course Franz is the most emotionally distorted amongst them, primarily by loss, anger and fear. I do not want to intrude on his thoughts. It makes me too sad.

Gertrude, sitting there in the middle, is convinced the production is about to be cancelled and all her diva dreams are to be dashed.

As for Guido, he is fatalistically convinced that *all will be well, all will be very well.* He cannot imagine that like an armoured knight on a charger heading for the tournament, he could ever be unhorsed.

Feddy, like his fiancé, is riddled with thoughts of doom. With one of his cast dead and another seemingly about to be arrested for murder, there can be no future for Rodelinda. He awaits the sword of Damocles without the slightest fatalism. His predominant thought is *Why Me. Why does this happen to me. Is it a curse, is the ghost of Handel trying to stop this production. This is not fair. Does Gertrude love Guido. If so he will kill himself. Or her. Or perhaps not. He could never kill anybody. But he will certainly descend into the depths of the deepest depression ever invented. Or is this for the best.*

Capo is thinking: *if they arrest the boy I am finished for now. I have very little money. I cannot live in this cultural cul-de sac. These Limburgers have the creativity of a dead rat. Will this Dwarf give me money. What if the boy is right. He is dreaming. He will be hanged or shot. That will be good and bad. Good because he deserves it. But bad! God I have never heard such a voice. This is the voice of a God. This is the most incredible voice in Opera. In the cosmos. This voice alone can slaughter Europe. Never mind the knife. The knife. That is the voice. A knife. Sharp, dangerous. I must protect him. I must save him at all costs. We must get out of here. Can I find a lawyer. This is a university. They will certainly have lawyers.*

The thoughts of the others though certainly important to themselves at the time, are of no relevance. (Although I should mention that Lucia Dell'Isola was feeling fantastically – ach – aroused.)

Enter Polizeiobermeister Adalbert Weber stage left. The Polizeiobermeister has made an attempt to tidy and spruce himself up. His uniform has, incredibly, been ironed. Though not cleaned. He is extremely conscious of the extent to which these people awaiting him are dependent on his opinions, decisions and actions. So he is certainly in his element. A provincial policeman in a German University town seldom has any excuse to enjoy his power. The most dramatic moments of the job are to do with drunken students misbehaving, although in this particular university town their drunken revels seldom reach a pitch beyond the mildly amusing. Certainly panties have been stolen and placed on statues' heads. Students in stupors have been decanted from gutters. Females have been placated or paid off, their complaints generally ignored and the male student involved gently reproved. Boys will be boys. There has never been a violent rape – the gentlemen are far too studious and gentlemanly for that. Or so their parents think. So all we can say with certainty is there has never, in the two hundred years of the University, been an incident which would raise more than an eyebrow of any local news reporter.

Apart from the duels.

There have been only eight duels resulting in deaths in the history of the University. Usually someone gets a couple of picturesque scars across the cheek, something to boast about to peers and grandchildren. Badge of honour.

One of the deaths being, of course, that of Franz's unfortunate brother Hans.

Which was a subject of intense annoyance to the Polizeiobermeister. He had worked hard to suppress any scandal, especially when Herr von Bülow expressed a fervent desire to hush up the entire episode. Herr von Bülow was a minor official in the Weimar Republic, a powerful man in the province and an influential member of the Assembly. He feared nothing in life. Except his wife, his sons and the loss of reputation.

Besides von Bülow had been a participant in a duel in 1880 at the same University, in which he had killed a rival for the supposed affection of a prostitute. *His* father had suppressed that scandal, and he had suppressed this one. With an appropriate payment and a quick funeral, of course. Like father like son. Duels seemed to run in the family. And to be honest, the Herr had never liked Hans. Too smart, too arrogant, too argumentative. Too beloved of his mother.

So when Adalbert Weber entered stage left he had all this in his mind, smudged, it is true, by several swigs of Schnapps he had taken for fortification.

His first word was 'You!' spat out on entrance like the thrust of a lance. This is directed straight at Franz.

'Me?' Franz said.

'I told you there were to be no more duels! I told you!'

'It is not my fault – '

'Why did you not stop it? Prevent it! Your friend it was. You nearly lost me my job with your stupid pride and killing people.'

'I was not there!' Franz mutters.

Weber sees Guido. 'You! You think you are ok to go and kill someone because he insults you or whatever. What did he do? Call you a freak?'

Guido stares as if the policeman has interrupted a well-deserved snooze.

'You *are* a freak! He was right to call you that! I am here to arrest you!'

'Signor police! You are insulting an artist!' Capo has stood up, ready to defend the boy. 'Probably the greatest artist you will ever see in this town. You can never arrest him.'

'An Artist is he! An Artist! A piss artist!' Herr Weber is tired now, seeking somewhere to sit. 'I have had enough of you. I have had enough of you all. This is a respectable town! We have law and order here. Which is me. I am law and order here.'

Capo goes to the piano. 'Boy! *Se potessero i sospir miei!!!'*

Guido strides to stand beside the piano, and the voice, that voice that cuts sharp as a tanto through a throat storms the stage and enters every mind like a brain-eating leech…
(YouTube Se potessero. Put yourself in the smelly boots of the flatfoot. Listen.)

'Stop! Stop!' the policeman howls, his hands clasped over his ears 'Stop! I beg you!'

Capo caresses the keys into a seductive glissando and stops. 'Do you understand?' He asks.

'I understand that this boy is dangerous!' Weber replies.

'He is dangerous,' Feddy agrees. 'But he is perfect. He is a genius.'

'Explain to me. To me it's like a shrieking of a demented creature. I do not understand this music. Explain to this provincial policeman.'

'Her Polizeimeister. This is the greatest voice I have ever heard,' says Feddy.

'I am a Director, I have directed Opera all over the world Herr Signor. When this boy came to me I became the manager of the most magnificent voice I have ever heard.' Capo says.

'He sings like a woman!' The policeman says.

'That is the divine voice, Herr. That is the special and divine voice, as rare as an honest banker, as a divine diamond from the soul of the Virgin. People will come to Fohlingen from all the world to hear this voice and to see my Opera. It will, as they say, put this town on the map.' Feddy says.

'Is this true?' He turns to the cast. There is a stir of nodding heads. A mutter of agreement. 'But he has killed a man. Your friend, Franz. What do you say?'

There is silence. Franz' face is a flurry of emotions.

'I agree.' He says almost inaudibly.

'What? What do you agree? Speak louder.'

'You cannot arrest him. You did not arrest me.'

'What?'

'For dueling. If you arrest him for dueling you will have to arrest me. You know what my father says.'

Polizeiobermeister Adalbert Weber now does something he is not used to doing. He thinks deeply. He thinks, my pension. That pile of marks from Herr von Bülow I may forfeit. Putting this town on the map. But. 'There is also the suspicion of another murder,' he says. 'An Italian on a train. Probably pushed by this - this - degenerate - " pointing to Capo.

'He fell off,' Guido says. 'I saw him!'

'Yes!' Capo interjects. 'He was drunk. He fell off the train.'

'You saw him. Would you swear to that?'

'Of course I will!' Guido snaps. 'In any court!'

More silence.

'This dead boy, ' says Capo. 'Self-defence! Suicide! Whatever you like.'

Polizeiobermeister Adalbert Weber shrugs. 'You!' he says, addressing Franz. 'You! You will make sure there is never, never, *never* any trouble here with these people! There will be no murders, there will be no fights, there will be no need for me ever to see any of you again! Is that clear? Because let me tell you young man if there is any trouble whatsoever, the first person I will arrest is you, the second is Herr freaky genius here. Both of you will stand trial for murder. I don't care if your father is the chief justice of the *world*, understand?'

And in a miasma of threat and Schnapps-flavoured spittle, exit policeman stage right.

KITTENS FOR KATSOUMI

One of the strangest aspects to this Opera Seria, this tale of blood and sweat and also sperm, though not that of our Hero, is the role of Katsoumi Tabatabee. Perhaps you remember him - the lanky Persian whose father was Prime Minister of Persia.

Personally I would have given the role to Fleischmann. A big wide boxer built like a brick schoolhouse, no doubt he could produce a deep and possibly enthralling bass, perfect for Garibaldo. The Persian frankly looks like a tenor or more likely an alto. About 6 foot four, all lanky incompetence, certainly in matters like walking and standing still. His beaky nose, dull brown eyes, shock of unmanageable hair and terrible skin make him someone you would not like to share a bath with.

Mind you he is certainly the one you would like to share your essays with. In fact the popularity of this young man comes from his willingness to edit or even write essays for his classmates, generally for a very affordable fee. A good man to have on one's side.

Interesting that he always carries a knife. I do promise to explain that eventually.

Not that Fleischmann didn't audition, he certainly did, at Franz' insistence. Franz after all was in mourning and churning with hatred for Guido. He needed a trusted lieutenant at his side, just waiting for the opportunity to wreak terrible revenge on the boy who had killed his trusted 'brother'. And as he had to watch every step he took he wasn't ready to wreak revenge without the use of a proxy.

What made Katsoumi audition? Remember, this boy was consumed with the desire to please his friends, classmates and colleagues. He had a hunger for acceptance, for friendship and of course for women. Like a puppy always soliciting love. And so in the completely mistaken idea that participation in the Opera would bring him the admiration of his peers (and possibly, women) he turned up at the audition, tongue hanging out and tail wagging.

What made Feddy and Capo choose the Persian and not the German? Guido of course. Having just disposed of the other real singer in the Opera, he wasn't about to agree to another one.

Aha. You may just have spotted the reason for the joy with which Guido had entered so readily into the idea of a duel with Karl. Karl had a deep, powerful, resonant bass/baritone voice. Karl could have gone into professional Opera. He could act as well as sing.

Puccini, had he heard the man, would have created Scarpia for him. Verdi would have cast him, without hesitation and despite his youth, as the Grande Inquisitore in Don Carlos.

And Fleischmann was almost as good. Not as good an actor, but a damn good voice.

Katsoumi Tabatabee, on the other hand, had to reach deep into his admittedly capacious lungs to find the deep voice which was not even slightly natural for him. He had growled and rasped through the audition, convinced that he had no hope of securing the role – but, he was sure, he would get the immense respect of his peers for trying.

Guido had insisted on being present. 'I have to work with him! I insist!'

Poor Katsoumi, was told to prepare *Sibilar gli angui d'Aletto* from Rinaldo. Cliffs, crags, plenty of trips stalls and falls available. Listen on Youtube.

Feddy listened in transfixed horror, as Fr Müller clattered her way through the accompaniment on the piano. Difficult enough, if the singer you are accompanying has a different idea of the *tempo* to the pianist's. Almost impossible if the voice feels as if it's sandpapering one's inner ear.

But Guido sat as if entranced, and on the last note, clapped enthusiastically.

'Thank you!' Feddy said, utterly relieved when the torture was over. Please go and sit in the auditorium, wait.

Sweating and shaking, Katsoumi wuffled his way out of the room.

I admit Fleischmann's performance wasn't his best. Convinced he was perfect for the role, the brick schoolhouse (you may substitute an alternative syllable before 'house', should you wish. I never use that word except when I need a shit.) had not rehearsed the aria. Whereas the Persian had rehearsed himself silly. So Fleischmann had decided that volume and bombast would see him through the audition.

Guido did not clap.

Twenty minutes later, (the volume of dispute from the office almost reached a crescendo greater than Sibilar had ever reached), Feddy went out to the apron of the stage and announced the decision.

Imagine Katsoumi's surprise at the good news.

Fleischmann went off to get drunk.

5

ACT 8

Scene 1: The Substitute

'You must explain yourself to me!' Franz von Buhlow has Katsoumi Tabatabee by the ears in an alley off the Lindengasse. His face is inches from that of the frightened boy. 'Why on earth did you audition for Garibaldo? WHY?'

---

[5] ***Illustration - Handel Festival***

'I'm sorry I'm sorry' he is almost in tears.

'How could you DO that! How could you DO that to me! After everything I have done for you?'

'I thought you would be pleased?'

Franz twists him by the ears and tosses him into the gutter. 'You have betrayed me! You have betrayed the Brüderschaft! You will stand trial! You will pay the penalty!'

'Please no. Please no Brother.' Katsoumi has witnessed a 'trial'. He knows how humiliating it can be to have to stand naked in the *Jungbrunnen*, the fountain in the middle of the University's quadrangle, while being interrogated by whip-yielding Bruder. 'What do I have to do? It was my mistake! I would never betray the Brüderschaft!!'

Here Franz kicks him in the ribs. Once, twice, then again from the other side. Again. Again. During this beating- which I do not need to describe, as so many other writers have done this job so effectively – Katsoumi is obviously crying, bawling for mercy (he is no hero) promising anything, just anything, including money and his sister. Franz is making bully noises, cursing, all the usual.

Then Franz is tired. And remembering, suddenly, as his fury dissipates, the Policeman's warning: 'if there is any trouble whatsoever, the first person I will arrest is you!'

'Very well.' He says eventually, 'You have had your punishment.'

The Persian has not experienced physical violence since his schooldays. Remember he comes from an aristocratic Persian family, tremendously rich and pampered, more used to reciting poetry than conforming to the ancient Persian stereotype of horse-riding and shooting arrows from the saddle. This is the reason, in fact, that his father – ostensibly on the advice of his Uncle - sent him to Germany to study.

'Now you listen to me you slimy Untermensch. You have betrayed me, and you have betrayed the Brüderschaft. From now on, you are working for us. You owe us, understand?'

'I owe you.'

'You owe me your life. I could have killed you.'

'I am grateful.'

'You will tell *nobody* about this, understand?'

'Nobody.'

Exit Franz, leaving Katsoumi to experiment with standing up.

Scene 2: A Rehearsal

And so the factions begin to coalesce. Never has any Opera production been so riddled with dramas and agendas, so full of hatred and peppered with love. In fact, it is as complicated and full of potential violence and sex as most Baroque operas. Take Rodelinda, for one. Read the Synopsis and see if you can make head or tail out of it.

Compared to that! Well, we are now on the brink of the most incredible event in the History of Opera – the revival of Handel right in the middle of Germany, his homeland. Perhaps, like the Opera, we will have a happy ending, with celebrations all round. The villain relents and surrenders his kingdom. The hero is reunited with his beloved wife and his kingdom. Everybody happy.

Knowing Guido as I do, I doubt it.

We will now visit a rehearsal. The cast has been augmented by Katsoumi, who, while he can't move terribly well (a problem when he has to wield a sword in Act 2) he makes a brave attempt at the singing. Despite breathing problems. He certainly had a cracked rib, poor boy. If asked (and nobody did) he would have said he fell downstairs.

Feddy just assumed that the Persian was useless and despaired often.

The stage of the Konzerthalle, afternoon. This rehearsal is of Act 2, Scene 2.

Feddy: Plot Points. Please listen. Here is the conversation between the bad ones: Grimoaldo (Franz), who is the usurper of the throne, and his sidekick Garibaldo (Tabatabee). Now Garibaldo is trying to persuade his boss to kill the Hero, Bertarido. It's all very sinister and dramatic.

Feddy is standing by the piano from which Frau Müller mechanically churns out an approximation of the Handel music. Capo is sprawled on an armchair stage R, bored. In the audience sit various cast members waiting for their scene to be rehearsed. They include Guido.

Feddy: Useless! (steps to stage centre, waving the music in the air,

despairing) There is no tension! No threat! No passion!
Franz: I am doing my best.
Feddy: No you're good. It's this idiot.
Tabatabee: I am doing my best.
Feddy: You move like a tree! You sing like a bee! You're supposed to be a *baritone!*
Capo: Excuse me Maestro, a word? (He beckons Feddy aside.)
Capo: (Sotto voce) It's fine.
Feddy: I'm sorry Maestro, (exasperated) how can you say it's fine? Why could I not cast the other boy, that lunking Flesh man. *He* was fine.
Franz: That's what *I* said.
Capo: (Annoyed, starting to lose his temper) You know why! We have this beanpole boy now! We are stuck with him! We must make do.
Guido: (from the auditorium) Excuse me, can we do my scene now?
Feddy: Just wait. (Turns back to Capo) He can't sing, he can't act, nothing! Tabatabee! Perfect name!
Guido: (hearing) Excuse me! He acts and sings fine! Why are you nasty to him?
Tabatabee is shrinking and squirming with embarrassment. He doesn't like being demeaned again. He has indeed been trying his best, within the limits of his beaten body and his basic incompetence at acting and singing. As I said, he is SO like a doggie that just wants petting, poor dear. And just like a kicked dog, he wants to howl.
And now someone is defending him. Gratitude rising.
Guido: You need to give him a chance! Can't you see he's ill?
Feddy: Useless! *I'm* ill! I'm sick of *him!*
Franz: I told you he's useless. Get Fleischman back.
Capo: Are you ill, boy?
Tabatabee: I – I fell down stairs. I have pain.
Guido: You see? He will be fine tomorrow. Can I do my scene now?
Feddy: Oh my God.
Capo: We can do Act 3 Scene 1. (Claps his hands imperiously) Piano! Act three Scene 1! Go away boy. Get the girl!
Exit Tabatabee, hastily. Enter Gertrude.
SINISTER MUSIC.
The rehearsals proceed like a leaking ship through a stormy sea. There is always the possibility that some storm or rock or drunken pilot will sink the vessel. Storms abound. Rocks leap out of the waters and smash themselves against the hull, or leap onto the deck, or fly into

the helmsman's face. The greatest danger, of course, is that while captain and pilot know the destination, both have different ideas as to how to reach that Promised Land.

Capodimonte is used to the traditional rehearsal schedule, Feddy is not. In Capo's world, rehearsals start with the *sitzprobe* - sitting with the cast and going through scenes. There would be five different phases of rehearsing. Sectional rehearsals, for example, would be for each section of the orchestra.

So at least two Sitzprobe, a three hour sectional for each, four 'blocking' rehearsals with singing, then one pre-dress, one dress rehearsal and then - performance!

Feddy had never done any of this before. Poor Feddy. He just wanted the Opera on the stage. No pre-dress! 'They will be ready! You will see! I am going to do this my way, Maestro.'

So far so chaotic.

On the day the musicians joined the singers, the destination, like a harbor winking its lights at you from across a leaden ocean seemed at least to exist. You will remember they had been rehearsing initially without the cast, so that by the time Feddy brought everyone together they had a very good grasp of the music.

Rodelinda is more of a concert piece than a full fat and round Opera. The orchestra is a trim little thing, a mere 2 recorders, flute, 2 oboes, [bassoon] 2 horns, strings, continuo (cello, lute, harpsichord).

The feeling of singing an aria or duet is so very much more life-enhancing with an orchestra, however small, rather than just a piano. At last it begins to feel as if the performance is real. Now with three weeks to go, Feddy has begun to rehearse the piece in sequence, and so the performers are beginning to get an idea of the actual plot. Let's face it, most of them wouldn't have read the entire libretto and if they did, they would most likely have no idea whatsoever as to what is actually going on.

But all of a sudden everything begins to come together. (The Synopsis is on Wiki – type Rodelinda synopsis, but really it's not essential to read it. Just if you want to. It is not necessary to understand the plot to enjoy the music, as a great man once said. I think it was me. It's true about life, too. I once thought I had understood the plot, about the time I wrote Messiah.) Guido becomes Bertarido, the king without a country, and Gertrude, as his beloved Rodelinda, and her real self is beginning to fall seriously in love with him. Not the character, the Castrato. Not a great idea when her husband-to be is the conductor and Musical Director. And again, the object of her affection is lacking the two attributes which would make him the ideal husband. Feddy cringes and flinches whenever he sees his intended on stage in the arms of the misshapen Guido.

Don't forget the fuming Franz, suffused with hatred and the desire for revenge, having to watch his once-beloved in the arms of the freak. He has indeed become every inch his character, Grimoaldo, the usurper and lover of Rodelinda.

Tabatabee, who has gained some idea as to how to produce an acceptable baritone voice, is inserted uncomfortably into the role of Grimoaldo's counselor Garibaldo. Who hates and loves his boss.

So far so typecast.

The others: Eduige, played by Beatrix Müller. Bless her. There was no way Beatrix could ever fit into her role. Supposedly the sister of Bertarido and betrothed to Grimoaldo,you could well understand his lack of interest. This obese hausfrau, who, you will recall was both pianist for the initial rehearsals and part financier of the whole production, had the sex-appeal of a potato. She rather saw her role as the substitute mother and protector of Feddy, his sidekick and helper in all things. She was also there to protect and defend her daughter Lisa, who is playing Flavio, Rodelinda's son. Believe me, Lisa needs no protection whatsoever.

Enter Lucia del'Isola to play Unulfo, Bertarido's friend and counselor.

Lucia arrived late, with less than two weeks to go before the Dress Rehearsal. She had been awarded the part in absentia, and without consulting her initially, by Feddy. He knew her well as a singer and a student. He was confident that she would accept the role, that she would fit into Unulfo's trousers as if she was made to wear them and would sing the role as if she'd been doing it all her life. Which in a way she had.

When rehearsals started, Lucia was in Italy at the side of *Il Duce*, as his security chief, spy, assistant and official lesbian. She had taken her summer break from the University as her perfect opportunity to slither her way into the Fascist government of her home country and had been eminently successful in this endeavor. Her path had been oiled by her oleaginous father, who had provided Mussolini with his entire wardrobe for the whole of his political career. While the Nazis were designed by Hugo Boss, the Fascisti in Italy were visually at least the creation of Gaetano Del'Isola, the chief designer at the 'Opificio Militare' and the personal tailor of the boss.

And so, when the formidable Lucia arrived at last it was to a minor fanfare, at least from Feddy.

He was conducting Act One at the time. On the stage Franz as Grimoaldo is trying to persuade Gertrude as Rodelinda that she should love him. After all, he has defeated her husband (Guido as Bertarido). He is probably dead. Franz is now king. Marry me and be my queen. I don't fancy my intended, Eduige. (Not surprising. If you were a heftily masculine possibly closet homosexual would you fancy a fat lady called Eddie?)

Gertrude angrily rejects him. *L'empio rigor del fato* she sings.

Stop! Cries Feddy as she comes down the aisle of the auditorium like a crowd. Lucia never does anything by halves.

'*Caro Maestro*!' she caws as she flows past rows Q and R, 'Do not panic! Lucia *è arrivata!*'

'Precious one!' Feddy, never given to extreme expressions, knows exactly how this rare bird should be treated. In the *Frülingskonzert*last year he had coaxed a marvelous alto voice out of her, a voice she didn't know she had, and it had transformed her life. She was hugely grateful to him and would be until she died in New York at the age of 101 as a well-known Opera star who featured in almost every production Feddy had anything to do with until he retired.

She adored him as a teacher and a mentor.

Which was why, despite her having taken her vacation to prop up the Mussolini regime, he had cast her so confidently in the role of Unulfo, Bertarido's great friend and counselor. Frankly, had Guido not arrived and climbed into his mind with his incredible voice, Lucia would have had the lead role. For which he felt somewhat guilty, but as he had never told Lucia of the possibility of her singing Bertarido, he knew she wouldn't be hurt.

'You made it!'

She leaps up to the podium and they embrace. Gertrude stares uncomprehendingly. Well, it certainly is a strange sight. Her diminutive husband-to be in his motheaten frock coat and ruffled shirt, enveloped in the embrace of a vast tall thin bony woman with very short hair, dressed in a pinstripe suit, bright yellow cravat and spats.

'Ladies and gentlemen,' Feddy says, stepping aside and turning to the orchestra and the stage, 'I present Lucia, our Unulfo. She has come all the way from Torino, from the side of the beloved Duce, just to be here with us and sing in our Opera. Applause please!'

Some applause from the cast on stage and those scattered in the auditorium, or backstage waiting for cues.

'Please please Maestro, anything for you' She bows to the stage, turns and bows to the auditorium.

Capo had been warned, to some extent. 'She is eccentric, but with a marvelous voice', Feddy had assured him

'But Maestro, surely she needs to be here for the whole rehearsals? Will she know the music?'

'Ahh, Maestro, you must not doubt my judgment. I assure you, she will know the entire Opera, long before she arrives!'

And so she did.

Entr'acte (or, more appropriately, *Zwischenspiel*)

And so now, my dear audience, we are approaching the Dress Rehearsal. Everything is getting into order. All the characters are in place, their roles defined, ready to thrill all of us with a performance of a lifetime.

Before you plunge into the remainder of our story I suggest you watch the whole Opera on YouTube, preferably in English or with English subtitles.

Not compulsory! If you want to get on with the story, continue, with guilt.

Scene 3: Marketing

The conventional wisdom in the theatre, as Opera, is that in order to ensure a magnificent Opening Night the Dress Rehearsal should be a total disaster. As a result few productions invite critics to a Dress Rehearsal, they may put on a Preview performance instead – which is a dress rehearsal with all the problems, theoretically fixed in the pre-dress Feddy did not know this. And Capo, by now totally frustrated, did not tell him.

So the damned fool invited some of the greatest most pompous pedantic egotists in the Opera world to the dress rehearsal of his Rodelinda.

There was Foure, of the Berliner Tageblatt. Mannheim of die Zeit. Halshoffer of Volkischer Beobachter. A long shot, Pecarino of La Stampa. And several others, whose names I don't have. At any rate, these were the gentlemen whose reviews appeared the following morning. The same men, incidentally, mentioned by the Baron and Sebastian years ago. Critics live forever, damn them.

Why on earth would such an august group of connoisseurs of the Opera bother to travel miles to the barren heart of Germany, to a university production of an obscure Opera? The reason probably lies in the brilliance of Feddy's letter of invitation.

Here it is:

My dear colleague in Music
THE HANDEL FESTIVAL PREMIERE
This is a tremendously exciting time for German Opera! The works of our wonderful modern composers such as Wagner are everywhere, but remember that the tradition of great Opera goes back many more years. In the early 18th century German music conquered Britain. One of the greatest of our great composers, Georg Frideric Händel, moved to London, abandoned his umlaut, changed his name for the English taste to George Frederic Handel and completely delighted and amazed them with his genius. Since then, we have criminally forgotten this great man's operas and it is time for his resurrection as one of the heroes of the German people.

We are therefore launching what is to be an annual Opera Festival in the beautiful University City of Fohlingen, which will feature the magnificent visions, and the thrilling music of Handel's, RODELINDA, one of his earliest and greatest operas.

SENSATIONAL DISCOVERY
The lead role of Bertarido is to be played by the sensational discovery, Signor Guido della Roccaporca , a genuine Castrato. This will be the only opportunity this century to thrill to the exact sound of a male voice, as heard by the adoring Opera goers in the eighteenth century! Those who have heard Sr della Roccaporca sing will never forget the experience.

Because you are one of the most noted critics in the entire country, we are inviting you to the Dress Rehearsal, to take place on 24th June 1920 at 8pm, at the Konzerthalle of Fohlingen University.

Your tickets are enclosed. I sincerely hope to see you on the evening.

Yours in Music
Federich Arshlock

Well, who could resist such an invitation.

Feddy had prepared advertisements in all the local newspapers, lauding the lead singer, extolling Handel, Germany, music and the town itself. How fortunate he had secured an immense budget, not just from Frau Müller, determined that her adored daughter would be in a famous production of a fantastic Opera. I am certain that a beloved diamond ring went into this project but I am not going to tell that story as you are perfectly capable of telling it to yourself. (Hint: a furious husband, a midnight mammoth contretemps of epic proportions, a dyspeptic apoplectic gentleman of considerable size exiled into the night)

ADVERTISEMENT IN NEWSPAPERS

The FIRST INTERNATIONAL FESTIVAL OF GF HANDEL'S OPERAS!

Begins with
RODELINDA
An Opera in 3 acts
FEATURING the ONLY TRUE Castrato of the 20th Century
The Magnificent singer **GUIDO della Roccaporca**
Fresh from his success at the BERNE Opera
In the heartwarming and heartbreaking story of love and loss by the greatest German composer of the 18th Century, **Georg Frederich Handel**

AT The Konzerthalle Fohlingen University from the 26th June 1920 at 8pm every week night and Saturday until 5th July.

Music Direction: Hr F Arshlock, Stage Direction, fresh from productions at the great Opera Houses, Sr Capodimonte of Naples and Milan.

Tickets: From Fr B. Mueller Ganzstrasse 14, Bullersdorf bei Fohlingen or apply at the University.

You can well imagine how furious Capo was at seeing the emasculated status of his prodigy used to aggrandise the production. No surprise for you then, as I play for you the scene when Maestro Capodimonte, joint Director of the production, confronts Maestro Arschloch, joint Director of the production, waving in his fist a copy of the Fohlingen Zeitblatt.

Capo: What is this! What is this filth! You told me you would not –
Feddy: Maestro! What is amiss?
Capo: This! This! (He spreads the newspaper out on Feddy's desk and stabs at the advertisement with his finger.) Castrato! You have written here, *Castrato*!
Feddy: (Calm) Certainly I have.
Capo: You agreed not to do this!
Feddy: And how else am I going to fill this great big Konzerthalle? Do you think anybody on earth would bother to come and see an ancient Opera no-one knows, performed by nonentities from a University

amateur drama group, with a conductor no-one has heard of, eh?
Capo: (Defensively) *I* am heard of! I have had productions in great houses –
Feddy: Yes Maestro, I have mentioned that! See? 'Under the Stage Direction of Sr Capodimonte, from the great Opera Houses of Europe, with Musical Direction from – '
Capo: Stage Director! I am Director of the production!
Feddy: *Joint* director. With me.
Capo: You are the Conductor! Why don't you say so!
Feddy: Musical Director, it says –
Capo: I am the main Director. Everything that happens on stage is me! My vision!
Feddy: And mine!
Pause while two egos tangle up like drunken wrestlers. Straining here, there, doing throws, leaps and slams, the Maestros battle for dominance. Frankly Capo has completely forgotten the original reason for his anger, and perhaps that's exactly what Feddy was relying on. Because the next time the ad appeared, not just in the Fohlingen Zeitblatt but in several newspapers with far larger circulation, it said:

The FIRST INTERNATIONAL FESTIVAL OF GF HANDEL'S OPERAS!

Begins with
RODELINDA
An Opera in 3 acts
FEATURING the ONLY TRUE Castrato of the 20th Century
The Magnificent singer **GUIDO della Roccaporca**
Fresh from his success at the BERNE Opera
In the heartwarming and heartbreaking story of love and loss by the greatest German composer of the 18th Century, **Georg Frederich Handel**

AT The Konzerthalle Fohlingen University from the 26th June 1920 at 8pm every week night and Saturday until 5th July.

DIRECTOR: Sr CAPODIMONTE, *fresh from productions at the world's greatest Opera Houses including La Scala, Vienna, Berne*
Music Direction: Hr F Arshlock.

Tickets: From Fr B. Mueller Ganzstrasse 14, Bullersdorf bei Fohlingen or apply at the University.

Scene 4: The afternoon of 24th June 1920

A DRESS REHEARSAL

At last. This dress rehearsal is the final act of my story, which is both a tale of innocence corrupted and also, genius restored by such a weaving of lives and deaths it could be an opera. Yet it is such a painful birth!

A few brave clouds attempt to obscure a sun bored to death with sizzling the world, without mitigating the waves of heat that reach up in a lazy attempt at reunion with their source. Butterflies. Birds. All the dust and detritus of early Summer.

1pm
The Bierkeller, Fohlingen.
Brimming steins of Fohlingerbrau. Bubbling students, bursting with the joys of Summer and youth and overfilled crotches. An occasional raucous drinking song. I have no intention of regaling you with one or many of these: Operas are full of them. Pick any one and you will get yourself an ear-worm.

Franz is uncharacteristically subdued in the company of his brothers. His eye keeps seeking Karl and not finding him. The absence is like a ragged hole in the fabric of his reality. And as the Dress Rehearsal approaches (it's supposed to start at 6pm, the cast is due to arrive at 3 for makeup and costume) Franz is getting depressed. And the beer is not helping.

Katsoumi Tabatabee sits at his elbow. Franz' withdrawn detached cold shoulder has depressed him too, so that the only solution appears to be stein after stein.

Stein after stein.

Franz von Bülow and Katsoumi Tabatabee are getting rolling, catastrophically drunk.

MEANWHILE...

1.25 pm
The Maestros are already at the Konzerthalle. A final scoot through the score for Feddy, and an extra music rehearsal. For Capo, there are a few last-minute adjustments to the flies, a couple of licks of paint for some backdrops, a tantrum or two to be had at poor Abigail Feste and her crew of three backstage. No real reason, just nerves. Capo finds stress to be something to inflict on others: it's his way of getting his

way.

Not a great time for Frau Adalbert Foche to come storming in to explain why her Jakob (oboe) could not possibly play this evening. 'His throat is *vekrank!'* she spurts. 'Full of germs! Big ones! You can see them with your eyes! Coming from that stupid devil's implement, a man should never put such a thing in his mouth, it gives ideas! Next thing it's Sodom and Gomorrah!'

'What – ' Feddy manages.

'Full of germs those things. I put in bleach yesterday. Did it kill them?'

'You stupid woman!' Feddy erupts. 'Your bleach is what has caused the *kranke* mouth! Now what am I going to do for an oboist? Signor Capodimonte!' he calls. Capo emerges from behind a backdrop dripping with paint. 'Signor can you play the oboe?'

'I play everything. Why.'

'I have an oboist down with bleach-induced mouth ulcers.'

'Are you *mad*? A Direktor playing oboe? Have you lost your senses? Who Maestro? I am needed here!'

'Jakob. Maestro, what shall I do for an oboe?'

'Maestro! There are two in the orchestra are there not? Tell the other one to play like two.'

'I cannot alter the score now! Impossible!' Feddy throws his hands up in the air in a very good imitation of a Maestro giving birth to an egg. 'There is only one thing to do! I will play!'

'You cannot play maestro! You are the conductor! You are going to conduct with an oboe? In between tootling?' Capo is pretending to be amused. Actually he's furious.

'*You* can conduct! You have conducted before I presume?'

'Never!' Capo responds with great huff. 'I am the Direktor! Not the conductor!'

'It's easy,' Feddy says, pretending to be amused. 'So my instrument is clarinet. But I will play oboe. Your instrument is directing. So you will conduct! All you have to do is wave your arms about. My Orchestra is wonderful. They know the score. The cast knows what to do. They have rehearsed. It will be fine!'

'This is amateur! This is children trying to be adult! I have directed at some of the greatest Opera houses in Europe! I have never seen such a mess!' at which he storms out.

2.22 pm

Gertrude is feeling a growing sense of panic. She is convinced that unless she gets some of her 'special', her essence of man, her man-juice to lave onto her face, the makeup would look shabby and her face would sag. Feddy had been far too stressed this morning to comply with her demands. After a hurried breakfast during which he had practically ignored her head's persistent intrusion onto his lap, he had rushed off to the Konzerthalle in a mood only a few centimeters removed from despair.

And so off she goes on a hunt. Guido? No! Dammit! Juiceless!

Damn. Who else? Who else?

She ranges up and down Pflaumenstrasse, eyes flitting from male face to body to face. Careful! This one knows Feddy. They all know Feddy! Or too old, too empty, too fat to find it, too dirty!

Aha....only one person she can think of full of juice.

Franz.

She knows where he will be at this time! He could only be at the Bierkeller.

The only women generally in the Bierkeller are the waitresses or the occasional whore brought in by an unwise student, who would invariably regret it. Though not half as much as the whore would!

Aware that the clock is ticking, Gertrude lurks outside the Bierkeller. The sound of raucous singing comes in waves out of the open windows, the words are scarcely distinguishable and those which are vaguely intelligible are better not understood.

Ein Prosit! may have been one of them. Or, God forbid, *Der Schwanz von Hans* which is worse.

I have no idea why the Gestapo needed to torture people during the Second World War, which was of course just being invented at this time. They only had to play drinking songs. Slightly messy but less blood.

All that man-juice! And all she needs is just a little bit. A mere blob of liquid, enough to spread lightly over her cheeks. Men always seemed so grateful giving it to her, even Feddy had provided a supply when they managed to find some privacy. After the marriage it would be easier. Miserable fellow he was becoming!

She needed Franz. He wouldn't tell anyone. He and his brother had kept the secret when she used to meet with them ages back. Sad he'd killed his brother, but that was part of University life.

She was interrupted in her musings by the sudden appearance of the very man she had been musing about. Franz von Bülow, drunk as a skunk, emerged from the Bierkeller like the explosion of a storm cloud, followed closely by little Tabatabee, sticking like a Pilot Fish to a hydrophobic shark.

'Wait wait – Miss Gertrude!' Tabatabee is thrilled to see her. 'Thank God! You must help me! He's drunk! Dress rehearsal – '

'Oh my dear God – ' Gertrude said, more in joy than despair. 'So he is!'

'What shall we do!!' Tabatabee on the other hand was in deep, terrifying despair. Probably Franz had warned him not to allow too much drink to pass his lips.

'My liebling!' Franz said, as he recognized her through his blurred eyes. 'I love you! Why has thou deserted me!' slurring, staggering, the stereotypical drunk.

Gertrude wound an arm around his waist, holding him up. She was a big girl, remember. Wagnerian.

And it was as Brunhilda that she said 'Mr Tabby. Go ahead! You leave him to me! I will get him there.'

'But – Fräulein – I can help – '

'No! You don't want to be late, yes? Go! I will get him there. Sober or dead.'

'Dead???'

'Dead sober!' she said. 'Just go!!!'

'Yes of course!' he said, and scuttled off.

I think we should allow this couple a little privacy at this point. After all, Gertrude had to find a very secluded place in which, despite the dread Brewer's Droop, she would coax from the flopped tenor some of that juice which renovates and refreshes. She would not be happy if we were there staring.

But it can be recorded that Gertrude and Franz were only an hour late for Makeup, and while Gertrude was fresh-faced and happy, if rather tired, Franz seemed a little subdued but at least he was walking.

Mind you, Gertrude had almost lost her voice.

3.35 pm

Guido is stuck in his chair in the tiny Gasthaus room he shares with Capo. A statue. Rodin's Thinker perhaps.

This is going to be the most important night of his life. Tonight, the critics. Up to now the only critic who had heard him was the writer for the Berne Blattet, but who was he and who in Opera ever read the newspaper of a pompous Swiss city in the backwoods of culture? Tonight, all the most powerful men in Opera would be listening, watching, assessing, criticising.

Feddy had been astonished thrilled and terrified by the volume of acceptances he had received from his invitations. Only Peccarino had refused, stating with regret that he was attending a premiere at La Scala. (This was a lie, incidentally, as La Scala was closed. Research would no doubt reveal something far more salacious. No time for that.) But those who did accept had obviously done so out of curiosity. A Castrato! A Castrato on a stage for the first time in a century!

This evening he would know if everything had been worthwhile.

Everything. Cast into a world he had not chosen. Driven by the ambitions of other people. Used to prove other people's theories.

They didn't know him. No-one knew him. The Ragazzo still, in his heart. An urchin without love. That girl, that Brunhilda type, she could not love him. She was due to marry the Jew in a month, he would give her children. Guido could give no-one children.

No-one children.

Look closely at his face as he thinks this. It is a very beautiful face. Not handsome, beautiful. He is so young, but you can see lines around the eyes and a slightly sulky downturn of the mouth. It is a disturbing face. Beauty and cruelty. And as these thoughts flit through, it changes not a jot. To read his mind we must step inside.

I am alone. I have always been alone. My mother did not want me. The Ragazzi only wanted me to make their boring lives full of adventure. The Baron didn't want me. Gramaschi was afraid of me. That bitch tutor, hated me. Capodimonte, only wants me for his own glory. Same, the Jew. All of them! They take away my manhood so they can glory in theirs! What do they give me? A voice. A voice only good for old-fashioned music nobody listens to any more -

But tonight they will see the brilliance of Handel. Tonight with my voice I will empower the Baroque anew. Here starts the Baroque revival and I will lead it! The return of the King!

Two weapons.

Scene 5: The Gasthaus

Enter Capo, L.

Capo: Guido! What are you doing! We need a run-through of the end of

Act 3! I am conducting tonight –
Guido: (Looks up, frowns)
Capo: What is wrong with you boy! You are due in makeup. We have to do the run-through!
Guido: What do you mean you are conducting?
Capo: That blasted idiot, that apprentice Maestro, that – he is going to play oboe. Oboe! Is he mad! He is the conductor –
Guido: (sighs) Handel conducted from the harpsichord.
Capo: The harpsichordist? Burstein? She cannot conduct! She's a cretin. Mediocre harpsichordist. Nothing else.
Guido: Can you conduct?
Capio: My God you are so stupid sometimes. Right! That's fine! You don't think I can conduct! Pack your things.
Guido: What?
Capo: Pack up. We're leaving. This is a farce. If it goes ahead you will look ridiculous. I will look ridiculous. These are amateurs! Why did I let that ugly little gnome persuade me he can produce an Opera! A conductor! He could not conduct an organ grinder!
Guido: We are not leaving.
Capo: (exasperated) I know what you think. I beg you. This will fall to pieces in front of the greatest critics in Opera….!
Guido: (Forced patience) Tonight is my first starring role. If the others look ridiculous, I will look better. I will sound better. I will consume the stage.
Capo: The critics will consume both of us! We must leave!
Guido: I was too good in Berne. Everyone applauded like they applaud Caruso in Milan. Only you swore at me.
Capo: Milan! Fine, Milan! We will go to Milan. You watch. I have contacts –
Guido: I don't want to go to Milan. Not until I have sung Bertarido. There are no Castrato roles in Milan. Not yet.
Capo: Fine! Get up! Either pack your things or go to the Konzerthalle. Now! Decide!

Scene 6: Backstage

The cast are all in their dressing rooms, either being made up by Frau Feste or doing their own. The smell is greasepaint, Leichner of course. Only the best for Feddy. And old sweat, clinging to the sweatpads of costumes which any warmth liberates into the dusty air backstage. Shoes, some of them harboring unnamable tiny horrors. Wigs, made of hemp and redolent with the bacteria of anxiety.

Costumes are being assembled and tried, retried, fitted, refitted by the trio of backstage dressers (who are also the stage hands), under the occasional control of the formidable Abigail Feste. Despite the costume call yesterday there are so many last-minute adjustments! Buttons pop, trousers are too long, people obviously have changed size overnight. 'This doesn't fit!' 'It was fine yesterday!' 'It couldn't have been!' Pinning, tweaking, tidying, adjusting.

The sounds are the fluffing and crackling of cloth, the clanking of swords, mutters of dissatisfaction. Bangs of last-minute scenery adjustment. Shouts of 'heads!' Distant calls from the fly tower. Occasional tweeps from musicians tuning up, with some of the harder passages playedover and over...

Guido – Bertarido, *usurped King of Lombardy* - has dressing-room 1 to himself. There is even a tattered copper star nailed to the door. Perhaps Gertrude did that. Franz – Grimoaldo, - *Duke of Benevento, Bertarido's usurper* - has been escorted by Gertrude - Rodelinda, *Queen of Lombardy-* to dressing room number 2, which he shares with Tabatabee - Garibaldo, *Grimoaldo's counsellor, duke of Turin.* 'Get coffee!' says Gertrude, and the Persian scuttles out. 'So Liebling,' she whispers teasingly, before slipping off to dressing room 3. 'Remember what I said. Not one word. Not a sentence not a paragraph not a whisper. Or you, Liebling, -' she gently twists his balls, 'become the second Signor Guido. Yes?'

In dressing room 4, Beatrix Müller – Eduige, *Bertarido's sister, betrothed to Grimoaldo* - and her daughter, Lisa - Flavio, *Rodelinda's son* are dressing and Beatrix is doing makeup for both. For Beatrix, this is a massively important evening. A mediocre contralto herself, she is a better pianist, which was why she provided the music in rehearsal. She is relatively nervous about her own performance but far more concerned about her money. While the University has been generous in part-financing the production, her contribution has been critical. As for her daughter, she has no concerns. The girl seems to really enjoy dressing as a boy. Perhaps she should have more concerns.

Lucia Dell'Isola - Unulfo, *Bertarido's friend and counselor-* is in dressing room 5, dressing and being made up by the divine Abigail Feste. The appellation 'the divine' is Lucia's. Let's face it, she has the hots for Abigail, a pasty-faced overweight young woman whose careless pose of efficient competence is belied by the downward curve of a mouth which Lucia regards as cute beyond imagining.

Poor Lucia cannot work out if her hots are returned. As much as she has strutted in her tight Unulfo trousers, as much as she has pouted and waved her sword, Abigail has looked on expressionlessly. Apart from the maddening downturned mouth.

'What do you think? Does it suit me?' Lucia demands.

'Yes, good. Adjust that belt, make it tighter.'

'Won't you do it for me *Schatz*?'

'You can do it. Just one notch.|'

(Lucia adjusts the belt. Her disappointment flits over her face.)

'Look. I draw the sword! Isn't it exciting?' Whoosh. Whoosh.

'Exciting. Are you done? I need to check the others.'

'….(sigh. *Sotto voce*) if only….

'Break a leg!' Abigail drops the words into the room like an imprecation. 'Toi toi toi!'

'Fine!'

Exit Abigail. Lucia, to herself, 'I'll break yours. Wait.'

In dressing room 6, the Bruder. Schmidt, Krause, Fleischman, Nekker are the extras. Guards, populace, anything required. They have only just rolled in from the Bierkeller, stinking drunk. They are half-dressed, play-fighting with their stage swords.

Tick. Tock.

Tick tock.

The orchestra trickles into the orchestra pit. The tweeps and tootles of tuning-up rise and fall in waves. A few harpsichord plunks. A squeaking of strings, zizz zizz.

Tick tock.

They are waiting for the conductor. And for the oboe players.

The critics trickle in. The most influential critics in Germany! The only similarities between them being the air of pomposity, the aura of ego surrounding each like the most clinging of perfumes. They are shown to seats in the front row, as is their right. Like men in a urinal, they ensure that there is a gap between each one.

In the second, third and fourth rows, local journalists and celebrities, University bigwigs, some musicians and a small scattering of relatives of the cast and orchestra.

Feddy enters the orchestra pit. The musicians stand, the first violin extends his hand for shaking. Feddy waves them to sit down. He is carrying an oboe. They are confused. Feddy mutters an explanation. 'Signor Capodimonte is to conduct' he hisses.

They wait.

Gertrude (Rodelinda, I won't keep reminding you), Franz (Grimoaldo) and Tabatabee (Garibaldo), are waiting casually for the overture to begin, and start to wander to their places, their parts hesitating at the border between mind and mouth.

'You miserable worm,' Franz whispers to Katsoumi, 'You left me!'

'*Chol Bukhor*!' Katsoumi responds.

'What did you say?'

'*Haroomzade*!'

Abigail seats herself in the flies L, one hand on the turning handle which operates the curtain.

They wait.

Gertrude goes to the armchair backstage L and sits. She stares at the lining of the red plush curtain, in deep concentration, doing her deep breathing exercises, *sotto voce* scales.

While we wait, feel free to browse through the program

RODELINDA

Regina De Longobardi

An Opera in 3 Acts by Frideric Handel
Libretto by Haym, based on an earlier one by Salvi.

The CAST

Rodelinda, *Queen of Lombardy*	Gertrude Hassler, Soprano
Bertarido, *usurped King of Lombardy*	Guido della Roccaporca , Alto
Grimoaldo, *Duke of Benevento, Bertarido's usurper*	Franz von Bülow, tenor
Edulge, *Bertarido's sister, betrothed to Grimoaldo*	Beatrix Müller, Contralto
Unulfo, *Bertarido's friend and counselor*	Lucia del'Isola, Alto
Garibaldo, *Grimoaldo's counsellor, duke of Turin*	Katsoumi Tabatabee, Bass
Flavio, *Rodelinda's son*	Lisa Müller Silent
The Orchestra of the University of Fohlingen conducted by Musical Director R.F. Arschloch 2 recorders, flute, 2 oboes, 2 horns, strings, continuo (cello, lute, harpsichord)	

DIRECTORE: Sr CAPODIMONTE *of La Scala Milan, Vienna Oper, Opera Berne*

Scene 7: THE GRAND FINALE

Or, the Stranger in the Back Row

Synopsis

The argument:

Prior to the opening of the Opera, Grimoaldo has defeated Bertarido, King of Lombardy, in battle and has usurped the throne of Milan. Bertarido has fled, leaving his wife Rodelinda and his son Flavio prisoners of the usurper in the royal palace. Failing to secure support to recover his crown, Bertarido has caused it to be reported that he has died in exile, a ruse to be used in an attempt to rescue his wife and son.

ACT 1
The Overture
8.20 pm.

The overture is 20 minutes late already. Feddy's annoyance at Capodimonte's non-appearance is mounting into fury. Fine! He had stormed out. But the man was a professional. Surely he shared the Show Must Go On philosophy of every person who has ever been involved in a stage production? Surely he would eventually come? All that was required was to make a decent pretense of conducting. Anybody can do that.

The critics are restless. Foure is irritatedly doodling on the programme. Mannheim is angrily writing in a notebook. Halshoffer is picking his nose.

Mannheim stands, shouts. 'What is happening here! Do we have a production? I have not come to listen to an orchestra tuning! Where is Herr – ' consults his invitation letter - 'Herr – Arshlock? Where are you?'

'Yes, mein Herr, ' Feddy says, standing in the orchestra pit. Only his head can be seen above the parapet. 'So sorry! The conductor is not well! Indisposed!'

'You had better start now. I have an appointment later. Understand! Start now. I want to hear your famous Castrato!'

He sits.

'House lights!!!' Feddy shouts, and the house lights dim. Feddy stands. Using the oboe as a baton, he conducts.

The overture is a mess. The musicians are all good at their job – they are usually Feddy's pride and joy, but for some reason everything is off, tonight.

Rodelinda Act 1
Scene 1

The apartments of Rodelinda. Rodelinda is weeping. Enter Grimaldo and Garibaldo with guards.

Our heroine Gertrude, is actually weeping. She fears the audience will sense or intuit her sperm foundation beneath the stultifying clinging Leichner She is terrified of smearing it, of making her overdrawn kohled eyes run, of looking stupid. She knows she looks stupid.

Strangely enough, she remembers her entire part! People should not jump to conclusions.

Enter Grimoaldo, to tell Rodelinda that her husband the King, whose throne he has usurped, is dead and that he is passionately in love with her. Translation: Enter Franz, to lasciviously and drunkenly paw Gertrude whilst throatily scratching his lines like a lion's claw on a vinyl record. He is declaring his undying love. Gertrude is repulsed by him.

Neither of them are acting.

Act 1 steams on. Stumbles on. Staggers and spurts on. Franz is faced by his betrothed, the fat and fulsome Frau Müller as Eduige. He plots with his buddy Tabatabee as Garibaldo, to get rid of her, so that he can marry Gertrude (Rodelinda)

The critics are getting distinctly restless. Almost 30 minutes have gone by and still no Guido. No Castrato. Nothing worth writing home about – Amateurs! What a waste of a great critic's time!

……Rodelinda **Scene 6:** At last. Enter Guido, as Bertarido. The scene is a cypress-grove, in which are seen the monuments of the kings of Lombardy; and among them, the urn, newly erected to Bertarido. Grimoaldo has usurped his kingdom by claiming that Bertarido is dead, and has even erected an empty tomb and monument to him.

First, in a tinky-tonk bit of recitativo, he bemoans the fact that he's been mourned. He reads the inscription on the tomb: 'Bertarido was King, but he, defeated by Grimaldo, fled - And amongst the Huns he died. Rest his soul, and peace to his ashes.'

The man standing at the back freezes. He knows what's coming. The Aria, *Dove Sei*. Where are you.

Where are you, my lovely treasure,
Come to your husband, console me,
Bring me some comfort, bring me some pleasure,
Bring me balm to ease my wearied soul….

(Et seq)

In the wings, L Gertrude gasps as if stabbed.

In the wings, R, poor Franz almost emerges from his woozy stupor. He feels a wave of love flowing through him, across the stage, enveloping Gertrude.

In the front row the massed ranks of critics cease breathing. Almost long enough to prevent their being able to breathe again.

The man at the back sits, stunned.

(I confess, even though I have heard Guido give this aria before, this time my dry ghost tears burst through the dust of my eyes. I thought Senesino's rendering divine, I remember so well almost two hundred years ago how the aria was greeted by storms and wails from the audience, by flowers from the galleries, by ecstatic applause which raised the roof)

Enter Lucia as Unulfo, Bertarido's best buddy. S/he pledges eternal fealty to his/her liege. Bertarido asks after his beloved wife, Rodelinda. Gertrude in the wings is rapt. She is ravished by his love. Especially because he sees her there, continually looks toward her. Their eyes meet. Franz feels as if his guts are protruding through his mouth.

From the orchestra pit, Feddy watches, the oboe flying about in his hand. A question repeats itself in his head....but the boy is Castrato! Surely not!

When Rodelinda emerges and sings *Ombre Piante*, one of Handel's heartbreaking arias of a woman bereft, Gertrude has finally found her voice.

Feddy is amazed. This is not Gertrude. *This* is Rodelinda!

Life has become Art. Art has become Life. And as it proceeds, as each singer begins to become their parts, the tiny audience becomes transfixed. They can see the developed love between Gertrude and Guido. They feel Franz' yearning for Gertrude as his drunkenness evaporates, as his singing improves. The hatred between Guido and Franz crackles.

By the time Bertarido sings his final aria of Act 1, the line between Art and Life has dissolved.

Confusa si miri

Yes, let my faithless wife still think me dead,
Pledge to her new spouse the same

Faith she kept for me.
Then let her know I live, and, blushing, find
the fickle promise of her female mind
light as a leaf, that's sporting in the wind.......
.........Tho` she won my belief,
when she acted her grief,
tears, false as my reported death, she shed,
An kill`d the living, while she mourn`d the
dead...

END of ACT 1
Interval
The curtain descends. The Critics sit frozen for a moment. None wants to show his thoughts or feelings. Then, almost at a cue, each begins to write in his notebook frantically, as if attempting to blunt his pencil, or set it on fire. Desultory applause erupts from Beatrix' aunt.

Trays of tea, coffee and wines negotiate their way between the seats, borne by nervous members of the University Entertainments Committee, whose best efforts to see what the critics are writing are frustrated by the need to keep trays balanced.

The stranger in the back row sits impassive, except for the occasional coughing fits, which he is trying to suppress by frequent sips from a brown-papered bottle. He waves refreshments away imperiously, as if somehow the performance is personal, for him alone, and no distractions are tolerated.

The performance is indeed for him alone.
[6]

Rodelinda Act 2. Curtain up
Grimoaldo is challenged to kill Flavio by Rodelinda - he refuses. Amazing! The villain has principles!

It's not until scene 5 that Bertarido reappears on stage. By this point, despite the fact that each performer is giving the performance of his or her life, ennui has begun to set in for most of the audience. Let's face it, the complications as to who loves whom, who is the betrayer,

---

[6] *If you must,, read the Synopsis of Act 2 in Wiki https://en.wikipedia.org/wiki/Rinaldo_(Opera)*

who are the goodies and who are the baddies are of no interest except to Feddy, who has decided to ignore the second oboe part altogether and concentrate on conducting, and the two people in the audience who actually know the story. One of whom is Beatrix' aunt, who has carefully studied the Opera her adored grand-niece is acting in, albeit mute, to ensure that it does not in any way offend the basic principles of the Lutheran Church.

Scene 5 is supposed to be 'a delightful prospect' – in the sense of, a pretty bubbling stream in a beautiful landscape which in this production consists of a flat painted by Karl Lorenz, later a famous expressionist painter, in the manner of a black-and white woodcut. Which manages to give this delightful prospect a distinctly funereal air.

The curtain rises as Bertarido insinuates himself onto the stage and slides his aria, *Con rauco mormorio*, into the consciousness of the audience like a ghost sneaking through the ears into the mind.

It's one of Handel's most heartfelt arias, all about the raucous beauty of the (black and white) stream, about how much the Hero has lost. Remember: this is 1920, when melodrama is huge. The silver screen drips and pulses with excessive emoting. No surprise, then, that the audience is in tears, as are the actors in the wings.

As is Guido.

Guido is singing from the bitter depths of his heart. For Guido has lost so much. Too much. Beneath the sorrow, the anger, like a pebble in an expensive shoe. Guido has finally realized that the loss of his manhood means the loss of women too.

And to those who know that this man is Castrato, his pain is searing. Feddy, who had not understood what this song would mean to the singer in rehearsal, suddenly understands it now, and even the conductor's eyes are annoyingly moist.

Con Rauco Mormorio
With the rough murmuring of streams,
each brook, each river, running on,
Makes such mournful music, seems
Sighing, to give reply
To my sighs.
In choked accents, and with broken sound,
the mountains seem, relenting,
to echo my lamenting,

from the caves resound.

Except of course for the now sober Franz, who, as his sobriety has advanced, has been regaining his contempt for Guido.

So when the Opera decides that Bertarido is to be thrown into prison, Franz' relish at his discomfort is not feigned.

INTERVAL

Another man has entered the hall. He is portly, dressed in a grubby uniform. He goes to the man in the back row and starts an intense conversation in whispers. He is Polizeiobermeister Adalbert Weber.

We now recognize the man in the back row as Sebastian Amore Geillis. The men are arguing.

Our critics, meanwhile, have moved to be next to each-other, a chittering phalanx on the front row. 'Did you – ' 'Ach liebe Gott!' 'This voice! This voice!' 'I feel like I am in the eighteenth century!' They are intensely agreeing. Nodding. Writing. Excited. They are like birds together on a wire in Spring, spotting a fabulously fat and delicious worm.

Just time to have a last look at the Synopsis in the Appendix. 'You don't need a weatherman to tell you which way the wind blows.' Bob Dylan

Rodelinda Act 3

The curtain rises suddenly, well before anybody – including the cast – is ready. Feddy knew that unless Act 3 happened now, it would never happen.

The act starts with recitativo. Unulfo and Eduige rush and stumble onto the stage and conspire to free Bertarido from prison.

This is the *sotto-voce* discussion between Sebastian and Weber:
Weber: I have to find him! Now!
Sebastian: Wait! You must wait! Until the end! I have to know what the critics are writing!
Weber: Herr – this is police business now. Another man is dead. Do you understand! Another man!
Sebastian: So what! He is dead, yes? So he can't run away.

Weber: Yes but –
Sebastian: So what do you want? Arrest him now? I promise you, he will stay until the last note of the Opera. Who is dead?
Weber: His fluttery-fancy man. That Italian. Capodimonte. How do you know he won't run!! This one is so slipperish!
Sebastian: I know! This is the performance of his life. He will sing.
Weber: He draped – he draped the man's – his eggs! – his sack! – and the tail! On the neck! -!'
Sebastian: Shush! Shush!
Weber: I'll not –
Sebastian: Two thousand.
Weber: What?
Sebastian: Three thousand
Weber: You cannot –
Sebastian: For Heaven's sake man! Ten thousand! Ten thousand marks! You can arrest him straight after the performance! He cannot escape!

*

I need to remind you of that bet. Way back in February 1909, Sebastian Amore Geilis bet his best friend Baron Heinrich von Schweinstein that however good a singer a Castrato may be, he would never be better than a modern countertenor, or an alto, and that any modern singer, male or female, with an appropriately high voice could take any role in a Baroque Opera written for a Castrato and do a damn good job. Hence the purchase of young Guido and his Operation.

Your question: who is to decide?

Thank you for asking. The agreement was related to the reception the singer received from critics and public. The agreement was that at least 5 critics of high reputation should be delighted astonished and awed. What if, for example, the young man, Castrato or not, was just crap at singing?

Guido was not crap.

What if he was simply mediocre, a moderately good singer, Castrato or not. After all there were thousands of Castrati in the eighteenth century who stayed unemployed.

Guido was not mediocre.

Ok, fine. So what if he was just a damn good singer Castrato or not? How do you compare him directly with a great mezzo or alto or counter-tenor?

Guido was better than that. Better than all of them. Guido was eye-wateringly, soul-batteringly heart-stoppingly beyond belief brilliant. Which is why, just as in the eighteenth century, women swooned and men died when they heard his voice.

But there were few who had heard him. You have met most of them. And Sebastian had never seen him, until now, playing the hero in a full Opera, with a real audience.

So he was in limbo. As was the Estate of the late Baron – because as long as there was no resolution to the argument, the Castle remained unclaimed. Should Sebastian be proven right, the Castle would be his. If wrong, the Castle would become Guido's.

Now add to this Sebastian's conviction that Guido is a murderer, responsible not just for the five deaths described heretofore, but also for the death of his beloved friend the Baron.

This is horror pending. As Churchill or someone said much later in different words: the clouds were gathering in Europe

*

Weber sits straight and silent.
Sebastian: You will be a hero. Just let him finish!
Then, Weber: What's happening in this crazy Opera?
Sebastian: If I tell you, will you be quiet?
Weber: Yes.
Sebastian: So that woman, dressed as a man, Unulfo, and the fat woman, Eduige make a plan to get Bertarido out of prison: they will smuggle a sword to him and the key to a secret passage under the palace.
Weber: Oh my god. This Bertarido is the boy Guido, yes?
Sebastian: Yes.
Weber: He will escape! It is to prison he must go!
Sebastian: No he won't! Not until he sings!

(Exit Eduige and Unulfo. Enter Garibaldo and Grimoaldo. Scene 2)

Weber: So now?
Sebastian: And now the slimy one, the scrawny foreigner Garibaldo advises the villain, the nasty one, Grimoaldo to put Bertarido to death even though he doesn't know who he is. So this Grimoaldo as you can see is full of anger!
Weber: I don't understand.

Sebastian: Nobody does. You don't need to understand. Just enjoy the music.

CURTAIN

Weber: (stands) Now I can get him?
Sebastian: (restrains him with a hand on his forearm) Wait! Two more scenes to go!
Weber sits, reluctantly.

Curtain up!

Rodelinda Scene 3: A Dark and Dreary Prison.

The critics tense. Lean forward. Entranced.
(Bertarido, seated in semi-darkness. Deep music. Then he sings. Semi-recitative, moaning, bemoaning...)
Bertarido: *Chi di voi....*
Weber: It is him! Hah! Now he is practicing for real life.
Sebastian: Shush!
Weber: What a racket. When he is finished singing can I arrest him?
Sebastian: I'm paying you to stay here until the end! Now silence!
Bertarido: (sees the key and sword left for him. The music changes, becomes more urgent, dramatic)
(Enter Unulfo. Bertarido, thinking he is the executioner, stabs him)
Weber: (Stands) Dear God! He has done it again! Murder! (rushes out of his seat, dashes to the stage. Can't get over the orchestra pit. Finds his way to enter stage L via the wings. Hauls his huge bulk up to the stage)

Guido is stunned. Lurches away. Flight or fight?

Lucia, covered in fake stage blood, raises herself into a sitting position. She laughs. 'It's a play! It's acting!' she whispers, highly amused by the policeman's apoplectic fury.

Guido raises the stage sword. The policeman, overcome with terror, cringes back. Suddenly Weber falls back into the wings, just out of sight of the audience. Guido steps back into the wings stage R, confused and indecisive.

Panic in the orchestra pit. Bertarido has just exited several bars before he was meant to. Feddy, having been very concentrated at the music, hadn't seen or heard the unscheduled stage invasion. As far as he was concerned, there was no reason for the sudden exit of the singer. So, in a flurry of irritation and agitation, he is frantically turning pages of his score, as the members of the orchestra follow suit. '*Scena quarta*!' He hisses. '*Scena quarta*!! *Attacca!!*'

The critics meanwhile are thoroughly confused. Was this eruption onto the stage some peculiarly modernist addition to the Opera, to make the audience more aware of the injury to Unulfo? None of them know the Opera well at all. None realise the scene was foreshortened.

Enter Rodelinda Followed by Eduige. They ignore the policeman shaking with terror stage L, in the wings. He has suffered a massive episode of Atrial Fibrillation. He thinks it is a heart attack.

Feddy, sweating, conducts the orchestra and singers into the scene. Idiots! He thinks.

Rodelinda sings, Eduige sings. She sees the blood. Oh! She cries, My Bertarido is dead! She sings the terribly sad aria *Se 'l mio duol non è si forte* which means, where is my life and strength (I think) and bemourns the husband she thinks dead.

Meanwhile, in the wings, only just out of sight of the audience, the huge bulk of polizeiobermeister Weber writhes. 'I am dying…' he moans. 'Help me…'

Sebastian has tiptoed his way to the front of the auditorium, L where he is trying to mount the stage. All he wants is to shut the policeman up, so that the Opera can continue.

On to the stage he goes, and as Rodelinda continues to sing, vaguely aware of the drama in the wings, he firmly shakes Weber. 'Get up man. You are making a fool of yourself!'

'I am dying! My heart – '

'Don't be ridiculous!'

'He could have killed me! This murderer!'

'Nonsense!' Sebastian withdraws a bottle in a paper bag from one of his capacious pockets. 'Drink this!' With a combination of coercion and care, he forces a few gulps down the man's throat.

From the wings stage R, Guido stares anxiously at the tableau across the stage. What to do! In the darkness at the edge of a dark scene he doesn't recognise the man tending to the policeman. He knows there is great danger here. Fight or flight.

The aria takes forever.

It ends. Curtain.

The man tending the monstrous bulk of the policeman lays the porcine head of his charge gently onto a folded piece of rotting canvas. Is he dead? And then slips down the stairs L into the auditorium, seating himself as quietly as he can (not quietly enough) in the second row, behind the critics.

Rodelinda Scene 5
A Garden

Enter Bertarido and Unulfo. Guido and Lucia, Bertarido supporting the apparently injured Unulfo.

The short scene ends with Guido's opportunity to free the caged raptor in his throat, to soar and dive on the breath of his lungs *Se Fiera Belva Ha Cinto* 'Now it's time to hide and conceal myself'. The critics lean forward in ecstasy, every now and then scribbling a sentence or two. Behind them, Sebastian stands shamelessly reading their notes over their shoulders.

Bertarido
I'll conceal myself; no longer fear
the harsh commands of an imperious tyrant.
Since heaven has set me free, I wish no more
Than to trust my fortune to my courage.
Thus when a savage beast in snares is caught,
he fiercely roars and bites the rattling chain,
but when, to liberty restored, he roams,
the trembling prey their safety seek in vain.

From the wings, stage L, the aria is punctuated with stentorian snores.

Exit Bertarido and Unulfo, stage R

Enter Grimoaldo. Franz. A turgid recitative, followed by the aria *Pastorello d'un povero armento*.....singing of his three furies, Love, Jealousy and Anger. Wishing he was a shepherd, with no cares, and he falls asleep.

Meanwhile Guido has rushed to his dressing room. He has packed the few possessions he had brought with him, a handful of money taken from Capo's briefcase into a small suitcase, ripped his costume off, dressed. He heads for the stage door.

Bumps into Katsoumi Tabatabee who is heading for the wings as Garibaldo. Almost knocks him down.

Katsoumi: What are you doing? Where are you going?
Guido: I – I have to go.
Katsoumi: You can't just go! Act 3 isn't finished! You have to wait for my scene! You have to see it!
Guido: You don't understand – that's a policeman there – I won't even be able to give my *Viva Tiranno!'*
Katsoumi: *'You MUST!* It is the greatest song ever. You will make the critics scream and shout. The policeman is asleep! What would he want with you?'
Guido: My friend you are right…I have trained since I was eight for that moment.
Katsoumi: And you must see me get my revenge! He shows Guido his Kris, all shivering light quivering like a white snake.
Guido: You have to use the stage knife. That's dangerous.
Katsoumi: Exactly! I will get my revenge in full public! I will show them. I will show them my ancestor was Cyrus of the Persians. My ancestors were kings! That pig –

Guido: Wait wait now. What are you going to do?

Katsoumi: He has insulted me once too often! Just watch!

Katsoumi has had enough. Franz' constant bullying, his arrogance, his hatred of the 'little Persian' has awoken something in the man's breast. Finally, his ancestors have spoken to him. Cyrus! Xerxes! Darius! His domineering father, whose taunts had led him to go to Germany, to escape his responsibilities. Katsoumi is going to show them all! And the ghost of Ardashir, dear Babak, whispers in his ear: 'NOW is your time. NOW use everything I taught you! KILL HIM!'

He evades Guido's restraining hand, is onstage. He approaches the 'sleeping' Franz. His Kris, the knife his father gave him, raised to strike.

Guido dashes onstage. He knows the little man will kill now, on stage, for real. His antique Japanese Tanto leaps to his hand.

Feddy freezes - raises his baton. The orchestra stops playing.

'Stop!' Guido shouts, and the Persian turns to face him. 'I've had enough!' he shouts in German. 'Let me kill him! He has insulted me enough!'

'You can't do this! Please Katsoumi. Leave it. I hate him too – '

'Go away. Run away. It's time for me!'

Guido takes a knife man stance, and Katsoumi raises his knife in readiness. *Sotto voce*: 'Let me give *Vivi Tiranno* at least! Then you can kill him!'

Hoarse whisper: 'Let me kill him first! Get out of the way!'

'You can't kill him! It's not in the script!'

'Then I will have to kill you! Then I will kill him!' And Tabatabee leaps like a cat high into the air, his knife like the claw of a tiger raking downwards.

Guido side-steps, trips over the prone Franz who screams.

Again, Tabatabee attacks. There is no option but to fight.

Stage directions here would read, 'A knife fight ensues'.

The critics are speechless with joy and fear. Convinced this is all part of the production.

Franz, seeing these two men who hate him wielding knives very close to his throat, crawls into a fetal position, terrified.

A knife fight ensues. Secretly I'm rooting for Katsoumi, even though I know he hasn't a hope against our hero. I want you to see the tears of frustration in his eyes as he fights. Finally, he is ready to shrug off the years of bullying. He has been trained, after all. And Babak is watching.

But Katsoumi is facing Guido della Roccaporca .

I have already described a knife fight, so I will leave the description to the foremost critics in the world at that time.

*

Extract from the review by H. Mannheim in Berliner Tageblatt Monday 25th June 1920

RODELINDA G. F Händel

University of Fohlingen

G. Hassler,

L. dell'Isola, G. della Roccaporca, F. von Bülow; K.F. Arshlock, L. Capodimonte

BAROQUE IS BACK

'And della Roccaporca is the new sovereign of the style!

'You may well wonder why a critic of my reputation should be commenting on an obscure opera in an unknown University with unknown singers. Suffice it to say I was attracted by the promise of the century: the opportunity to hear a Händel opera with the hero's role being sung by a genuine Castrato.

'......Guido della Roccaporca in the role of Bertarido did not disappoint. His astonishing voice is capable of soaring way into the upper register with the confidence of a well-equipped mountaineer. Sometimes the voice is close to that of the counter-tenor, at others, like a perfect mezzo soprano. And yet the voice is different to either: in summary it has the clarity and crisp quality of ice. As transparent, yet with a sharp cutting edge which can enter the heart and there dissolve, leaving only the fear of death behind.

Händel's arias for the character of Bertarido, the deposed King of Milan, range from the introspective to the angry and della Roccaporca excels in both. But the combination is utterly indescribable. His breath control during the coloratura is almost incredible: it seems as if his chest contains lungs at least four times the capacity of the ordinary man. He commands graceful runs and delivers a spinning pianissimo. This young man, I have no hesitation in asserting, will one day be the greatest performer of the Baroque in Europe....

'....Gertrude Hassler was adequate as Rodelinda, considering her lack of experience. She leans into her notes, and manages to project the tragedy and longing of the role. Her voice has a trace of the *bel canto* which could develop in her future. ....'

He goes on to be moderately unenthusiastic about the rest of the cast. Then:

'...I can't say the same for the Direktors of this production. While Herr KF Arschloch did a workmanlike job in conducting a competent small Baroque Orchestra, the Stage Production left a great deal to be desired...

'...There is a poisonous fashion which pervades Opera productions in this century: the passion for modernism, and interpretations of beloved old operas in modern dress. The first three acts of the Opera were fairly conventionally staged, with the props and scenery appropriate to the average amateur production. However, in the final scene of the third act, the Regisseur, a Signor Capodimonte, saw fit to costume the hero in modern dress. In the plot the hero Bertarido kills Garibaldo, who is trying to kill the usurper Grimoaldo, thus regaining his kingdom from a repentant usurper. In this production there was a most bloody fight onstage, in which eventually poor Grimoaldo, who, I may say, fought bravely, was finally put to death. The fight lasted only four minutes, four horrifying minutes of excellent acting, which frankly would be much better in Verdi or Puccini, but not in a mannered Opera of the Baroque.

'...Thank heavens for the aria *Vivi Tiranno*, Bertarido's final aria of the Opera. I must say this was one of the greatest moments of my life as an Opera critic. There stood the misunderstood hero, his hands covered in blood, singing the last of the marvelous treats from this Opera, a cry from a wounded heart... This left me in no doubt whatsoever: Guido della Roccaporca has the greatest voice for Baroque Opera I have ever heard...'

He ends his piece with:

'...The final triumphal chorus, in which husband and wife are at last reunited and the villain defeated was very strangely performed by a solo singer, the redoubtable Frau Müller, who had been performing the role of Eduige....and this was done on the apron, in front of the curtain. All-in all, the last scene of the final act was quite extraordinary. Disturbing, frustrating and more in the spirit of the librettist than in any way the desire of the composer. No wonder it was decided to skip curtain-calls altogether....'

And in Paris Match, Norbert Foure: '....astonishing voice of Sr. della Roccaporca, as Bertarido....transfixing...the Baroque Opera is back! With voices and acting of this quality....'

Giovanni Halshoffer, Berliner Herold: '....the knife-fighting climax had me clutching my seat as if to prevent myself being pitched into the darkness of Hell, with the emotional intensity of the truly magnificent voice of the Castrato G. della Roccaporca . I believe the magnificent Herr Wagner himself, were he to have heard this performance, would write a part for this man.'

*

The day after the critics had filed their reviews, the whole world learned what had really happened. How I would have loved to have seen their faces!

FINAL CURTAIN

The Opera is over. The fat lady sang. Everybody died. On stage, the corpse of Katsoumi Tabatabee lies splayed out next to the corpse of Polizeiobermeister Adalbert Weber. The Atrial Fibrillation the policeman suffered earlier, combined with the Schnapps from Sebastian's flask triggered a massive stroke when he witnessed the lethal knife fight and, to his credit, tried to arouse himself to intervene. This was too much for a heart which had so gamefully propelled all that flab and ego around for so many years, and it just went pop.

Back at the lodging house, the corpse of the popinjay Signor Capodimonte lies on the blood-muddied bed, slit from nave to chaps, his testicles draped about his throat like earmuffs.

Well, not everybody died of course. There is an epilogue, a short scene you may wish to see. Wait. Let the critics excitedly wrap up their pieces, recover their composure, leave the theatre in a chittering mass of self-congratulation, so relieved that they have survived the most harrowing Opera of their lives. And yes, most of them have seen Madame Butterfly's suicide, Aida's suffocation, Carmen's slaughter.

Sebastian knew already, even before the newspapers were out, that he has lost his bet. Here all about him and strewn in a bloody trail all the way back to Castle Schweinstein are the victims of that afternoon at the Slachthausgasse. Guilt, anger and hatred become Sebastian's constant companions. His life's mission was now, to save Schloss Schweinstein from the man he was now calling the Dissolute, to find him and kill him before he claimed the Castle.

EPILOGUE

The way this story ends is irredeemably corny. An immense cliché. So tell me, how else could it have ended? Like an Opera! No apologies. Here it is.

Fohlingen Railway station. A train sits amidst its escaping steam at the platform, where the sign ZURICH displays its intended destination. Leaning out of the window, Guido della Roccaporca . Bidding him farewell, Franz von Bülow.

Franz: You have enough money? You will be fine once you cross the Swiss border.

Guido: I don't understand you. You had nothing but contempt for me. Why are you helping me get away?

Franz: You saved my life. The von Bülow family motto is Honour Above All. You saved my life.

Guido: I didn't want him to stop the Opera before *Vivi Tiranno*.

Franz: You were leaving! You were running away! Before Act 3.

Guido: I thought I was going to be arrested – then when the policeman passed out –

Franz: Arrested? What for?

Guido: Ah. You will find out.

Chuff!

Franz: If you need money write to me.

Enter Gertrude L. She is carrying a small case of personal belongings.

Gertrude: Guido! Wait!

Guido: Gertrude! No!

The train starts to move.

Gertrude: Guido! I love you! Stop the train!

It speeds up. Gertrude runs after the departing train.

Franz runs after Gertrude.

Eventually, the train has gathered too much speed, Gertrude cannot possibly get to it.

Franz catches up with her and with a mighty shove pushes her onto the tracks.

END

Another Epilogue

The show went on two weeks later, as you would expect. As a result of the publicity once all the deaths were known, people fought for tickets. Just like when I first came to London, the whole populace swarmed to my operas! Now, they will again!

The blood was scrubbed, the cast replaced and rehearsed. The role of Bertarido went to Lucia Dell'isola who magnificently made it her own. Fleischmann took Garibaldo, performed brilliantly and would have gone on to a great career in Opera if he hadn't died in a concentration camp in 1942.

As for Gertrude, she didn't die on the railway tracks. Stupid Franz didn't realize that in order to kill someone on railway tracks you should push her in front of the train, not the back. So she went on to sing the role of Rodelinda, 'acceptably', according to critics. Franz went back to his role of Grimoaldo. He is, after all, the perfect villain. Gaps in the cast were filled by various members of the University Choir by people you've not heard of. And won't.

Franz and Gertrude married in 1922, to Feddy's great relief. Franz joined the Gestapo after 1935 and was a big hit with Hitler. Happy ending...

If you think this was the end of the Handel Festival, and of all Feddy's ambitions for making the operas of Handel live forever, you would be wrong. Of course you would! How could those 42 operas with their magnificent plots, their visionary mise en scene *and above all my heavenly music – disappear for ever? The Handel Festival continues every year growing ever more popular. Well, you try to get tickets! (But remember:* 'Fohlingen' *is an invented name for the real place)*

Feddy, as I have already told you, ended up in New York and to great success at the Metropolitan Opera.

As to Guido? Ah. I may tell you in the next part of this story. Suffice it to say, ever pursued by Sebastian.

THE ACTUAL END

***Note:** All names of people and places except one, are a lie. Forgive me for having fun with names! And if you think you are in this book, welcome.*

THANKS to my wonderful Beta Readers, my marvellous editors and friends, to my dear Esthers who are both and to my exceptional Publisher for putting up with me.

Dedications

Dedicated to all the Fat Ladies who sang as they died, to the Heroes whose lust flied, to the betrayals and twists and turgidity, gods and traitors of the librettists, the divine sounds created by a genius and translated into scrapings of catgut, blowings of wood and brass, tapping and booming of drums by genius composers, the gallons of stage blood, the rafters shattered by top c's, the armies of the brave in the flies, the scene artists, the stage directors, the thousands whose tears and tantrums make that most perfect of the arts, that divine creation of love and art, that is Opera.

Btw: My team of 10 Beta Readers were extremely helpful. They were recruited from applications online, did not know me. They read (selected) chapters as they were written, then the whole ms. Their comments and criticisms were invaluable.

Printed in Great Britain
by Amazon

48154679R00108